The Curiosity of Scrooge

Scrooge's determination to solve a mystery
brings about a serious crisis.

by

Judy La Salle

The third book in "The Scrooge Years" series

Book One - Scrooge The Year After
Book Two - The Society of Scrooge
Book Three - The Curiosity of Scrooge

To all Scrooge lovers, every one

"... crime, like death, is not confined to the old and withered alone. The youngest and fairest are too often its chosen victims."

Charles Dickens
Oliver Twist

ACKNOWLEDGMENTS

Once again, my husband Rod, my sister Nancy and my friend Lynne supported and helped me as I accompanied Scrooge on his latest adventure. Rod provided the technical and formatting support for publication well beyond my limited knowledge. Nancy kept me in her prayers and read anything I asked her to read, always checking on my progress. Lynne offered editorial advice on a regular basis, even though it meant hours of reading and re-reading.

Margaret Forbes, Search Engine Assistant with the National Railway Museum in York, England attempted to help me as much as possible. I am grateful for the information she was able to provided even though she was working remotely because of the COVID-19 Virus pandemic.

I am also grateful to my friends and relatives who kept me in their minds and prayers and gave me moral support.

THE CURIOSITY OF
SCROOGE

PROLOGUE – 1836

The boy was far too young to understand what was actually taking place, and he hadn't the maturity to discern the motivations of those around him. One thing was very clear however, even to a child who could not articulate his feelings. He was in the clutches of evil – unlike any he had ever encountered, and his discomfort and confusion were compounded by an intense fear of the unknown.

It had now been a week since he was kidnapped from his nanny in Regent's Park, but his mind could not grasp the passage of time, and it seemed an eternity. In this place there were always people coming in and going out, but he knew by instinct and recent experience, which included severe threats, that he was not safe here, and he was, for the most part, very much alone. The few small rooms were dark and very dirty, and he was cold since his nice suit of clothes had been taken from him and replaced by worn-out rags.

He remembered the warmth and security of his parents' home, and he desperately wanted to be returned to that place of sunlight and loving care. There, if he cried for his mother during the night he would quickly be engulfed in warm arms and hear soothing tones. Last night he had called for her and been struck for making noise and for being "a baby" even though he was, in fact, not so long out of the cradle that he could be expected to act more like a man than a baby.

Tonight, there had been a decided change in the activity and mood of the people in the house. There were more of them and their urgent whispers were occasionally broken by a loud oath of disagreement. Even the occasional shrill laughter was evil and frightening.

When the boy had first been brought there, the Father and the sons were more patient, more friendly, but their patience and small kindnesses waned as the days wore on, other than one or two, and the boy seemed not to understand how he should behave. Apparently, his worst offense was the shedding of tears. Hadn't they warned him time and again? Wasn't he cuffed about the head and shoulders repeatedly, which only brought on the very behavior they so loathed?

The boy did his best, truly he did, but his efforts were useless. He consistently gave in to tears and sobs, and tonight was the limit. The boy attempted to bury his head in a pile of rags, cowering and wailing like a wounded animal, when the Loud One suddenly turned in his direction and bellowed, "He's no good to us. He'll never be worth nuthin' 'coz 'e's got no brick!"

With that, his huge hand clamped onto the boy's arm, quickly yanking him to his feet, where he stood trembling at the horrible possibilities that awaited him. Without another word the boy was dragged from within that smelly prison and into the mysterious dark night of London. He prayed he was being released to somehow find his way home – if only he could.

As the boy was pulled across the threshold, one of the other boys yelled something that he could not quite make out – a warning perhaps, but to whom? Amid the commotion the Father also whined, "'Ere now, there's no cause for violence, my friend. No cause. 'E'll come 'round, you'll see. "E's only got the morbs," but it was too late. The Loud One had reached his very short limit. He did not answer, nor hesitate.

The night was unwelcoming, and as they progressed toward the River the boy noticed faint candlelight from nearby dingy windows, each one hinting at the evil he now knew could lurk behind rickety doors. The Loud One was in a hurry, but where were they going? Their pace increased even though the boy was unable to keep abreast. He tried to run, fell, and was then dragged along over cobblestones until his knees bled and he felt as though his arm would be ripped from his shoulder.

By the time they reached the River, the Loud One was no longer in the throes of fury, but his determination remained intact. The boy was a weakling. He had no brick. He had become an unproductive mouth to feed and must be got rid of. No, he could not simply be put out on the streets lest he blab to someone. As the Loud One thought on these things he slowed his pace somewhat, unaware that he was allowing the boy to regain his balance.

Unfortunately, just at that moment the Loud One changed his direction, causing the boy to once again lose his footing. As he fell, the man impatiently jerked him up and swung him around like a rag doll, unintentionally striking his head on a post at the entrance of the bridge. The force of the motion proved instantly fatal to such a small and weakened child.

The poor little body lay there, its spirit already received into Heaven, leaving the man with a job he considered easier now that his burden was little more than a light sack of coal. Picking the boy up, he looked both ways. Seeing no one, he easily chucked the sad bundle into the murky water, and the pitiful remains were quickly swallowed by an insatiable inky current.

Relieved and satisfied with his completed task, the man quickly made his way off the bridge and back to the bleak lodgings, unaware that he had been followed and the entire incident observed.

CHAPTER ONE – 1846

A Wish Is Spoken as Fact

It was inevitable that Honora Purdy would eventually be at the root of a certain amount of trouble. She did not possess any depth of wisdom concerning herself, nor was she one to curb her tongue in order to hide those sentiments that would best be left unrevealed amongst polite society.

Mrs. Purdy was not wicked nor impolite, it was just that where Ebenezer Scrooge was concerned, she had no governor on her conduct, much less her tongue. Her heart was his, and the whole of London Town might know it because she was not of a mind to hide it. She was, in fact, totally and very publicly besotted.

Poor Honora. She was destined to seek a lover in one whose hopes lay elsewhere, meanwhile spurning other gentlemen who would happily become her suitors, and not only for the lucre the wealthy widow might bring into their lives. A Mr. Blythe was one of those, and he had no doubt that Mrs. Purdy would suit him exactly. He wouldn't have minded had she not a tuppence. In his eyes she was a goddess – too good for those who failed to see her virtues.

Honora Purdy was pleasant enough, and partially attractive in a hue that was somewhat faded. She was also well-schooled in the social graces, if one could get beyond her peculiar noises. Being in the company of Honora Purdy often resembled a stroll through the mews. It was her braying laughter that made it so. She was prone to release the occasional snort that suggested a horse had made its way into the room. Her sense of humor thereby worked against her, since it was certain to bring on one or more of her equine emissions!

Most denizens of Town suspected, with good reason, that the widely venerated Mr. Ebenezer Scrooge did not return the affections that Mrs. Purdy so desperately wished to shower upon him. In point of fact, most people suspected, again with good reason, that his own affections were settled elsewhere. Had they not seen him time and again in the company of the lovely widow, Rebecca Langstone? Had not Honora Purdy also seen him? She most certainly had but, alas, she hadn't the discernment, nor the wish, to believe her eyes.

At any rate, that same lack of perception kept her from the mortification any other woman may have suffered by being the victim of her own socially unsuitable behavior. That lack was the impetus that kept her pursuing her love object, to his annoyance and dismay.

Scrooge knew it was unkind, but more than once he had allowed himself the delightful thought of placing a feedbag over Honora's mouth and leading her to a stall, where he would shut her in for the evening, to end her braying and the horrid incessant flattery. At the same time, he admitted there was nothing inherently wrong with the infernal woman other than that, like a hungry poacher, she had him perpetually in her sights. He was weary of having to be on his guard lest she bag him like some poor unsuspecting pheasant!

On occasion, Honora found it difficult to separate her desires from the truth, and it was at just such a time that she erred in her conversation. Whether she was aware of her gaffe, or not, no one would ever know since she could be quite vague in her replies when questioned regarding her one-sided attachment.

This time, while having tea with the three Broadslipp sisters, Mrs. Purdy made a simple yet fateful statement as she dabbed the outer corners of her mouth with her serviette. One of the sisters, Harriet, mentioned that she had seen the very eligible Mr. Scrooge on Corn Street, and everyone heartily agreed that he was a fine figure of a man and what a shame it was that he had no wife. Whether it was a fantasy or an outright lie, no one, including Honora herself, could tell, when she pursed her lips and said, quite matter-of-factly, "I happen to know that Mr. "S" is soon to wed, but it is a secret, so you musn't say a word!"

The women were agape. Cups and saucers clattered as the sisters all spoke at once. None of their queries was discernible from the others, but the general noise contained the questions, "How do you know such a thing" and "Who is the bride-to-be?" followed by the demand, "Mrs. Purdy, you will not remove from these premises until you impart all that you know!"

Naturally Honora was pleased to be the center of all of the commotion and perhaps that is why she veered even further from the truth. Setting aside her cup and saucer, she gave in to the delicious urge to continue and said, "Mr. Scrooge and I, that is to say, well . . . I could say we have somewhat of an understanding." Here she demonstrated the art of rolling one's eyes slightly to the left, while, at the same time, raising her eyebrows just a bit. Relishing the shocked expressions on her companions faces, and completely unable to stop herself, she continued.

"Mr. Scrooge, whom I often refer to as 'Ebenezer,' is definitely in search of a wife and, after all, who could fault him for marrying the appropriate widow?" She attempted to appear to be deflecting any hint that it might be she, herself, and continued.

"Even though he does not need a widow's wealth, he can certainly appreciate it." Honora did not elaborate on the fact that she only used Scrooge's Christian name in her daydreams, but what was the harm? Surely someday she would, in fact, be intimate enough with the dear man that she would use his Christian name whenever she liked. As far as having an understanding, Honora had never quite comprehended that the understanding on Scrooge's part was nowhere near her own. He understood only too well that any energy put in to avoiding her company was energy well spent!

Honora Purdy did not realize the unseen firestorm she had ignited with her idle talk because she was enjoying herself far too much to consider any possible consequences of her words. When she declined to share further details, other than again to say she definitely should not be quoted to anyone, the sisters began bustling about and tried very politely to urge her to take her leave, at one point actually showing her the way out. They could scarcely abide her presence another moment since she, the source of a most surprising bit of information, was preventing them from dispersing it as long as she remained in their drawing room!

After successfully shooing Mrs. Purdy into her carriage, the ladies paused only long enough to heave a unified sigh of relief, and they immediately began devising plans to make social calls beginning on the morrow – even today, if possible! They would, of course, only speak with those few women whom they could trust to utter not a single word – not even a breath of what they were about to relay to them!

CHAPTER TWO

The Rumour Takes Wing

It was the very next day that the Broadslipp trio made their way to several homes, barely touching their tea. They were too busy feigning modesty and reluctance as they hinted at knowing some earthshaking news, then finally allowing it to be pried from their bosoms. Without admitting so, even to themselves, they knew they must act quickly, before the word got around and they inevitably lost their position of being the only ones in possession of a new report.

The Broadslipps' last call was to the home of Dick and Priscilla Wilkins who, unbeknownst to the sisters, were long-time intimate friends with Ebenezer Scrooge. It would be misleading to assume that the women were totally ignorant of the bonds that connected people in their society, but they were currently blinded by their zeal to impart such a remarkable secret. In short, they conveniently ignored the probability that the Wilkinses and Scrooge conversed often, or that they were well-enough acquainted that they even used their Christian names when they did so.

It was Theodocia Broadslipp who first broached the subject, speaking as if her audience were a total stranger to the subjects of her discourse.

"My dear Mrs. Wilkins," purred Theodocia. "It is such a pleasure to find you at home. It is always pleasant to see people from time to time and exchange pleasantries, particularly when we have not spoken in some weeks."

Priscilla nodded as she handed a plate of biscuits around and responded with a simple, "Yes, it is indeed." Annoyed, Theodocia tried another tact. She must be successful before the other two put their noses in and claimed the conversation. She wanted to be the one to "break the news" since she had not yet had the pleasure of doing so. Sometimes Harriet and Lilias could be so selfish and thoughtless!

Without comprehending the fact that Priscilla Wilkins was no gossip, Theodocia pressed on, but not before she cast a warning glance to her sisters to hold their tongues. She would not allow them to be the only ones to have the joy of sharing someone else's secrets!

"As I was saying, these little visits allow us to catch up on so much news – some of it very surprising. Why, just yesterday we were given such earthshaking information that we could scarcely believe our ears!" Pausing, she added, "But then, it is not something we are at liberty to share, so I should not have mentioned it."

Priscilla wisely agreed with Theodosia and offered more tea. Oh! It was too much! Lilias could stand it no longer and leaned forward, ignoring Theodocia's narrowed eyes.

"But have you no interest in what we know, even though we must not share it? We did get it from the horse's mouth, so to speak." She suppressed a giggle as she suddenly pictured Honora Purdy sounding off with an equine nicker.

It was Harriet who could resist no longer, and interposed next, speaking before Lilias could continue. "Most people like to hear about their acquaintances, since it gives a more complete picture of their characters and their activities, don't you agree?" She paused, but not for long lest one of her sisters invade the silence. "You have no doubt met Mr. Ebenezer Scrooge? He is certainly a well-known personage about Town."

With that remark Priscilla realized it might be virtuous to ignore gossip, but it might also be reckless to ignore information her friend Ebenezer should know. Closing her eyes and taking a breath, she relented enough to learn the gist of the tale the sisters were so anxious to tell. She would not, however, make it easy for them.

"I have indeed met Mr. Scrooge and have never found him wanting in his character."

The sisters' patience was waning. Had Mrs. Wilkins no curiosity about those in her society? Was she so dull of mind and breeding? All of the others had greeted the sisters' new secret with impatient anticipation, leaning forward and plying them with questions, their mouths set in mischievous smiles as they waited for the "truth" to be revealed. Some had even squealed and huffed with delight and disbelief, or disapproval, as they voiced their opinions concerning Mr. Scrooge and Mrs. Purdy's reported relationship.

Theodocia was clever, or saw herself as such, and tried a different tact.

"Well, since we cannot repeat the matter, it is just as well you are not interested." She sat back and took a bite of pastry, pleased with herself and secure in her belief that the statement would reveal Mrs. Wilkins' natural curiosity, if she could keep her sisters mute long enough to let her statement have the desired effect. Priscilla was curious, but not for herself. She sought to protect her friend Ebenezer and she could only accomplish that if she were armed with the truth of what these women were spreading around like jam on a crumpet. Silly, unprincipled women!

"I can't imagine that Mr. Scrooge has done or said anything that would be worthy of gossip." She meant to use that word, which took the three gossipers somewhat aback, but not for long.

All three spoke at once, until Harriet waved her hand at the other two, quelling their enthusiasm to speak, and wanting to draw things out just a bit longer since Mrs. Wilkins had not been a willing partaker of their game.

"It is not gossip, I fear," said Harriet. "It is –" but she was interrupted by Lilias, who quickly blurted, so as not to be interrupted herself, "Mrs. Purdy told us, herself –", but it was no use. Theodosia seized the moment and delivered the news before anyone could stop her!

"Mr. Scrooge and Honora Purdy are pledged to wed!" There! They had succeeded in revealing their news and could finally bask in Mrs. Wilkins' disbelief and awe. Now they could share further details and discuss the happy couple, even declaring a bit of disapproval, if the conversation led in that direction.

Priscilla somehow managed to conceal her utter shock, and simply said, "Oh. I had no idea. Well, if that is the case, I pray they will be very happy."

"Oh, it is the case, for we heard it from Mrs. Purdy, herself, not but yesterday," retorted Lilias. Goodness, but the Wilkins woman was trying!

It soon became clear that the Broadslipp sisters would be unable to engage Mrs. Wilkins in any sort of meaningful remarks on the topic, and they took their leave politely, but quickly, sorry to have had their rewarding day so thwarted at the end.

Priscilla was aghast. She was certain the report was untrue because she knew Scrooge and Rebecca Langstone had been intimate friends for nearly two years and were no doubt in love. So why would Mrs. Purdy put such a thing about? Or had she? Dick would know something. He always had his ear to the ground and knew the goings on around Town. She spent the time waiting for him by pacing the floor and wringing her hands, trying to make sense of the purported news, and failing with every new thought.

Dick Wilkins was laughing as he entered his home that evening. Yanking his hat off his head, and pulling off his scarf and coat, he announced, "My Dear, you will not believe the latest tittle-tattle I picked up at the Exchange today! It concerns none other than our dear friend and confidant, Ebenezer!" A knowing countenance was her only response and he pulled his head back on his neck as he retorted, "You don't seem in the least interested in my report. Are you not at all curious? No, I can see that you are not."

Leaning toward her he said, "You know something, don't you? Yes! I can see that you do. Share with me immediately what you have heard, and from whose lips the report has come!" She remained silent and as he sank into a chair he added, "We shall put our heads together and compare our information. Perhaps we can make sense of it, or at least discover how and why this report has come about. I'll begin, and I will attempt to entertain you by repeating the report to you just as I heard it this afternoon." Settling further into his favorite spot, he began.

"It seems that our dear friend Scrooge is planning to wed. Yes! And to Honora Purdy, of all people!"

Here he laughed heartily, forgetting altogether that two years earlier Priscilla had thought Honora a possible match for Scrooge and had even introduced the two of them. She preferred to ignore that fact also, as he continued.

"Not only are they engaged, but they would have eloped not ten days ago, had his business demands not interfered. Poor Honora was left standing alongside her stuffed trunk, awaiting a groom who did not appear. He sent, in his stead, a short note of apology penned by his clerk and delivered by messenger. My informer states emphatically that he knows (since his information came from an impeccably reliable source) that the two have been secretly engaged for several months and have behaved almost as total strangers in public for fear of a report just such as this getting get out."

Priscilla then recounted her afternoon exchange with the Broadslipp sisters when she suddenly slapped her cheek and exclaimed, "Oh! You don't suppose Ebenezer has got wind of this, do you? Or, Heaven forbid – Rebecca!" As she said so, the damaging possibilities of such a report struck her and she truly feared for both her friends. Even Dick's gleeful smile disappeared as he seriously considered the harm such gossip could do. He was thankful he hadn't spread the report himself, except to his wife, but he would certainly seek out Fred Symons as soon as possible. Fred could share the rumour with Scrooge since neither Dick nor Priscilla wanted to be the ones to do so.

CHAPTER THREE

An Old Grievance

Ebenezer Scrooge was totally unaware of the fact that his name was being tossed about by many, and that he had been linked so closely to the object of his avoidance, Honora Purdy. The tale of Scrooge's betrothal to Mrs. Purdy had been spread by Londoners all day, but always ceased the moment he came within earshot. It is a practice widely employed by talebearers who prefer not to be credited with furthering the fuss. Fortunately, none of the men in the Scrooge and Symons counting house had heard the report either, so they did not have to feign ignorance or decide whether or not to inform Scrooge.

Scrooge's clerk Bob Cratchit had not gone outside the counting house walls all of the day. Cratchit's assistant, Homer Probert, dashed to the George and Vulture for some sausages at mid-day, but he was so preoccupied with some figures that he did not hear the man who asked him, "So what's the story 'bout your employer, eh?" The one employee who might have heard something while running constant errands would have been Cratchit's oldest son, but he was no longer employed at the counting house, having left some months earlier, to serve as an engineer's apprentice. He was now building tunnels and bridges to accommodate the expanding railway lines.

Fred Symons, Scrooge's nephew, was not, however, fortunate enough to avoid the idle chatter, although at least he first heard the tale from his intimate friend, Julian Thorne.

Fred and his uncle Scrooge had been at the Exchange earlier but went their separate ways following the conclusion of some business. As Fred passed a corner, Julian grabbed his sleeve and pulled him aside, glancing both ways to ensure they were not observed, although the move was, most likely, unnecessary.

"My friend," said Julian in a low voice, "I must share an unfortunate rumour that is being bandied about. It concerns your Uncle Scrooge, and I, myself, am finding it stretches the imagination just a bit." Before relating the details, Julian looked his friend in the eye and asked, "Is your uncle's heart set on anyone?" Fred's response was immediate. "Yes, I believe it is." "Then," returned Julian, "do you believe it is Honora Purdy?"

Fred was obviously taken aback, and an expression of humorous disbelief crossed his face before he began to laugh aloud. His response gave Julian permission to react in kind, and soon both men were creating a rumpus that required them to lean against the wall and wipe their eyes with their handkerchiefs. It was some minutes before they could compose themselves enough to return to their conversation. Neither man could say anything damning about the woman's character, but they admitted to each other that she was just a bit "peculiar," which sent them once again into a fit of hilarity.

Julian finally composed himself enough to relate the tale to Fred, which, incidentally, ran along the same lines as the information Dick Wilkins had received. Fred knew he was in possession of information that might seriously wound his uncle, as well as Rebecca Langstone and even Honora Purdy, herself. He would wait for a proper time to share it with Scrooge, but knew he mustn't wait too long because to do so made it all the more likely that Scrooge and more of his acquaintance would be caught up in the absurd chatter. In the meantime, Dick Wilkins caught up with Fred, who confirmed that he knew of the rumour and would see that his Uncle Scrooge was made aware.

The men employed at the counting house, including Scrooge, were all very loyal to each other and would not have taken kindly to the outlandish wildfire ignited by Honora Purdy's careless and wishful remarks. It must be assumed that anyone being included in the circle of whisperers would, in his or her heart, recognize the absurdity of the claim, and of the embellishments that had attached themselves with each sharing of the matter. Still, unfounded prattle has a pull much like gravity. It is strong and can only be resisted by an equally determined and more powerful force.

While the firestorm regarding Scrooge and Honora Purdy raged on, scorching the ears of anyone who would listen, all was calm within the walls of the counting house. Scrooge's life was in good stead and he was carrying on his business as usual. At least once a day Scrooge was thankful for the fact that the men who worked there got on so well.

Scrooge was particularly pleased with his nephew and partner Fred, although he did seem to be a bit out of sorts since returning from the Exchange. It was nothing Scrooge could put his finger on, but there was definitely a change in Fred's usual mood. He seemed . . . occupied elsewhere, as if a weight had settled on his shoulders and was requiring his complete attention. Once, Scrooge asked if everything was as it should be, and although it took an instant for Fred to realize his uncle had addressed him, he simply said, "Oh, no. I'm sure everything is fine."

"No" was a negative answer to the question, and Fred's inclusion of, "I'm sure" in his reply told Scrooge that there was, in fact, something bothering him, but it would not do to pry. Scrooge would bide his time and wait for a better opportunity to enquire. He might even speak with Fred's dear wife, Catherine, although he did not want to alarm her unnecessarily. No. Better to wait it out. Fred would come forward with any problems at some point in time. He always had.

Scrooge was the last man to leave the counting house that night, and he was walking alone down a darkened passage he often used as a short-cut to home when he sensed he was being followed. He stopped, heard nothing, and continued.

There it was again. The sound of footsteps tended to match his own, which was generally not the case unless two were walking together. When not in the company of another pedestrian, a person's footsteps tended to match the rhythm of his own thoughts, rather than another's stride. This was definitely someone walking "with" Scrooge, but staying back several yards, which surely indicated a sinister or, at best, a secretive intent.

To further test his senses Scrooge slowed his gait, then picked it up, and the footsteps' tempo rose and fell with his own. Curious rather than fearful, he turned the next corner and quickly slid into a smaller passageway. He stood still in the shadows, hoping to get a glimpse of whoever was following him as he went by. He heard nothing for several minutes, and when the footsteps resumed, they were headed in the other direction, growing more and more faint until they finally died. Scrooge looked both ways in the outer passage and, seeing no one, continued home.

Minutes later Scrooge stood before his front door, fiddling with his key. He heard no noises, so he had no warning prior to being struck soundly on the back of his head, which sent him to his knees. As he attempted to gain his footing another violent blow was delivered, rendering him senseless, and he was engulfed in total blackness. He lay in a heap on his front doorstep, resembling discarded clothing intended for the ragman.

It was later that night when Scrooge awoke in his own bed. Pain roared in his head and he was somewhat dizzy, but he could make out his nephew; his housekeeper, Mrs. Dilber; and his physician, Doctor Easton, hovering over him.

"Oh, my, Mr. Scrooge, 'ow you did give us a start, 'n that's fer certain!" cried Mrs. Dilber as she wrung her hands. "We was that afraid fer your life!"

Dr. Easton interrupted what may have become a longer dissertation of a loyal housekeeper's fears by explaining, "No, I did not expect you to die, my good man, but I do expect you to have a gruesome headache for a day or two."

Bending over his bag, the Doctor added, "I've had to suture a cut caused by the more serious of the two blows you received, but I expect it to heal nicely, if you do not bother it." Looking at Fred, he nodded and took his departure by saying, "I'll check on the patient tomorrow, but you know where to reach me, if need be."

Fred then gave Mrs. Dilber permission to return to her bed by saying, "Thank you, Mrs. Dilber. I don't think we'll need you further tonight, and Ollie will be wondering what's become of you." Unwilling to leave her employer just yet, she nevertheless obeyed the directive while delivering several comments regarding his care as she quietly closed the door.

"Now, Uncle," said Fred, drawing his chair closer to the bed. "I came to speak to you tonight and found you in a pile on your doorstep. Please tell me what happened."

"My boy, I wish I knew. I most likely know less than you, since you have observed my wounds, and I can only feel them." Scrooge attempted to move, but was prevented by the pain, so he settled back with a resigned sigh and added, "It did seem I was being followed after I left the counting house, but whoever it was gave up the idea when I ducked into a smaller alley and waited for him to pass by. Instead, he went in the opposite direction.

Naturally I continued on my way, but as I was unlocking my door, someone, presumably my pursuer, coshed me from behind." Touching his fingers to his wounds, he winced and gave up the exploration.

Fred was truly in a quandary now. With his uncle wounded and abed, having suffered violent injury, it was not a good time to tell him that the entire population of London thought him betrothed to Honora Purdy. His headache would be bad enough without adding such an idea to the mix! However, there was something else he must address.

"Uncle, I came here tonight to speak with you about a matter than can now wait – but this cannot." As he spoke, Fred retrieved a somewhat worn sheet of paper from the bed table and presented it to Scrooge. "This was pinned to your coat when I found you." Scrooge held the missive before him, but could not quite make it out, so he handed it back to Fred, saying, "My vision is somewhat blurry nephew. Please read me the contents."

"It says, in a rather child-like scrawl, which could be a disguise, '*I do not desire your life at this time. I mean to make you suffer first.*'"

CHAPTER FOUR

The Nuisance of Rumours

As she entered her carriage Mrs. Sotherton instructed her driver, "Quickly, Thompson! To Mrs. Langstone's residence. Hurry!" Her haste was genuine and was founded in what she had learned within the past half hour while paying a call. Two others were in attendance, and the conversation had naturally turned to bits of the most recent and fascinating gossip, which meant that Mrs. Sotherton was made aware of the rumour concerning Scrooge and Mrs. Purdy. She did not want to fan the fire, but she did ask enough questions to be convinced that it was a report that was being widely circulated and was emphatic in its insistence the two were to marry soon.

After managing to politely take her leave, Mrs. Sotherton was now careening through the streets to her daughter's home, to inform and arm her against the account. She prayed Rebecca had not yet been told, and that their social acquaintances had had the good grace to spare her the information.

A servant answered the door and Mrs. Sotherton dashed to the morning room, where she found her daughter. Rebecca's expression was nothing out of the ordinary, which gave her mother some small relief, even though it now meant that she would be the one to break the news to her.

"Good morning, Mother. It is wonderful to see you, but what brings you here in such a huff?" Mrs. Sotherton was unaware that she had entered on the run and was even puffing, but it was small wonder. Seating herself, she gasped and said, "Oh! My dear! It is insupportable, but I have news. No, I have gossip. Untrue, malicious twaddle those horrid busy-bodies are repeating and expanding, even as we speak!"

Rebecca was surprised to see her mother in such a state since Mrs. Sotherton was a formidable rock on which many people relied. She ruled her arena of society with a kid-gloved iron hand and was a pillar of strength who was known to be steady and composed. Yet, here she was, actually flapping her hands in an agitated effort to fan herself.

Rebecca was confused as to what on earth may have brought on such a change in her mother. Sitting down across from her, she asked, as calmly as possible, "Mother, would you like something to drink? Would that help?"

"Oh, bless me, no. Thank you, but I have already washed down too many untruths this morning with an abundance of tea, and I could not face another cup!" She paused, then conceded, "However, a few sips of sherry or brandy would be helpful." She continued to fan herself and let out a heavy sigh.

Within minutes Rebecca handed Mrs. Sotherton a small glass of sherry and stood over her as she took two sips, closed her eyes, took a deep breath and ordered her daughter, "Sit down, please do! Tsk, tsk. You may need to be seated when I share my information." Mrs. Langstone tilted her head to one side as her mother, still in an uncharacteristic dither, blurted, "People are saying that Ebenezer Scrooge and Honora Purdy are to marry!" There. She knew she had been far too blunt, but the plain fact of it needed to be exposed, for Rebecca's sake. At least she hoped so. Almost involuntarily, she took another gulp of sherry.

Rebecca's spine straightened and her face paled. She could only stare at her mother in disbelief. "But how can they be saying that, Mother? I realize Ebenezer and I have made no hard and fast commitment, but we do have an understanding, unless I have totally misread our situation. Why would they be saying such a thing?"

Seeking a kind way to ask her mother what she was truly thinking, Mrs. Langstone continued, "And why Honora Purdy?" A second later she repeated, *"Honora Purdy?* Why, I have never seen him exchange more than two sentences with the woman, and he always seemed anxious to be relieved of her company. Unless, of course, it was an act with design."

"I do not know how or why it should be the very unusual Mrs. Purdy," replied Mrs. Sotherton, "and I was too anxious to remove myself from their company to ask that question. They would not have known, at any rate, since I am certain the story is many times removed from its source. It now has a will of its own that does not require any amount of proven fact in order to keep moving. To enquire regarding any detail at this point is to invite more fabrication." She took a smaller sip of the sherry, cleared her throat and suggested, "There is, of course, a way to clear this up." Setting the glass on a table, she said, "You could ask Ebenezer himself."

Rebecca shook her head. "I cannot believe that Ebenezer has been deceitful. Perhaps the gossip is untrue, and he is trying to protect me until he can find a way to put an end to the talk. Or is it true and he simply does not know how to approach me with the matter?" She tugged one hand with the other and continued to take steps in each direction.

"If he wouldn't want me to know, why would he allow others to know?" An idea struck and she said, "Or did Honora herself reveal it? And what if it is not true and he is not aware of the story? Do I want to tell him? Or am I not the best person to do so?" Again, she sat, not knowing what else to do. She continued to give voice to her thoughts while her mother allowed it.

"My impression has always been that Ebenezer does not care for Mrs. Purdy, although he is too much of a gentleman to make rude or unfeeling remarks. I simply cannot believe that he has toyed with my feelings as a cover up for a liaison with Mrs. Purdy. I know he is a better man than that, as do you!"

At some point in their exchange mother and daughter agreed that the rumour would be proven untrue were no marriage to take place, but how long would that take? Barring an immediate diversion, such as another Great Fire of London, the gossipmongers could stay with this topic for weeks!

As she departed, Mrs. Sotherton shook her index finger and said, with more assurance than she felt, "You and I will think on this and we will come up with a way to approach the situation." Patting her daughter's shoulder, she used soothing tones. "Do not worry. I believe Ebenezer loves you and no one else." Then she wrapped her daughter in her arms, lowered her voice and promised, "All will be well."

Rebecca certainly prayed so, but at this moment she was more shaken than her mother realized.

While Mrs. Sotherton and Rebecca Langstone fretted over Scrooge's alleged betrothal, Fred arrived at the counting house after spending much of the morning with Scrooge. His entrance was unusual since he did not wear a smile nor give a cheerful greeting, and it did not go unnoticed. Once he had settled into his chair, Cratchit and Homer both approached him, having obviously conferred with each other. Cratchit spoke.

"Mr. Symons, we couldn't help but notice you seem somewhat less than your usual chipper self, Sir. Without putting our noses where they don't belong, is there anything we can do? And where, pray tell, is Mr. Scrooge today?"

There was so much information to relay that Fred could not decide what to share, or where to begin. There was no fear in sharing it all with Cratchit and Homer because, other than his wife and uncle, he trusted no one more than these two. Hadn't they always come through in a pinch?

"Men, there are evil winds blowing around Mr. Scrooge, and I am convinced that we must be alert and on guard, for his sake." They had never seen such an expression on his face, and they knew that what he was about to tell them was deadly serious. Having been asked to sit, they did so, and stared intently as he shared the current crises Scrooge was facing.

Cratchit and Homer were appalled at the rumour regarding Mrs. Purdy, although neither was acquainted with the woman, but their simple disbelief turned to genuine fear when they learned of the violent attack on Scrooge and the threatening note which he had received in such an injurious manner.

Fred appreciated the men's attitude and knew they meant well, but at this point he was unsure of what, if anything, they could do, barring alerting the City of London police. He made the suggestion but was met with definite refusals, at least for the time being. Cratchit insisted they must first put their heads together and make some sort of sense of what was occurring. Then they could proceed with clear minds.

Against Dr. Easton's wishes, Scrooge insisted on returning to business the next day. He did not want to neglect his duties, and he also wished to speak with the men about how to proceed in the face of the threat on his life. Many clients stopped in however, and there were a great many transactions, which meant that by mid-afternoon they had not yet had the opportunity to discuss anything other than business.

At precisely 3:00 of the clock, George Purtell-Smythe, a friendly acquaintance of Scrooge's, and Rebecca Langstone's first cousin, entered the offices of Scrooge and Symons. He announced to Homer that he was there to see Scrooge, and him only. Once seated before Scrooge's desk he came directly to the point.

"Now, see here friend," he spouted. "I know a man's actions are his own, but when he has friends he must expect them to put in a word here and there when they believe he is headed in the wrong direction." Scrooge was not responding because he was completely baffled with regard to whatever it was Purtell-Smythe was referring. Was he trying to warn Scrooge not to walk down dark alleys?

Purtell-Smythe's countenance was serious – almost angry. "Scrooge, my man, I stopped by to tell you to take heed. I'll do what no one else will have the courage to say to your face." He leaned forward, slapped Scrooge's desk and cried, "I am imploring you not to marry Honora Purdy!" Without noticing the confusion on his friend's face, Purtell-Smythe continued, giving a dismissive wave as he did so. "Oh, she's a good enough sort, but not for you, my friend – not for you."

Scrooge did not reply immediately, so Purtell-Smythe took the opportunity to also ask, "And what have you done with the lovely Rebecca Langstone, eh? Why on earth would you *ever* forfeit *her* attentions?" He shook his head disgustedly. Although he did not say so, Purtell-Smythe had at least had the good sense not to report the rumour to Rebecca.

Scrooge was leaning back in his chair, unable to comprehend what he had just heard, so he simply said, "I am not marrying Honora Purdy. Believe me, my friend, the thought never entered my mind!" Purtell-Smythe was caught off guard with such an absolute denial, so naturally he didn't believe it. Why, it was contrary to common gossip. Purtell-Smythe responded with obvious surprise, "But, my dear man. Why deny it? Everyone *knows*!"

It was true that now everyone did know, since Scrooge himself had finally been included in the circle of chatter. After Purtell-Smythe departed, still shaking his head over Scrooge's inability to understand that he must not marry Honora Purdy, Scrooge marched into Fred's office and demanded to know if this was truly a tale that was being bandied about by "everyone."

Fred had no good answer and replied, instead, by saying, "Uncle, I heard it yesterday and came to your home to tell you about it, but I found you lying on your front stoop with a threatening note pinned to your waistcoat. I think you can see how the gossip about Mrs. Purdy was suddenly of lesser importance."

"I beg your pardon, my dear nephew, but it is of the utmost importance to me, even though I appreciate your desire not to increase my pain at the time. How on earth could such a story ever be hatched? Imagine! *Honora Purdy*! Why, I can barely tolerate the woman when she is thirty feet from me in a social setting, much less in a state of matrimony!" He was in such turmoil that he could not control his tongue and ended by adding what he believed to explain everything – "She *snorts*!" It fell to Fred to calm his uncle, which he somehow managed to do by reminding him that the rumour was simply that, and that it meant nothing in terms of changing Scrooge's life or obligating him to the woman in any way. He then suggested that they all discuss the matters at hand as soon as there was some relief in the day's activities. That had always proved beneficial, and Scrooge readily agreed that he was definitely in need of good counsel!

CHAPTER FIVE

An Accusation of Past Sins

A t 4:30 of the clock that afternoon the men of the counting house finally gathered to confer. Dick Wilkins had also been summoned since he could always be counted on to give loyal and valuable support. He was also their best source of information regarding the activities in Town.

Once they had reviewed the known facts of the gossip surrounding Scrooge, and the violence he had suffered at his own front door, Scrooge asked, "Alright men. What do we know? Perhaps that is where we should begin."

Cratchit put the question that was on his mind. "I cannot help but wonder if the two – the rumour and the attack – are somehow connected."

"I have been considering the same thing," agreed Fred, "but I cannot see how a silly rumour could be tied to being bashed on the head by an unknown person who is seeking revenge, for that is obviously what it is, given the contents of the note. Did he not say, 'I do not require your life *at this time*?'"

The men nodded in unison, realizing the seriousness of what had been scribbled on the note. The intimation was that Scrooge was meant to suffer before being taken out of this world altogether.

It was Scrooge himself who suggested the attack upon his person could perhaps be an isolated act and would not reoccur. "The note may be only the ramblings of an unbalanced person and mean nothing. Perhaps we should look to see if the blackguard makes another attempt. If not, I believe we can relax a bit."

That was perhaps going too far for the rest of the group, who wanted to catch the attacker as quickly as possible, regardless of whether or not he repeated his behavior. He had, after all, nearly killed Scrooge once and threatened his life at some future time!

Cratchit, who was known for his sensible approach to matters, spoke for each man when he insisted, "I, for one, am not willing to ignore such a dastardly attack on Mr. Scrooge, and I believe we should do all that we can to bring the fellow to justice."

Looking first at Homer, then at each of the others, he suggested, "Perhaps we can compromise with our employer and do as he says. We can wait for our miscreant to make another move, but we must do so with a solid plan. I suggest, therefore, that you, Mr. Symons, Mr. Wilkins, Homer, and I take our turns following Mr. Scrooge home of an evening. If we accompanied him, our fellow would, of course, not make a move, but if we follow at a distance, we may be able to protect Mr. Scrooge and apprehend the rogue if he does make another attempt."

Scrooge was horrified at the idea of having keepers, and he remained adamant that he was not in need of being guarded. He did not see the expressions the men shared behind his back, which said otherwise. In fact, their glances were a silent agreement to the plan, and they would proceed accordingly, regardless of his protests.

So, the plan was adopted without Scrooge's permission and in spite of his refusal. Fred, Cratchit, Homer and Dick Wilkins would act as Scrooge's "protectors." However, they were careful not to use that particular word at any time, lest they give themselves away and he take offense. They spoke only in terms of a common effort between Scrooge and themselves to apprehend a criminal, carefully omitting the bit about trailing Scrooge as he made his way home.

Prior to ending their meeting, Dick Wilkins made a suggestion that agreed with the conclusion drawn by Fred, Cratchit and Homer the previous day. "I feel strongly that we should not be hasty in bringing the police in on this matter." He held up his hand as he said, "I have a great deal of respect for Constable Rollo Norris, but I am convinced that we can embark on a successful investigation without abdicating the handling of the matter to the local constabulary." To further argue his point he added, "Besides that, we have no real clues as to the attacker's identity or his specific motive." The others concurred and the police were, for the time being, barred from any reports.

With regard to the gossip of Scrooge's impending nuptials with Honora Purdy, it was also agreed that the less said, the better. Hopefully the thing would quickly be crushed under its own weight and if any of them was asked to comment, they would simply state that it was a false report. If need be, they would also remind others that they were in a position to know!

At the time they did not consider the fact that any denials would generally fall on deaf ears. Gossips, and those who encourage them, usually choose to believe the rumour, no matter how unlikely it might be, over any rebuttal by the person in question.

That night Dick Wilkins lingered around a nearby corner for Scrooge to take his leave of the office. He then followed him at a goodly distance, ensuring that he was not interfered with. Once Scrooge was safely inside his front door, Wilkins made his own way home, relieved and yet disappointed that the attacker had not shown himself.

Some days passed with no discernable interference from busy-bodies or ruffians, which gave Scrooge and his men a chance to return to their routine and almost forget the trials of the previous week.

This particular morning was sunny, which resulted in a brightening of the interior of the counting house. That was due, in part, to the fact that the windowpanes were now kept clean, and dust motes that tended to float in the sun's rays were also kept at a minimum by the hired cleaner. It was one of those details that neither Scrooge nor Marley would have considered necessary years ago since they were not interested in the sunlight at that time, and they certainly did not care to connect with anything outside the walls of their money-making enterprise. In those days, seeing through windows was an unwelcome nuisance and the glass was best left covered in as much soot as possible.

Today's warm brightness lightened the mood of everyone and proved the adage that things truly do look better in the morning. That was, until Homer stood before Scrooge's desk, holding a missive. He seemed rattled.

"Please excuse the interruption Sir, but I have been going through the morning post and . . . well . . . I came across this."

"What is it Homer? Is someone closing an account? That isn't the end of everything, you know. It happens." Homer shook his head and reluctantly handed him a letter with a broken seal addressed to Scrooge, which Scrooge quickly unfolded. It read, "*You cannot escape the sins of your past.*" He looked up at Homer, who was clearly unsettled, and remarked, "Well son, it looks as if our miscreant has not given up the chase, after all." As he refolded the letter he said, "Homer, please get Cratchit and Mr. Symons in here now. We need to discuss this."

Both men appeared quickly and Cratchit had already begun to apply his thinking to the problem. Scrooge could see it in his expression. He bid them all to sit and he asked Cratchit to state what was on his mind.

Cratchit shifted forward in his chair. "It seems to me that we now have two clues in this matter. The first was the reference to wanting to make you 'suffer' before doing you harm. I believe that points to a grudge this person holds for some injury he believes you have perpetrated at some point in time. The second validates that supposition by saying you must pay for the 'sins of your past,' which indicates an earlier connection to you.

"Unfortunately, we do not know if his grievance is real or imagined, but it could even be a combination of the two. You may have had a business dealing that did not go well for him and in his disillusionment he allowed his imagination to twist and magnify it beyond the truth of the matter. Add to that what may be a propensity to blame others, and you may have a man who hates beyond reason and feels compelled to act on it." Homer and Fred nodded in agreement.

Scrooge smiled. "My dear Cratchit, you never disappoint me, and I believe you are on to something." He did not say so, but he was stung to the heart because he knew Cratchit spoke the unvarnished truth. Once again, his greedy past was being thrust into the present day, and he was reminded that there was so much that could never be undone. He hated the man he had been for so many years and he could not find fault with others who continued to despise him.

It would be unfair to say that Scrooge had never had a conscience. It was just that it had been seared during the years when his greed and selfishness grew. Then, following the visits of those dogged spirits on Christmas Eve 1843, his renewal included a totally refreshed conscience, albeit one that was unable to make reparations to all he had injured. Many of his transgressions occurred in his youth and were beyond record, either on paper or in his memory. Still, in his initial determination to honor Christmas in his heart and to try to keep it all the year, Scrooge had directed Cratchit and Homer to revisit old records in order to find those who had been unfairly used by Scrooge and Marley, and to make reparations.

There was one unexpected result of that effort. Scrooge had made a great deal of money during those earlier decades, but records proved that his shrewdness had also made a great deal of money for his clients. Satisfied investors sent new customers his way, and the business was extremely successful. In fact, Cratchit and Homer found only a few individuals who had been outright ruined by Scrooge and Marley. When discovered, each one, or his heir, was recompensed, with interest, whenever possible. But it seemed he had missed someone – someone who was now determined to take his revenge by repaying ruination with violence.

"Ahem." It was Homer who interrupted Scrooge's thoughts. "Perhaps we could once again study our records for a client who had bad luck or felt he was mistreated, in the chance that we missed him the first time around." Then, as an idea occurred to him, Homer continued.

"I beg your pardon, but I suppose it is also possible that this is not connected to business, at all. Perhaps someone felt he was dealt a different sort of injury?" It was possible, of course, but the four of them decided it was highly unlikely since Scrooge's life prior to 1843 consisted only of business, and he had essentially no social contacts at all, other than Marley.

CHAPTER SIX

Another Walk Home

That night it was HomEr's turn to follow Scrooge home. Scrooge still had no idea that Fred and the other men were carrying out such a thing simply because they were his friends. Of course, he would have been appreciative, but discomfited, to think he was in need of protective covering. In fact, *he* did not think he was in need of such oversight at all, but he could not have borne the fact that *they* believed he needed it. It was perhaps that small measure of pride that kept him from simply hiring a cab to take him home, rather than making his way through the dim streets after nightfall.

Since having his scalp ripped apart by a faceless enemy, Scrooge had varied his route home each night. He had also got into the habit of occasionally glancing over his shoulder, even when he did not hear footsteps or sense another pedestrian in the area.

Tonight, it was a challenge for Homer to keep Scrooge in sight, particularly since he seemed to have stepped up the pace of his usual stroll home. While keeping him at least partially in view, some blocks from Scrooge's destination Homer noticed a dark figure step between himself and Scrooge, keeping to the shadows. The man's movements were furtive, and he was so intent on his prey that he did not notice that he was, himself, being followed by Homer.

Homer knew that every moment he delayed, the danger to Scrooge was increased, so he made his move just as Scrooge was nearing the far end of the passage where the way would again be lit by an occasional gas lamp. Homer was tall, but more lean than stocky, which gave him both an advantage and a disadvantage. He could move swiftly, which he did, but when he leapt on the man, he did not have the weight to hold him down. Instead, he found himself clutching the man's neck and riding his back as if it were a bucking pony.

Scrooge was too far ahead to hear the grunts and snarls made by both men and was even further away when Homer began pummeling the man's head and face with his right fist. The noises from both men were beginning to resemble those of a Puffing Billy locomotive, but Scrooge remained ignorant of the fisticuffs, even though he was the cause of it all.

"Ow!" the man yelled before he managed to slam Homer against a brick wall, knocking some wind from his lungs. "Oof!" was all Homer could manage, but he rose quickly enough that he was able to pursue the man and make a leap. He landed near the ground, clutching the man's shins with both arms, which brought him down with another yelp of pain.

The two exchanged furious blows until the villain managed to get to his feet and kick Homer in the ribs before Homer could rise from the cobblestones. As the toe of the man's boot made contact with Homer's ribs, he slid on the damp stones, lost his balance and fell hard onto his left ankle. He hoisted himself up but was limping terribly as he fled the way he had come.

Homer got to his knees and slowly managed to stand, even though he had received enough of a blow that he was finding it difficult to do so. He was unable to pursue the fellow, which meant he had failed in part of his mission, but what worried him more was how he could hide his obvious injury from Mr. Scrooge!

Scrooge's would-be attacker was also having difficulty making his way back, but he would bear any amount of pain rather than stop and perhaps be apprehended. He must protect his identity. Anonymity was a large part of his power over Scrooge and he planned to maintain it for some time, just to keep the old miser disquieted. Yet, he would now need to wait a bit before making another move on the streets since his ability to walk or run had been curtailed, and someone evidently knew what he was about.

In addition, he did not know who had attacked him. He feared it may have been a constable, which meant he must be very careful, or even forego his plan altogether, but he was not of a mind to do that. Never! He would not give up the revenge he had planned. His father's blood demanded it.

Scrooge reached his home safely and without any inkling of the commotion that had transpired in his wake, leaving two men with scrapes, bruises and possibly cracked bones. His house was welcoming, and Scrooge's cook, Mrs. Haiter, earlier prepared a nice supper for him, which Mrs. Dilber left by the fire in his room. He smiled as he thought on how mistaken the men had been concerning his safety, and he was of a mind to tell them so on the morrow.

Yes, it seemed to him that the attack he had suffered was most likely a one-time occurrence with myriad possible explanations, most of which did not include a true threat to his well-being. Since he no longer felt a need to thumb his nose at fear in order to prove his mettle, he would perhaps forego walking in the dark and take a cab home tomorrow night.

It was after Scrooge crawled under his bedcovers and had drifted near to sleep that Marley appeared. Scrooge was aroused by the sense of being observed since Marley had long since ceased making himself known by moaning, "Scroooooooge!" In fact, it had been Scrooge who suggested to the apparition that it was no longer necessary to do so. These days he was never surprised to see Marley manifest himself since they had met so many times during the past three years, and their conversations now were just relaxed exchanges, for the most part.

Scrooge noticed several months ago that he was not the only one who had changed. Marley was more a friend now than simply his old money-grubbing partner. In fact, Marley seemed more at ease. More . . . friendly. He also appeared somewhat luminous, which gave off a very pleasant radiance to the space, and many of his chains had disappeared. His frown and the scowl were gone, and he even laughed once or twice. Scrooge liked this newer Marley much better than his old partner, who was still definitely quite dead.

Tonight, Marley was not of a mind to converse. He simply said, "Scrooge, you have been reawakened to life for the third year now, but you spent decades living for only the amount of silver you could palm." His essence floated several feet closer to Scrooge before he finished with, "It takes time to repair damage, but you have made reparations where possible, and that is all that is required. Do not be bullied by the misconceptions of others."

Before Scrooge could respond or ask a question, Marley faded, resembling a slow whirlwind as he disappeared. Once again Scrooge was left sitting up in bed, dissatisfied with the exchange, and staring at an empty room. Whereas Scrooge applauded Marley's improved character, he sometimes wished he could grab him by his transparent shoulders and shake a few more manners into him.

Several minutes later Scrooge was near to sleeping when he bolted upright, his heart in his throat. *Rebecca!! Oh, blast! I wonder if she has been told that I am betrothed to Honora Purdy! Dear Lord, don't let it be so.* The thought so upset him that sleep was now impossible. Instead, he paced his bedroom floor for more than an hour before deciding he must visit her as soon as possible on the morrow. He must at least attempt to forestall any damage to their understanding, which had been so long in coming and was so precious to him.

CHAPTER SEVEN

In His Own Defense

It was far too early to make a call, but Scrooge must see Rebecca Langstone as soon as possible, to forestall any untruths she may believe with regard to him and Honora Purdy. He would admit, but only to himself, that he felt just a bit misused. Several months ago, hadn't he had to fend off the bold advances of that actress whose behavior came near to causing a very serious breach between Rebecca and himself? And now he was the subject of falsehoods that were being spread throughout the whole of London, which again threatened to separate him from Rebecca! Oh, it really was too much. His experience as a simple miser had not prepared him for these sorts of difficulties.

These were the days he would just as soon quit society altogether, retire to the counting house and once again bury himself in contracts and numbers. There, he could enjoy the company of his trusted men and carry on an honest business without having to deal with the silliness that seemed to be part and parcel of a greater society. But no, if he were honest, it wasn't his social connections that he wanted to quit, since he had many dear friends within that circle. It was, instead, the problems that seemed to arise whenever more than five human beings worked, played or lived within shouting distance of each other!

He was afraid. How would Rebecca react to such a rumour? Would she seriously believe he could do such a thing? She must know his opinion of Mrs. Purdy, and she surely understood his feelings regarding herself. Yet, it would be presumptuous to expect her to endure the embarrassment she might well be suffering when she could easily avoid it by severing her ties to him altogether.

Scrooge ruminated on the situation as the cab rumbled and jostled its way to her house on Russell Square. *If she has heard the rumour and should be upset, how will I approach the matter? What if she has not heard the rumour? I pray God she has not, but if that is the case, then I must be the one to tell her. How can I articulate that the man who cares for her is being said to have asked another far less suitable woman to wed him?*

By the time Scrooge reached Mrs. Langstone's front door he was in terrible turmoil. Not only was his brain in a muddle, he was now uncertain as to why he was calling on her at all, particularly at this indecent hour of the morning and with no plan of what to say! In addition, his head was aching from where that wretched stranger had had the temerity to hammer it open.

Mrs. Langstone was having her breakfast when Scrooge was announced, but she was pleased to see him, no matter the hour. She was somewhat confused regarding the current situation and was unsure of what to say to him, but he was so dear to her that she would never turn him away. Instead, she invited him to sit and share her meal. He sat, but he declined any food because his stomach was in turmoil. He did accept a cup of coffee, however.

"My dear Rebecca," he began, but he did not know how to proceed. All he could do was stammer, saying nothing. The expression on his face was one of abject misery for fear of hurting her or, God forbid, losing her affection altogether, and it was enough to twist his tongue into a figure of eight knot.

Mrs. Langstone could see his misery, but she did not understand. Was it guilt? Fear, perhaps? She recalled that bold-faced actress of the past year and would not repeat her error of making the same assumptions she made in that case. However, was this a pattern? Would being attached to Ebenezer Scrooge mean that there would always be questions about other women? That, she could not bear. Yet, in her heart, she knew him to be true.

"Ebenezer, I am always pleased to see you, but what brings you here this morning?" She sounded calm, but such was not the case. Her hands were visibly shaking, so she attempted to keep them out of sight. Somehow, she managed to pour him a cup of coffee without knocking the entire service to pieces.

Taking the cup and saucer, Scrooge began. "Dearest," he mumbled, "there is so much I must say, and yet I am uncertain of how to go about it." He took a drink, looked at her and realized he still did not know if she had heard the rumour. Perhaps it was best to assume she had not.

"I have heard a report that I find extremely upsetting, and although I do not wish to pass my misery on to you, I cannot leave you ignorant of what I consider a preposterous notion." She folded her hands in her lap and attempted to manage a natural expression. "Go on," she said.

Scrooge ventured to enquire, "My dear, have you been made aware of a certain rumour concerning myself?" Here he began to stumble.

"I refer to a rumour that includes another . . . what I mean to say is, it is a piece of absurdity that . . ." He could not proceed and opted, instead, to take a drink of coffee, even though he did not particularly want any.

Mrs. Langstone did not blame him, but she decided not to make it easy for him. She simply assumed a pleasant expression and said nothing. It was very unlike her, and she could not have explained her behavior. It must be the result of confusion and unease that only this man could engender. It was, of course, due to her strong attachment to him, but the strength of her fondness for him allowed for equally strong, yet unpleasant, sentiments when things went amiss. She was currently experiencing the latter.

"Ebenezer, are you struggling to relate a thing over which you have no control, or are you endeavoring to make a confession? There is a great deal of difference between the two, at least as far as you and I are concerned."

Scrooge took another long gulp of his coffee, swallowed and almost barked, "Of course it is not a confession, my dear girl!" Realizing that his tone of voice did not match his fondness for her, he said, as calmly as possible, "It is a rumour I heard of late which concerns me and Honora Purdy, of all people. It is bizarre in content and whoever came up with such an idea must be totally unhinged!"

Mrs. Langstone felt a pang of pity for this man for whom she cared so much, and she decided to assist him. "Are you telling me that you would never propose marriage to Mrs. Purdy? Is that it?"

So, she knew. She knew all along! Scrooge could not blame her for toying with him a little, since he imagined she must have suffered upon hearing the report, even though she must know that all of his affection was hers to possess. Still, he must say so. He took her hand, which was no longer shaking, and said, "Dearest, surely you know my heart is yours, and it will never be offered to anyone else. I cannot fathom who in his right mind would ignite such a rumour, but perhaps therein lies the answer. Whoever dared to utter such a thing must have been absolutely out of his mind!"

As with Julian Thorne and Fred Symons several days earlier, Scrooge's last comment brought on a smile from Mrs. Langstone which turned into a giggle, then a chuckle from Scrooge that quickly developed into full-blown contagious laughter. He leaned back in his chair with a roar while Mrs. Langstone doubled over, her face buried in her serviette. Poor Mrs. Purdy – the brunt of so much fun, but they were helpless in their mirth.

Finally, Mrs. Langstone asked, "But what are we to do, Ebenezer? How are we to deal with this lie?"

Still wiping his eyes, Scrooge thought a moment and suggested, "We are essentially helpless to disprove the rumour at this point, but it will die when no marriage between me and Mrs. Purdy takes place. I suspect our best move is to carry on as usual and show that nothing has changed between you and me."

Mrs. Langstone heartily agreed. After both confessed their guilt for laughing so heartily at Mrs. Purdy's expense, they promised that neither would ever reveal that particular unkindness to anyone else. Then they settled back as she ordered fresh coffee and a decent breakfast for the man whose heart still belonged to her.

CHAPTER EIGHT

New Friends Well Met

Every now and then Scrooge enjoyed reading a good book. It was a pastime he could pursue anywhere, provided, of course, that he remembered to tuck his current choice into a pocket as he left the house. Lately, however, he tended to do most of his reading at night, prior to falling asleep. It turned out that some books were better than warm milk, to make one's eyelids heavy.

Because of his interest in reading, Scrooge was ever on the lookout for a new title that might tempt him to lay out a few shillings for it. There were several shops that Scrooge perused regularly, and today he happened upon one of those. It sported a bookstall on the street, under an awning, which made it easy to choose one and glance at the first few pages.

On occasion, Scrooge could make up his mind within two sentences. Others were difficult to put down. Today he had finished almost half of the entire first chapter without realizing it and was happily unaware of his surroundings. Because of his reverie, he backed into another gentleman who was reaching for a book.

"Oh! I beg your pardon," said Scrooge before giving way to the man. The fellow looked over his glasses, paused and then cried, Why, I do declare it is Mr. Scrooge of Newman's Court, is it not?"

Scrooge was doing his best to place the man as he accepted his hand in a firm shake. Before he could reply, the man continued.

"Brownlow. Mr. Brownlow, but you may not recall the name or the face, although I do not believe I have changed so very much since our last meeting." Scrooge was struggling to recall that encounter when Brownlow explained.

"I happened into your offices several years ago for advice on an investment I was considering. A friend recommended you, and I found you to be exactly as he said. You were very knowledgeable in business and gave me specific advice. In short, you suggested I spit in the eye of the fly-by-night who was offering the deal! Ha-ha! I did so and have been forever in your debt since those who stuck with him ended up losing a great deal of money!"

Scrooge now recalled the man, and the meeting, and was about to say so when Brownlow commented, "Mr. Scrooge, I hope I am not rude when I say – and I mean to be complimentary – you seem altered in some way. Your countenance is changed from the man I met back then. I declare, most people would have aged in the interim, but you seem to have grown younger! Even happier, if I may say so." Brownlow realized he had not given Scrooge the opportunity to speak, so he took a breath long enough to allow Scrooge to reply.

"Mr. Brownlow, it is a pleasure to see you again, and I assure you I am delighted that you noticed a change in me. I am, in fact, a very different man from the one you met so many years ago. I am no longer the greedy miser I once was, and I have come to appreciate my fellow man, as well as the gift of life, in general."

"Well, and good," remarked Brownlow, nodding his head. "However, I trust you did not do away with your business acumen when you discarded an unsound philosophy!" He laughed, and Scrooge smiled in agreement.

"Here now, what am I thinking!" said Brownlow as he turned to a handsome young man standing behind him. "You must meet my son, Oliver. Oliver Twist, as was. We are in Town for a visit from the country, where we live a quiet and very rewarding life. Since we both love books, here we are, seeking more tomes to add to our ever-expanding library! In fact, this is the very spot where I first met Oliver. He is adopted you see, but that is quite a long story and we've no time to go into it here."

Oliver removed his cap and gave a slight nod to Scrooge. He seemed a nice lad, perhaps seventeen or eighteen years old? Suddenly, Scrooge was inexplicably curious about their story and found he liked Brownlow and this polite young man very much. He would venture an invitation.

"Brownlow, I dine this evening with my nephew and his wife, and I am certain they would be delighted to include you both. She is always encouraging me to bring visitors to their home, so I will send her a note, and I will give you the time and direction. What say you? Would you be amenable to spending an evening with strangers? I assure you they will not be strangers within half of an hour's time!"

Mr. Brownlow and Oliver were pleased to accept the invitation and they looked forward to meeting Scrooge's family. Then they all parted, each with at least one or two books under his arm.

Catherine Symons was, in fact, delighted that Uncle Scrooge was bringing new visitors to dinner. She and Fred enjoyed good conversation with interesting and varied people. They preferred a somewhat relaxed and easy conversation that included every-one at the table – sometimes all at once! It was never quite pandemonium, but each person was definitely allowed to speak. Catherine and Fred had been to too many opulent dinner parties where the conversation was stilted and dispirited, and the only animation came when the ladies stood up to leave the table – many with a huge sigh of relief!

It was also a fact that Scrooge had no hostess, and entertaining was not always easy for him, so including him in many of their social events served them all quite well. It was true that Rebecca Langstone, as a widow, might act as hostess for Scrooge without being sanctioned, but she had only done so with close friends and family, and very seldom, at that.

Everyone's arrival at the Symons home was jovial. Fred and Catherine made their guests feel comfortable and not only welcome, but as a valued addition to the gathering. Catherine's sister Flora was also in attendance and being senior to Oliver by a year or two, she took him under her wing. Scrooge's statement that Mr. Brownlow and Oliver would feel at home within the space of half of an hour proved prophetic. They were, in fact, at ease within ten minutes.

Dinner was simple and served without fuss. First, an excellent cream of asparagus soup with freshly made bread, then roast beef with potatoes and vegetables prepared with butter, followed by a berry tart with vanilla cream.

Mr. and Mrs. Symons preferred to concentrate on the quality of the gathering, with good conversation, rather than only the food, itself, and tonight was a particular delight. Mr. Brownlow and Oliver shared topics of interest and asked relevant questions, even listening to the answers! At one point, Scrooge asked Mr. Brownlow about the fact that he and Oliver first met at the very bookstall where they had spoken that morning.

"Ah, yes," replied the gentleman, while Oliver nodded in agreement as he replaced his water glass. All but Scrooge seemed bewildered by this information, and Mr. Brownlow added, "Yes, Oliver is my son, but he is adopted." Looking fondly at Oliver, he asked, "Is that not so, my boy?"

"Yes," replied Oliver, "and I will be forever grateful." Sensing that the others were interested, he continued by saying, "You see, Mr. Brownlow, now my father, took a chance on me when he had every reason to believe I was a thief and a scoundrel."

"Oh! But why would he think that?" enquired Flora, horrified.

"About seven years ago I was 'taken in' by a group of pickpockets and burglars when I found myself alone and friendless. Before I fully understood the nature of the group, and the great wickedness of their leader, I was falsely accused and arrested for one of their crimes. Fortunately, I was rescued by Mr. Brownlow, but they later found me, kidnapped me and forced me, once again, back into their band for a time."

Mr. Brownlow interjected, "Although forced into evil situations, Oliver never became one of them, either in habit or in character." He paused, then said, "Through a series of incidents which would be inappropriate to relate in this company, Oliver eventually became my son."

The group was astonished but applauded the happy outcome of such a woeful tale. Flora returned the group to merriment when she innocently remarked to Oliver, "I think you are the most interesting person I have ever met, and I hope we will be great friends!"

When the meal ended, rather than divide the men and women, everyone retired to the drawing room for coffee and more conversation. Flora was asked to play the piano, which provided the perfect entertainment to end a successful evening.

One thing remained. Prior to taking his leave, Scrooge climbed the stairs and tip-toed into the nursery, where he stole a look at young Frederick Ebenezer Symons, or "Little Freddie," as he had been nicknamed by his family. The baby lay sleeping soundly, unaware of the heartfelt adoration of the man looking down on him. Scrooge thanked God for the little fellow and had already determined to do the best he could in place of the boy's grandfathers, who were no longer living. He was, after all, his great uncle, and could easily become a grandfather in all that mattered.

As Scrooge smiled on the boy, he recalled a painful comment once uttered by Mrs. Langstone as she held the precious infant. It was a simple thing, but heart-wrenching, and he never forgot it. She whispered, "You remind me so much of my dear Peter." It was said without discernable pain, but it made Scrooge want to weep since it testified of the loss of her young son so many years before. Since then, he and Catherine had encouraged her to visit the boy as often as possible. After all, the child's grand-mothers were also gone, so he needed Mrs. Langstone as much as he needed Scrooge – and they both needed him.

Scrooge and the other guests were parting from each other on the street when Scrooge leaned his head toward Mr. Brownlow to ask, "May I contact you again? I would like to hear more of Oliver's story, if you and he would be of a mind to share it."

"Of course, my dear man, of course!" said Mr. Brownlow. "Unfortunately, we leave tomorrow morning for home, but you are most welcome to visit us there. Come and stay as long as you like! I will send our direction to your offices."

"Thank you, Brownlow. I may do just that. I have good reason, I believe, for wanting to speak with you both." An idea had occurred to him during dinner and he was set on pursuing it. Truth be told, the idea had been brewing for two years and he believed he may have finally met someone who could assist. Oliver Twist might be able to provide helpful information, or at least offer some direction.

Once home, Scrooge allowed himself to ruminate on Oliver's story. He should have realized that his thoughts would somehow summon Marley, because he appeared within minutes, just as Scrooge was pulling on his nightcap. Scrooge was still stinging from Marley's most recent abrupt departure.

"Marley, old partner, do not dare to drop a comment and then disappear as if you fear I may ask a question. Naturally I want to ask questions after you speak, but you seem unwilling to accommodate me in that respect!" He was angry, even though Marley had not yet uttered a sound.

"I have observed," remarked Marley, "that you become indignant when you do not have answers and I do not simply hand them over to you." Tucking his thumbs through his few remaining chains as if they were pockets, he leaned back a bit and stared at Scrooge, shaking his head.

"You are correct, Marley. You seem to have answers and I would be much obliged if you would share them with me! Instead, you seem to delight in dangling a piece of the puzzle before me, then flying off to wherever it is you go, leaving me to solve the thing." "And haven't you generally done so?" asked Marley. "And haven't I been of some help?"

"Yes, I have. And yes, you have." Scrooge crossed his arms on his chest. "Humph." That was all he would give to Marley.

"I know what you are about, old friend, but have a care," said

Marley. "Information is not always profitable when there may be no beneficial way to use it. I caution you regarding the thing you are set on discovering, unless you discuss it with Mrs. Langstone before you embark." Without moving his legs, he came closer. "I will speak plainly. You may uncover the details of Mrs. Langstone's son's death, but to what profit for either of you? You must think on that because it is important."

Having said that, Marley did not fade from sight. Instead, as if giving a slight ghostly rebuff, he disappeared in a quick puff of miasma.

Scrooge was not yet willing to answer Marley's question, even to himself. He had wished to solve the mystery of Peter's death for too long to give up on it simply because a spirit voiced some doubt. Scrooge could not say why he was so set on pursuing the matter, and he was now unsure as to how it would benefit anyone, unless he could bring the killer to justice. Was it for himself, and not for Rebecca that he was so set on detecting the truth? If he spoke to her, she might reject the idea.

He must think . . .

CHAPTER NINE

An Unexpected Informant

One morning, several days later, a street urchin banged the knocker on Scrooge's door, shoved a missive into Mrs. Dilber's hand and ran away, disappearing around a corner. She quickly took it to Scrooge, assuming it must be a business matter, although she did think the means of delivery was a bit out of the ordinary.

"This just come for you, Mr. Scrooge. I dunno 'oo delivered it 'cuz it were a young lad, one from the streets, no doubt. 'E scarpered once I took it from 'im. Didn't seem quite right, to me."

"Thank you, Mrs. D," said Scrooge as he opened the letter. He had nearly forgotten the man who cracked his head open since he had, instead, turned his attention to the mystery of Rebecca Langstone's son's death. The letter, however, brought it all back. It was written in the same scrawl and said, "*My father is dead these ten years because of you. He will be avenged.*"

Scrooge's first response was to wad the paper into a ball and toss it, but on second thought he opted to keep it and the other notes, to discuss with his men. This was another clue after all, and he was certain that Cratchit would have something to say about that!

The men at the counting house studied the three threatening notes, and they took them seriously since Scrooge had, in fact, been violently attacked. Homer also seemed to be moving about a bit slowly these days, but Scrooge was too absorbed by his own thoughts to question him. Both Fred and Cratchit knew about Homer's scuffle with the man in the shadows, but they had not yet said anything to Scrooge. Perhaps it was time.

"Uncle," said Fred, "There is a bit more to the story." He glanced at the others, who nodded their agreement that Scrooge be told.

"About a week ago Homer followed you home, at our urging. Now, do not be upset with him, because we had all agreed to do what we could to discover the identity of this fiend, and you were, shall we say, being a little less than cooperative." He did not add that they were also interested in protecting him, since that was the thing that seemed to offend Scrooge's pride, when it was first discussed.

"At any rate," continued Fred, "Homer observed this self-avowed enemy of yours following you home, but Homer prevented him from accosting you. There was a bit of a dust-up, and both of them came away with some bruises, but my point is that this is a very real threat. He is out there, and he is determined to do you harm!"

Scrooge was silent as he took in this new information and realized something must be done. He thanked Homer very sincerely and said to them all that he was not offended that they cared enough to look out for his welfare. With that, he looked to Cratchit for his thoughts on the matter.

Cratchit did, indeed, have something to say about the notes. Pointing to the third message, he said, "Mr. Scrooge, this last threat gives us a frame of time wherein we can search our records and find anyone we may have overlooked. It is a man who apparently lost everything ten years ago and died by causes unknown to us." He scratched his chin and suggested, "We can no doubt go back ten or eleven years, see who lost everything, or at least a great deal of what he owned. If our records don't show a death, we could search death notices, although I suspect the breadth of such an effort would be beyond our abilities. After all, we know nothing about the man or where he even resided."

It was agreed that Homer and Cratchit would conduct another thorough search of the records, which they began that very day. Unfortunately, the search, thorough as it was, revealed no one who fit the criteria.

The men put their heads together again, to consider how else to discover the attacker's identity, but they were at a loss for the time being. Homer had given as much of a description of the man that he could manage, it being dark at the time, but it was of no help whatsoever.

The men remained adamant in their decision not to report the matter to the constable, although their reasons seemed to be less compelling as time went on. There must be some way they could discover this man's identity! As is so often the case, the counting house was to become privy to the needed information when they least expected it, and from a source they could not have imagined.

Not three days later a gentleman entered the counting house and asked for Mr. Scrooge. He seemed a bit ill at ease, but very determined. In fact, he insisted that he see Scrooge as soon as possible, to impart information of some import. Fred was already sitting in Scrooge's office, discussing some business, so Scrooge bid him remain. He then introduced Fred and offered the man a chair.

"Thank you, Mr. Scrooge. My name is Stanbury. Aldus Stanbury. I have a few things to say, and I hope you will receive them in the spirit in which they are intended, which is, I assure you, kindly. I pray you will forgive me for waiting weeks to see you, because my hesitation has evidently resulted in your injury. I can only say, in my defense, that I did not realize the threat you were facing."

Stanbury seemed somewhat uncomfortable, as if he were a young schoolboy facing his headmaster, and that was exactly how he felt since he was about to tattle on a fellow. He took a deep breath and cleared his throat. He would go right to the heart of the matter.

"Mr. Scrooge, I know the identity of the man who has been sending you threatening letters, who has now even attacked you, and I know why."

Scrooge stood suddenly and interjected, "Let us pause here a moment, Mr. Stanbury. I need to invite my clerk to join this conversation." Scrooge did not tell Stanbury that he wanted Cratchit in on the exchange because of his ability to think clearly, since it might seem a bit odd to elevate one's clerk to the position of detective. Cratchit had an uncanny sense of reason and logic, and Scrooge did not trust himself or Fred to accurately repeat Stanbury's information. On his way back to his own office with Cratchit, Scrooge motioned for Homer to remain, unobserved, just outside the open door, within earshot.

Once everyone was assembled, Stanbury resumed his narrative. It was a distasteful task, but he was determined. He swallowed hard and did his best to assuage the guilt he was feeling by weighing it against the guilt he would feel if Scrooge met an untimely end because he had remained silent.

Stanbury looked directly at Scrooge and said, "The person who has been hounding you, and even attacked you, is a man by the name of Henry Martin, Jr. I believe you can find the name 'Henry Martin,' his father, in your records. I have known him my entire life, since our fathers were fast friends." He shook his head and added, "He is not an evil man, but he has, for some time now, been slowly slipping into a defective mental state. In fact, his landlady remarked to me recently that she believes he is 'one outburst away from Bedlam.' I can only assume he acquired the propensity from his father." He leaned forward in his chair.

"You see, his father began a slide into madness many years ago, but it climaxed following a bad investment that cost him what remained of his fortune ten years ago. Then, not long after, his wife packed her jewelry and moved to the Continent, never to be heard from again. Within a fortnight of her desertion, Mr. Martin shot himself."

Stanbury heaved a sad sigh and explained, "I'm very much afraid that was the beginning of Henry Jr.'s' downfall, and he blames you, Mr. Scrooge. He holds you responsible for his father's loss of fortune, his wife, and eventually even his life. Oh, I know it is unreasonable, but we are not speaking here of a reasonable man, even though he was not always in such a state of delusion.

"In stark contrast, my father lost a great deal of money in Martin's last debacle too, but he did not sink into despair. Instead, he worked doubly hard at employment that was beneath him, and he rallied in the end, both in his mind and his prosperity. Today he is an example of true success in the face of overwhelming obstacles." It was clear by his smile that Stanbury was proud of his father and his courage in the face of bad luck. He then continued to describe Henry Martin, Jr.

"The Henry I grew up with would avoid stepping on an insect, and certainly would never consider harming a fellow human being, but he is no longer that man. He is deranged by hatred and he needs to blame someone. In this case it is you, Mr. Scrooge. I'm certain you are wondering how I became aware of this.

"Several weeks ago Henry came to my home, and almost with elation he told me of his plan to avenge his father by making you suffer, perhaps even die. To be honest, I doubted that he would follow through with any threats. He had been imbibing, and I truly believed he was just relieving his anger by ranting.

Then, yesterday he reappeared and reported that, not only had he delivered written threats, he had actually attacked you. I realized then that his illness and his grief had reached a juncture that presented a very real danger, and I knew I must warn you!"

No one had interrupted during Stanbury's monologue, but now he sat back and invited questions. Fred was the first to ask. "Mr. Stanbury, have you provided any of this information to the police?"

"No, I have not. I wanted to bring the information to you and leave any criminal charges and resulting arrest in your hands. I am certain you can find the senior Mr. Martin in your records, and you will then have a full picture of the situation, to offer to the police."

Scrooge ventured to ask if Martin had shared with Stanbury any specific plans to carry out his revenge, and Stanbury shook his head. "No, Mr. Scrooge, he was unable to do so, though I did ask. My impression was that he is acting on impulses that come to him, day by day."

Scrooge enquired, "Why did your own father not blame me for the loss incurred? Do you know?"

"I do not, since my father never mentioned you to me. The first I knew of anyone blaming this office was when Henry said so the other day. If my father held you to blame, he never mentioned it to me."

Since no one else seemed to have questions, Stanbury rose, handed Cratchit the direction of the lodging house of Henry Martin, as well as his own, should any future contact be necessary. Then he bid everyone a good day. His mission had been an unhappy one, but it was the sort of thing required of anyone who considered himself civilized, no matter how much it might jeopardize a longstanding relationship.

Upon Stanbury's departure the men sat for a moment, contemplating the information they had just heard. Finally, Cratchit set Homer to work with the directive, "You now have names and the ten-year time frame, so get to it, my boy, and let's find this Mr. Martin, and Mr. Stanbury, in our records!"

Homer stood and immediately set about the task. Later that afternoon he reported back to Cratchit.

"Mr. Cratchit, I am unable to find any record of either Mr. Martin or Mr. Stanbury. I have searched 1835, 1836 and 1837 in the off chance that the ten-year mark was incorrect by a year, plus or minus, but there is no mention of either name at all, much less with a major financial loss."

Cratchit removed his spectacles, rubbed his chin and thought a moment before responding. "I believe Mr. Stanbury gave us correct information, at least as far as he knew. He knows Martin is the man who is hounding our Mr. Scrooge, but could he be incorrect in Martin's reasons for such intense hatred?"

"I suspect not," replied Homer. "It sounded as though Martin was very specific in his reasons for chasing Mr. Scrooge when he boasted of his actions, to Stanbury. He told Stanbury that his father had been ruined by an investment made through this office, did he not?"

"He did, Son, he did, so I don't know where that leaves us."

When Scrooge was advised of the situation, he agreed with Cratchit's last statement and said, "I do not know what to do at this point. I am not comfortable giving the police the man's name when all we have is hearsay to back up the charge. We certainly can't prove it was he who attacked me, and we can't prove that he wrote those threatening notes."

Scrooge added, "I cannot identify him, nor can Homer. We have Stanbury's testimony that Martin admitted the attack to him, but in court it might simply turn out to be one man's word against another. No, I would prefer to have a bit more to go on since a sharp barrister would destroy the charges, as they stand, within half an hour of the Court convening!"

CHAPTER TEN

The Narrative Is Completed

While the men were conversing about not finding the names "Martin" and "Stanbury" in their records, Edwin Carter entered the counting house. Carter's connection to the offices commenced years before, when Marley was still alive and had inexplicably loaned Carter the money to sail to America.

Prior to that, Carter had failed in every economic endeavor, but in America he prospered. He returned to England a wealthy man and sought out Marley, to repay his loan. Since that time, Carter had become a valued client and trusted friend to Scrooge and the men of the counting house. Along with Dick Wilkins, Carter was often included in what Scrooge considered "his men," and he was party to much that was privileged information.

Carter stood inside the offices long enough to overhear the names, "Martin" and "Stanbury," which piqued his interest. He said nothing, but instead stepped forward and stood with the group, continuing to eavesdrop in a perfectly obvious manner.

Finally, he put forth a question. He knew he would not be censored for doing so.

"I apologize for interrupting, but are you speaking of James Stanbury, and one Henry Martin, who died about ten years ago? They were friends of my father's, so I knew them both, as well as their sons, Aldus and Henry Jr., although they were somewhat younger than I."

His statement was heartily welcomed and over the next several minutes the men related the facts regarding the threatening notes and the violent attack on Scrooge. Their narrative left Carter speechless, which was a condition he rarely experienced. He finally managed to sputter, "Why, this is beyond belief! I am stunned that such a thing should occur!" He was even more flummoxed after Cratchit shared the rumour concerning Mrs. Purdy and Scrooge.

In response to such a ridiculous report, he simply said, "I am having difficulty receiving so much bad news, but I will, for the moment, set Honora Purdy, her gossip and her tea aside, and tell you what I know about your attacker's father, Henry Martin, Sr., who committed suicide." Homer again stated he could find no record of Martin's ruination in their books, to which Carter replied, straightforwardly, "Nor will you, because you, Scrooge, did not ruin the man!"

"But his son said . . ." interjected Fred.

"I can believe that is what his son believes is true, but either his father sold him a bill of goods purposely, seeking someone other than himself to blame, or he became so muddled that he truly believed our friend Scrooge ruined his business and his life."

Tapping his fingers on Homer's high desktop, Carter repeated the truth with emphasis. "Regardless of what he believes was your role in his father's demise, I am telling you that was not the case! In fact, I seriously doubt that the Senior Martin ever met the venerable Ebenezer Scrooge." Everyone looked at Scrooge, who shrugged his shoulders and shook his head, as if he couldn't say one way or another.

Soon everyone was seated and awaiting the full explanation from Edwin Carter. They knew him to be an honest man and he had a way of expressing himself that made others sit up and listen. He crossed his legs and began.

"I recall when my father entered into a business partnership with the seniors Stanbury and Martin. It was a joint venture and there were a few others, but I don't recall their names. Each one had guaranteed several thousand pounds, which most of them could not afford to lose. It was a risky business, so when one member of the group saw you, Scrooge, at the Exchange, he followed you back here and asked you about it. At least that is what my father told me later."

Nodding at Scrooge, Carter said, "You made some sort of off-hand remark and strongly suggested they remove themselves from the scheme, which you said was a risky gamble. My father and most of the others ignored your advice for two reasons: your reputation was not one of enriching others without including yourself in the profits; and they were confident that they were soon going to be as rich as Croesus."

Suddenly Carter snapped his fingers and cried, "Oh! I recall the name of one of the other investors – the one who had the good sense to listen to your advice. It was Barlow . . . Branley . . ."

"Brownlow?" asked Scrooge, recalling what Brownlow had said about coming to the counting house years earlier, to ask Scrooge's opinion of the investment scheme.

"Yes! That's it! It was Brownlow. I vaguely recall the fellow. In fact, if memory serves me, he met with you in person and you convinced him that the entire project was a ruse, which it was.

He heeded your advice and cleared out of the entire scheme while many of the others rushed to their own ruination.

"Now," continued Carter, who still had everyone's attention. "I need to make something clear. The Senior Henry Martin did not suddenly fall into a state of lunacy as a result of this one loss. It began years before that wretched investment. He always leaned toward melancholy, but it worsened with each hardship in life – those daily challenges that most people manage to get through, but he did not. He steadily deteriorated and began to seek someone or something on which to hang the blame. His son watched the process and accepted every excuse his father made for his own distress."

Carter cleared his throat. He was going to need some tea or ale after this soliloquy. He was amazed that he could recall so many details, but more came back to him as he spoke.

"My father found Martin in his study one night, fiddling with a handgun and ranting about the unfairness of his life. Somehow my father got the thing away from him and eventually gave it to Stanbury, for safe keeping. I assume Stanbury returned it to Martin at some point, because he managed to make good his threat to 'end the misery' ten years ago. Unfortunately, it was his son who found him."

"Tsk, tsk. Now that's a very sad thing," lamented Cratchit, who then asked, "Was it the failed investment that finally tipped the scale?"

"I believe that was the final straw, as they say, although he had brought on the majority of his problems, himself. For one thing, he had extensive debts, mostly due to gambling. He borrowed against his home and sold much of his property, but he still had not managed to overcome the urge to wager on anything from that day's horserace to the number of wild geese that might fly south in the morning. I was later told that one reason his wife left with her jewelry was to save it before he could sell it. I've often wondered if she reached the Continent only to find that he had already done so, and she was carrying, instead, very good copies."

CHAPTER ELEVEN

Surprising Compassion, and Admiration

Mrs. Sotherton was again on her way to see her daughter, Rebecca Langstone. Although she was not as shaken as she had been during her previous call, she was, nonetheless, upset. She had just called on Honora Purdy and discovered the woman's extreme talent for agitating those with whom she came into contact. Mrs. Sotherton was unsure of what she hoped to accomplish by making the call, but it did not matter since she had made absolutely no progress in terms of the truth, nor as far as Mrs. Purdy's own intentions toward Ebenezer Scrooge were concerned. Mrs. Sotherton was already speaking as she entered Mrs. Langstone's morning room and did not realize she was also waving her hands.

"My dear," she cried as she slid into her favorite chair, "that Purdy woman is not right in the head! Bless me, it is nearly impossible to carry on a meaningful conversation with her, and there is no chance at all of coming away from the encounter with any sensible outcome!" She removed her gloves as she continued.

"Why, at one point in our visit, if you can call it that, I asked her outright if she was, indeed, betrothed to Ebenezer, and do you know what she said? No, of course you don't, but I am about to tell you. She said, 'I should not answer that since so many details of my life are unsettled at this time.' There! She actually said that! Well, you know what the perennial gossips can do with that sort of reply."

Mrs. Sotherton plopped her hands onto her lap and declared, "Mrs. Purdy is discernably over the moon with joy because the rumour has not died down, and the more levity she displayed, the more snorts and brays I had to endure! Insufferable woman!" Mrs. Sotherton dabbed her nose with her handkerchief and lowered her voice as if to state something too shameless to be shared with anyone within earshot.

"It seems she has had so many visitors and invitations since this horrid tale began that she is experiencing a popularity the likes of which she had never dreamed. Everyone is curious and their curiosity fuels the rumour because, I am certain, they, having nattered with Honora Purdy, immediately call on their 'trusted confidants' to share the vague contents of their latest visit with her. Then, together, they bandy ideas back and forth until they have built the report into something more worthy of repetition. At that point they can pass it on to others who are waiting with itching ears."

Mrs. Sotherton shook her head and admitted, in clipped words, "She cannot help herself. Of that I am certain. So, she nods and smiles. Or, she says something that can be interpreted a number of ways, instead of simply refuting the story. She does not *want* to refute it!" Having said so, Mrs. Sotherton suddenly realized her daughter was not sharing her vexation. She stopped short and stared at Rebecca in disbelief.

"How can you sit there so calmly. Does this not horrify you?"

"To be honest, Mother, it does not, but you must already know that from the note I sent to you after Ebenezer and I spoke. Did you not read it?"

"Of course, I read it Dear, and I was glad to hear it. I was on my way to you today, to share your relief, but I decided to call first on Mrs. Purdy. Then, during my visit, I saw that we have a problem of greater proportions than we suspected. The fact that you and Ebenezer are in agreement does not put an immediate end to the trouble that is continuing to brew!"

Rebecca was not disturbed by her mother's fears. Instead, she replied calmly, "I readily admit the initial rumour did horrify me until Ebenezer and I spoke, and he reassured me of what I already knew in my heart to be true. Our conversation has relieved my mind to the extent that I now feel more sympathy for the woman than I did. Instead of undoing that resolution, what you have just told me gives me a fair idea of how bland Mrs. Purdy's life must be, for her to actually take delight in being the center of a rumour that has no basis in truth." No, Mother, rather than being vexed, I feel compassion." It showed in her eyes before she said, "It is a very sad thing, you know, and I pity her condition."

Tobias Blythe had always admired Honora Purdy. He had often engaged in business with her husband and observed the woman in many circumstances, most of them pleasant social gatherings, or the occasions when he called at the Purdy home to discuss a current contract. She had always treated him with politeness, but it was more than that. She was kind.

Blythe was a simple man who had never particularly succeeded socially, yet he was drawn to Honora's habit of making him feel that he had all of her attention whenever he spoke to her. Unlike most of his acquaintances, she did not hurry him along or let her eyes seek more interesting encounters as they conversed. It never seemed that she was seeking a good reason to excuse herself and escape from his company. He had no way of knowing that she felt the same about him.

Blythe had never forgotten the first evening he was invited to dinner at the Purdy home. The guests would be mostly Purdy's business associates, and Blythe felt, even prior to his arrival, that he would be like a speck of dust in the corner – present, but not noticeable, except as something to be swept aside once spotted. Mrs. Purdy had changed all that.

"Why, it's Mr. Blythe, is it not? My husband has spoken of you often. He values your acumen with numbers, you know." With that, she had led him to the drawing room, still conversing with him and asking questions as if she truly cared what he thought. She took the time to introduce him to several others before leaving him safely in the hands of a man with whom he was already acquainted, and with whom he could have an easy conversation. It was a small thing, but to Blythe it conferred a personal worth he had seldom experienced. She had actually bothered to make him comfortable!

There was nothing amiss with the basic character of either Mrs. Purdy or Mr. Blythe. It was simply that neither of them attracted the attention of others. He, because he felt inconsequential and therefore gave the impression of being so by offering little in the way of confidence, conversation or wit. She, because, although attractive enough, tended to melt into a crowd.

It was not Mrs. Purdy's appearance that put others off, however. It was her unfortunate braying and snorting. She could not laugh without doing so, and most people were repelled by such nasal and throaty commotion. Mr. Blythe, however, did not share their reactions. He did not even hear the noise. To him. Mrs.

Purdy was a flawless queen.

Mr. Blythe and Mrs. Purdy were, for reasons they failed to discern, drawn to each other at gatherings. They were pleased to enjoy a few moments of someone's undivided and freely given attention. It was true that their conversations were what others might label nondescript, but their exchanges were meaningful to them since they reflected the respect each had for the other – respect they did not receive from the rest of humankind.

Once, at a ball, Mr. Blythe approached Mrs. Purdy, offered his hand and said, with more self-assurance than he felt, "I would be very honored if you would grace me with this dance." No one else had made such an overture during the whole of the evening, and Mrs. Purdy was surprised. Gratified, she took his hand and let him slip it through his arm as they walked onto the floor. To the surprise of them both, they carried on an easy, pleasing conversation during the piece.

Blythe remarked, "Mrs. Purdy, I declare you look splendid tonight. That color suits you," and she had responded, "Thank you, Mr. Blythe, for the compliment." Then she added, "And I applaud your dancing ability since it enhances what little I have. You are talented in your steps. I admit that few partners are able to lead me in time with the music, and you see I have not stepped on your toes even once!" She gave a small laughing snort, which delighted him and made him feel like a giant among dwarfs. He boldly gave her an unexpected turn, which she followed flawlessly. It was a new experience for both of them, and quite gratifying.

Following her husband's death, Mrs. Purdy would have gladly received a romantic nudge from Mr. Blyth, were it not for a happenstance she could not have predicted. In early1844, not long after the three spirits had worked their miracle on Christmas Eve, Priscilla Wilkins introduced Ebenezer Scrooge to Mrs.

Purdy. From that time on, Scrooge dominated her thoughts, wishes and desires. Sadly, Mr. Blythe quickly disappeared from her sight and she no longer noticed him.

Without realizing it, Mr. Blythe became to Mrs. Purdy what he had always been to everyone else. She did not realize it, but by relegating him to such a status, she forfeited the only person who truly enjoyed her company. It was a choice that returned them both to their former wretched loneliness, but Mrs. Purdy had been unable to do otherwise. She was helpless because she could not quell the longing in her heart, even at the mere mention of Scrooge's name.

CHAPTER TWELVE

A New Policeman Is Assigned

T he men of the counting house were unanimous in their decision that the police should now be advised of the crimes of Henry Martin, Jr. They had their facts in order, even though there was no irrefutable proof that he was the person who attacked Scrooge. There was, however, the evidence that Mr. Stanbury brought to the table, as well as the damages that Fred and Homer and others had witnessed though, and all of that was surely enough to warrant further investigation.

From what they knew about him, the men expected that Martin would readily admit his misdeeds, once cornered, and they were confident that the police would quickly detect his questionable sanity. It was a sad case, but Martin's recent propensity to violence demanded that something be done. Homer dispatched a message to Constable Rollo Norris, outlining the particulars of the matter, and Norris appeared at the counting house the next day.

"Gentlemen!" cried Norris as he swung wide the door, to enter. It was more a proclamation than a greeting, and it left Homer rolling his eyes. He and Norris had at least finally reached a polite impasse since Scrooge's dealings with the canal boat last year, but Homer continued to be a bit wary in the constable's company. He seemed to be a little too pleased with himself. Still, Homer could finally get by all that, particularly now that Norris' interest in Martha Cratchit seemed to have cooled, but Norris continued to exude excessive self-interest, which kept Homer on his guard.

In truth, Norris was not quite the rogue Homer thought him to be. It is a widely known fact that men often find fault in each other when they have been in competition, and they had once been in competition for a woman's favor.

Norris was the sort of man who would scrutinize all possibilities prior to settling on anything in which to invest total constancy, including taking a wife. Perhaps it was that attention to detail and his refusal to settle until convinced of the rightness of his decision that made Norris an excellent policeman. He had successfully assisted Scrooge in more than one instance, and Scrooge once again requested that he assist with the current situation.

It was not Norris, however, who would be doing so this time. Another constable, who had accompanied him, stepped forward when Norris said, "Constable Lynch, here, will work with you to effect the arrest of your daft Mr. Martin. I brought him here to introduce you and to allow him to pose any further questions he has that were not covered in your report to me." With that, and before anyone could object, Norris apologized for having been ordered to return directly to the station, and he took his leave.

Constable Lynch seemed pleased to see him go and turned to Scrooge, his expression clearly one of annoyance.

"Mr. Scrooge, I have few facts and a great deal of hearsay in the notes that a Mr. Homer Probert prepared for the police. Which one of you is Mr. Probert?" Homer raised his chin and his index finger, and received, in response, an insult from Lynch, as he slapped the papers with the back of his hand. "I pray this office is more thorough than the preparation of this essay because, if it is not, you most likely will be losing many investors and a great deal of money." He scowled and said to Homer, "I can make neither heads, nor tails, of this ill-prepared text."

Homer was not the only one to stiffen at the affront since everyone in the room took offense and was immediately put on his guard. Even more so, each one questioned the constable's abilities to actually read and apply reason. They suspected that he had not understood the "essay" because he had not, in fact, read it, and they were correct. He had not.

The truth was that Constable Lynch did not like to do much of anything, and being directed by another officer, even one of higher rank, did not move him. During his time with the City of London Police he had learned that there were ways to appear to be occupied with police work when, in fact, he was not. One of those tactics was to accuse others of not providing what he needed in order to do his job. He was lazy, and he did nothing unless he was compelled by fear of being exposed for the sluggard he was.

It was, overall, a good thing that Constable Lynch did so little because he could not be trusted with power. He greatly abused his authority and peppered his few police contacts with affronts, threats, and improper arrests. One could only be thankful that he was so busy doing nothing that it kept him from making many arrests and therefore spared a great deal of unnecessary distress.

Having now provided himself with an excuse not to act on behalf of one Ebenezer Scrooge, Lynch announced that he might return when the counting house could provide a cogent outline of evidence, and that he would not dare to attempt an arrest on their current flimsy document. With that, he departed, slamming the door – another tactic he found useful in producing reticence in others, to keep them from questioning his behavior.

The room was in total silence until everyone spoke at once.

"Well! Did you hear that?"

"He doesn't plan to do anything, does he?"

Even, "The man is a liar!" This, from Homer, who had taken great pains to write a cogent list of evidence for the police.

When the hubbub died down and each man could take his turn, Cratchit suggested, "Perhaps we should all discuss this and see how best to proceed at this point, knowing that we are, for all intents and purposes, on our own. Unless, that is, we decide to report the man to his superiors." He sucked air through his teeth and admitted, "But I suspect we might wind up with even less police support in that case. No officer wants to assist a member of the public who makes accusations against one of his brothers, because he could be accused next!"

"That is quite true," agreed Scrooge. "Norris is obviously assigned elsewhere, so we cannot pull him into this situation, but I definitely plan to alert him to Lynch's behavior in the not too distant future."

Cratchit suggested, "It could be that Lynch would be willing to become involved once most of the investigation were completed, and the evidence compiled. At that point, all he would be required to do would be to pop in to make the arrest and receive the accolades for doing so. He has, after all, been assigned to the case. He would surely be delighted if it were wrapped up swiftly, and he got the credit, do you not agree?"

"Yes," said Fred. "He strikes me as the sort of man to do just that."

"I believe we concur, then," said Scrooge, "that we must do the investigating ourselves. So, what is next? Any more ideas?"

"Yes, Sir," replied Cratchit. "I believe the only avenue open to us is to locate Martin as quickly as possible and give Lynch his whereabouts, since he will not stoop to find Martin's last known abode in our memorandum." Here he must add, "Homer, you did a splendid job on our information, but it doesn't go far when the recipient won't take the bother to read it."

Homer smiled in appreciation, thanking Cratchit and the others, who all joined in to praise his work.

CHAPTER THIRTEEN

The Men Investigate

S tanbury had provided the direction for the boardinghouse where Martin was living, so it was decided that Fred and Homer would visit the place and see what they could learn. Scrooge could not go since Martin knew his identity. Hopefully he did not know the others'.

A Mrs. Picken answered their knock. She was about sixty years, well-worn and entirely unsociable. When they asked for Henry Martin, she looked them over and asked, "Now why would you two gent'lmen be askin' for the likes o' 'im, pray tell?"

They were ready for her question, and Fred replied, "He is a friend of an acquaintance of ours (which was true, considering Edwin Carter), and we have an important message for him."

Just then, Homer realized they had not made a plan of what to do should they actually find Martin at home. As he was trying to formulate something and somehow pass it on to Fred, the proprietress, having completed her assessment of them both, made it unnecessary.

"Well, 'e ain't 'ere. 'E scarpered 'bout two days ago without payin', so 'e won't be getting' any o' 'is belongin's back, if 'e shows 'is face. Not that 'e owns much, 'n what little he 'as, 'e took with 'im, mostly."

"In that case, Mrs. Picken, might we look inside his room? That might give us an idea of what to report to our mutual friend." She was hesitant, but when Homer placed several shillings into her open palm, they worked as well as the key she then produced from her apron pocket. The coins also freed her tongue, a bit.

To excuse the accumulated dust and grime in the house, Mrs. Picken said, "'Is room's not been tidied, but you'll get a good look at how 'e lived. Nat'rally I 'aven't cleaned it, sposin' 'e might come back in a day, or two. Wouldn't want 'im to think I was interferin,' like." She led them upstairs to Martin's door then turned back down with the admonition not to stay too long because other boarders "might not approve of such goin's on."

The sooty window hadn't been opened for some time so the air in the space was thick and stale. Ceiling cobwebs and a filthy wood floor testified against Mrs. Picken more than Martin, since the room had no doubt gone without proper cleaning for much longer than Martin's tenure.

There was no clothing in the wardrobe, and no hygiene products, but otherwise it looked as if the tenant might return that night. The bed was unmade, and a much-used towel hung on a hook beside a hazy mirror. Below the mirror was a washstand with a pitcher and bowl – one empty and the other filled with dirty water.

A small table was cluttered with papers, but there was no pen and no ink, and an empty gin bottle stood on the floor. Homer looked through the papers and said, "Mr. Symons, I think you should see this," pointing to several crumpled papers on the table and in an adjacent dust bin. Homer had spread two of them on the table. Neither was a complete sentence. One was inscribed, "You will regret what . . ." and the other, "Soon revenge will be . . ."

There were three more notes of similar nature, which Fred read. He then gathered them together, folded them and placed them in his coat pocket. Homer was still stinging a bit from Lynch's insults and wondered, aloud, what Lynch would do with this information. It wasn't a particularly fair question, since neither Homer nor Fred was sure what to do with it, either.

There was little else to be gained from the room, so the men returned the key to Mrs. Picken and asked if she knew of any visitors Martin may have entertained. Apparently forgetting Aldus Stanbury, she said, "I never saw no one come to see 'im. 'E seemed out o' sorts most o' the time, 'n 'e weren't very friendly."

"So, what can we conclude from what we know?" ruminated Scrooge to Cratchit after they had read the unfinished notes in Martin's room. "I'll tell you one thing we can assume – he must suspect that the police are after him, which is why he left his lodging."

Cratchit agreed that was most likely the case, although it wasn't clear how he would know unless Stanbury had confessed to him that he had informed, which was doubtful. He had exchanged blows with Homer, so he might suspect him of being a constable. Cratchit also suggested that it might no longer be convenient for Martin to write more notes if he was now "on the lam."

"We are making assumptions," said Fred, "but there is one more thing we can suppose, which is that, notes or no notes,

Martin may not want to leave the job unfinished. He set out to avenge his father, and he even threatened death, so he may still want to do you harm, Uncle."

Scrooge nodded in agreement but was at a loss as to how to proceed. The only logical tactic would be to request police protection, but Lynch would not want to put out that much energy. Perhaps, if they spoke to Lynch in the police station, where his superiors were within earshot, he would at least delegate some protection, utilizing constables who were on duty at night. It was worth a try.

Scrooge and Fred appeared at the station house and asked the sergeant for Constable Lynch. Naturally he was in, since it was easier to be there than to be out and about. Once again, he had found a way to remain inactive through some or other pretense. The sergeant sent Scrooge and Fred down a dingy hallway to the room where Lynch was idling, and there they found him, fiddling with his tall hat.

"Constable," cried Scrooge. "We have come to discuss the business of Mr. Martin with you, if you are not too busy." Lynch looked at them with a blank expression, as if he were attempting to recall who they were and how they knew him. "Scrooge and Symons," said Fred, wondering how in the world this policeman was holding on to his job.

"Ah, yes," smirked Lynch. "I hope you are a little better prepared than yesterday, or you'll get no help from the police. We can't operate on bad information, you know."

"Yes, we know," replied Scrooge, "which makes me wonder that you can operate at all, since you reject good information when it is handed to you on a platter!"

"I beg your . . ."

Scrooge was angry. "Don't beg anything from me, you malingerer. We have visited Mr. Martin's abode, which you should have done, and found him to have disappeared. We have also verified, by real evidence, that he was the author of the threatening notes I received, which suggests that he is very likely to continue his quest to do me harm."

Scrooge stepped close to Lynch, who was attempting to appear offended, and said, with a lowered voice, "Would it be too much to request that I have police cooperation, since it appears that he may make another attempt on my person?"

Lynch was about to make a response that would put these two in their proper place, and send them on their way, when a voice behind them asked, "Scrooge? Is that my old friend Scrooge? What in heaven's name brings you here? I haven't seen you since that evening at Purtell-Smythe's, last winter!"

"Ah, Inspector," interjected Lynch before Scrooge could answer. "We were just discussing the case of a fellow who is set on doing harm to Mr. Scrooge, and we are planning our next move."

"What's that, Scrooge? You? In danger? What's this about?" His questions required that Scrooge and Fred (rather than Lynch, who had not read a word of Homer's report) relay the facts to the Inspector. When they had shared all they knew, he agreed with their theory that the next move could only be police protection as Scrooge walked home from the counting house of an evening.

It was unlikely that Martin would strike during daylight, and there were constables on duty who could lie in wait for an hour or two each night, at least for a time, until the danger had been removed.

The Inspector turned to Lynch. Not knowing his propensity to avoid anything that resembled work, he directed him to "organize a watch over Mr. Scrooge for at least this week, from the time he leaves his counting house at night until he is safely inside his home." As if that were not bad enough, he worsened things by adding, "I want you to observe all, and ensure that everything works as it should. Now, see to it, and report to me how things come about!" Having said that, he bid Scrooge and Fred a good day, and went about his business, leaving Lynch in the most distasteful position of having to organize and oversee a certain amount of work.

CHAPTER FOURTEEN

A Somewhat Disorderly Arrest

As should have been expected, Constable Lynch appointed a newer Constable Stagg to assign officers to lag behind Scrooge as he made his way home, which was fortunate since the delegated constable was eager to succeed in any duty to which he was assigned.

Constable Stagg was an affable young man who was committed to protecting the citizens of London Town. He had not yet been on the force two years but had already solved a number of crimes and had demonstrated a character that allowed him to learn from his mistakes. For that reason, he was much wiser than when he was first employed as a policeman. Stagg was also adept at dealing with the populace of the City, be they criminals or victims. He knew what to say, to whom, and when to say it. His industry was in stark contrast to Lynch's laziness, as shown by his appearance at the counting house immediately upon being assigned to oversee Scrooge's safety. It was Cratchit who greeted him.

"Ah, Constable Stagg, you say? So, you are Mr. Scrooge's new protector." Stagg grinned and admitted he supposed he was, and Cratchit continued.

Well, we are all very pleased to meet you. Let me introduce you to each one of us." With that, Cratchit introduced himself, Homer, Fred Symons and finally Scrooge. The men were relieved that Lynch had wiggled out of the assignment by handing it on to a newer man. Lynch's laziness had worked in their favor, for once.

"Now, Mr. Scrooge," began Stagg. I have read Mr. Probert's extremely well-written and informative report, and I found it to be very helpful. We seem to be up against a man who is determined to make you pay for his own disappointments in life." Scrooge and the others had not thought of it in those terms, but it did seem to describe the situation alright.

"I believe we must assume that your walk home at night is the most likely time he will strike, since that is when he can hide in shadows and there is less chance of any witnesses. I do believe he will try again, so I suggest we place two constables, including myself whenever possible, to see to it that you not only get home safely, but that we actually capture this Mr. Martin." The men were in agreement and were prepared to take part in a definite plan.

"Mr. Scrooge, what time do you generally leave this office and what is your normal route home?" asked Stagg.

Scrooge gave him the routine, and it was agreed that the police guard would be implemented for a week. At the end of the week they would reconsider whatever action should be taken if Martin had not yet stepped into their trap.

Fred, Cratchit and Homer also volunteered their services, should they be needed, in the event that a constable might be called to another duty. The scheme seemed to be a good one, and the only fault anyone could find with it was the possibility that Martin might manage to act before they could apprehend him. For that reason, Stagg planned to ensure that the policemen were alert, and he promised that he would try to personally oversee them as much as possible, each night.

The first three nights Scrooge's walk home was undisturbed. However, since the policemen could not be seen in or near the counting house for fear of alerting Martin, there was no way for Scrooge to speak to them or to inform them of any last-minute changes in his routine.

So it was, on the fourth night, that two new constables were waiting nearby. Stagg had been called to another assignment and neither of the constables had ever seen Scrooge or his men, although they had been given a description of Scrooge. They knew the routine and were waiting a short distance away, for Scrooge to pass by them on his walk home.

Not an hour before closing, Scrooge received a missive that he was immediately required to sign a document at another place of business, which created a problem. Scrooge would not be able to leave the counting house at his regular time.

Scrooge could return by cab after completing the trade, but if he returned to his counting house, he would be late in starting for home, and the officers may believe they had missed him. If so, they would have moved ahead, leaving him behind and unprotected. The cab could, however, discharge Scrooge a distance from his office, inserting him into his normal route at the usual time, but there was no way to get word to the constables.

For that reason, Homer offered to walk Scrooge's route at the usual time until he could somehow locate the officers and alert them to the altered plan. Homer assumed that Martin would not recognize him, but he overlooked the fact that the officers, who were both new tonight, would not recognize him, either. They might keep clear of Homer, thinking he was Martin, which is exactly what occurred since he obviously did not match Scrooge's description.

Following Scrooge's meeting elsewhere, the cabbie discharged him at a spot that placed him where he would then be, had he been walking. However, Homer had not yet reached that point, having been slowed by his attempts to locate the constables. He could not understand why he hadn't yet seen one, not realizing it was because they were trailing *him*!

Martin, on the other hand, was prowling the streets just ahead of Homer, keeping to Scrooge's normal routine. He wondered where Scrooge was and assumed that he was merely keeping within the shadows. Martin was carrying a pin-fire pistol and had sworn to himself and his dead father that tonight he would make things right, or he would turn the gun on himself.

With all of their ducking and heeding of various movements and noises, everyone somehow converged under the dim over-hang of a building at the same moment the cab arrived. Scrooge descended from within, and the cab began to pull away just as a loud shot resonated, echoing off the close walls. The bullet passed through the top of Scrooge's hat, knocking it off his head.

In that deafening instant the cabbie shouted; the horse reared and began to stomp wildly; Scrooge ducked into a shadow; Homer grabbed Martin's shooting arm, and the constables leapt onto Homer.

There was just enough ambient light for Scrooge to catch a glint from the barrel of the pistol, and he had the presence of mind to move quickly and wrench it from the man's grip. He did so just before the constables yanked Homer off of Martin, thinking they had nabbed their felon. Martin was then free to dart away and into the street. Unfortunately for him, he ran directly into the terrorized horse and the crazed animal somehow managed to kick him into unconsciousness.

The following morning, Scrooge and Homer were regaling Fred, Cratchit, Dick Wilkins and Edwin Carter with their tale of the previous night, which ended with the capture of an insensible Henry Martin, Jr. The telling of the events was complicated, but they gave an animated depiction, which was entertaining and brought on laughter as well as disbelief over some of the antics. It was assumed that the police would find Martin to be quite mad, and he would then be dealt with in an appropriate manner.

As the group drank tea from the hob and enjoyed each other's company, the door opened, and the Police Inspector entered. Scrooge greeted him warmly, as did Wilkins and Fred, who were also acquainted with him. Scrooge thanked the Inspector for bringing about the arrest of Martin, and perhaps saving Scrooge's life, but the Inspector waved off the accolades.

"Tut, tut, my good man. I did little to nothing. It's Constable Lynch you have to thank! He saw what needed to be done, and he did it. When he gave me his report this morning, I was so pleased I decided to stop in here and make certain you knew of the role he played in all this." Taking the seat offered by Homer, he accepted a cup of tea from Cratchit and said, "You know, we could do with more men like him in the police. I can see him being very successful in future."

The Inspector did not notice the expressions the men exchanged, which was just as well. There was no way they would attempt to refute what he had said. He most likely would not have believed them, at any rate. He had read Lynch's impeccable report, after all.

CHAPTER FIFTEEN

A Suggestion of Admiration

The rumour of Mrs. Purdy and Scrooge marrying had lost most of its initial momentum since no marriage appeared to be in the offing. However, that, in itself, produced enough fuel to keep the gossip moving, only at a slower pace. The same characters occupied the leading roles, but now the tittle-tattle was an attempt to discover what on earth had occurred that changed things, or at least delayed them.

Neither Scrooge nor Mrs. Langstone was affected by the ongoing chatter, but Mrs. Purdy was finding it more difficult to answer questions with vague remarks. In some cases, such deflection had worked to her advantage because the gossips had been more than willing to attach their own imaginations to her answers. Now, more often than not, they simply lost interest and wondered if the report had ever been true. The talk was rapidly becoming an examination of the character of Honora Purdy, rather than an impending marriage.

Tobias Blythe realized that the rumour was waning, which actually pleased him, but he was highly disturbed by one or two insinuations that perhaps Mrs. Purdy had, herself, shamelessly put the thing about. He could not bear such an accusation being attached to her name. No matter that she did not care for him, he would not stand by and see her reputation sullied by the chatter of persons who did not know her, much less realize her value. He must do something to assist her, but what could he do? The answer came to him after he was stopped by a colleague who must repeat the latest.

"Ho, there! Blythe! I haven't seen you in weeks. I've been meaning to ask you about this Scrooge and Mrs. Purdy business. You're an acquaintance of hers, is that not so? Are they, or are they not, to be married? At our ages we can't afford to string things out for too long, can we? I'm beginning to wonder if it's true, or not, and whether Mrs. Purdy is going to be left out in the cold altogether!"

No, by all that's in me, she won't be! "Mr. Beakstone, I suspect that Mrs. Purdy will continue to be the 'toast of the town' as long as she resides in London, and I wouldn't put much stock in what is, or isn't, being said about her." Indignant, he continued by saying, "For all you know, people are also cackling about you, behind *your* back! Keep in mind, Sir, that if they are, it may be true, or it may be a fabrication."

He knew he had been unkind, but it stopped the blighter's mouth, alright. Beakstone sniffed loudly and tipped his hat to Blythe as he muttered something unintelligible, then moved on to more congenial company.

No, Honora would not be left out in the cold, and she would no longer be the center of gossip, for he finally had a plan!

That evening Mrs. Purdy received a note from Mr. Blythe.

My Dear Mrs. Purdy,

Although we have not spoken for some time, I desire to see you privately on an urgent matter. Would tomorrow at 2:00 o'clock be convenient? I will call on you then, unless you deny me the privilege by responding with a refusal. I pray you will not do so.

Yours,
Tobias Blythe

Tobias Blythe! Mrs. Purdy read the letter with interest and was pleased to hear from her old friend. It was true they had not spoken in some while, and she had always enjoyed their times spent in each other's company. Of course, she would see him, and since he had requested that the visit be private, she would turn away any other callers during that hour. There had been fewer this week, at any rate, so it should not be difficult. What could he have in mind that would require a private audience? She hoped he was not in any difficulty, but if that were the case, she would do whatever she could to help.

Mr. Blythe appeared at precisely 2:00 o'clock, having circled the area twice to cover the fact that he was early. He was finally ushered into Mrs. Purdy's drawing room, where he was received with fresh tea and biscuits. He accepted the tea, but found his stomach was a bit too jumpy to manage any biscuits.

Mrs. Purdy was easy in Mr. Blythe's presence, as she always had been, but he seemed a bit reserved. Where was the friend with whom she had shared so many comfortable conversations?

She had expected to entertain the man who had often rescued her from the boredom and anonymity of gatherings.

"Mr. Blythe, you seem somewhat preoccupied. May I ask if there is something amiss? Was that what you wanted to discuss?" He had never been good at confronting his sentiments, much less owning them to another person, but Mrs. Purdy was at a crossroads, perhaps in crisis, although she apparently did not realize it. It was no time for cowardice on his part.

"Mrs. Purdy, are you aware that you are the subject of recent rumours?" *Oh, my stars, did I ask that?* He hadn't meant it to sound so sordid, but there was no way to un-ring that bell, so he pressed on, albeit not very cleverly.

"By that, I mean, I believe society is finding you a very interesting subject lately, and I have even been approached regarding your future." *Goodness, that's worse!* He stopped and closed his eyes, to think, and heard her ask, "My future? In what way?"

All Mr. Blythe could do was take a deep breath and hold it. Should he just say he made a mistake in coming here, and leave by whatever means possible? He would, but he could not bear the thought of injuring her. In fact, it was precisely to prevent her injury that he had come. He coughed into his fist.

"Mrs. Purdy, are you betrothed to Ebenezer Scrooge?"

Neither of them could believe he had asked her so bluntly, and because it was put before her in such a direct manner, she surprised herself, and him, by giving the first honest answer she had given in more than a fortnight.

"No, Mr. Blythe, I am not!" She said it with more force than she meant to do, but it was a relief to actually speak the truth without attempting to fool anyone, including herself. As soon as she had spoken, Mr. Blythe's shoulders relaxed, and he was able to think more clearly. He took a sip of tea, considered having a biscuit after all, and leaned back a bit.

Setting down his cup, Mr. Blythe remarked, "I can't think, then, how such a rumour began, and I must say, I do not approve of anyone speaking of you so carelessly." His words of concern and his protective attitude touched Mrs. Purdy, for she had rarely been the recipient of such support. No, that wasn't true. She could not recall having *ever* been the recipient of such interest. Her husband had been very polite and was a good provider, but he had never thought her to be special in any respect, or as needing greater consideration than the latest horse he was purchasing.

Scrooge was no different. He had no use for her, and she had always known it. She had pretended that since it was Scrooge's friend Priscilla Wilkins who introduced them, Scrooge must have some interest in her, but of course he did not. The revelation of being so insignificant to so many for so long brought tears to her eyes. Not for itself, but because of the contrast between the painful truth and this man of such noble character who sat before her, voicing his genuine concern and loyalty. She could not speak, which gave her guest an opportunity.

"My dear Mrs. Purdy, I will not tread upon your hospitality by overstaying my welcome, but I do wish to speak with you further. May I call on you again?" He began to bite his lip, and when she saw it, her heart nearly burst with the joy of being valued by someone who cared enough to be unsure of himself in her presence. Yes, he could call again, as often as he pleased!

"Come for tea tomorrow," she said, surprising them both.

"Priscilla, you are a friend, and I am appealing to you to do your best to find out what is going on with that Purdy woman!"

Mrs. Sotherton had called on Priscilla Wilkins to enlist her aid, and she was resolute in her intent.

"We both know our dear Ebenezer does not return, nor desire, her affections, but somehow this chatter about whether or not they are a couple has not ceased. Can you speak to her? I tried, but I got no information and can see how she has, herself, been putting these suggestions about."

It did not matter to Mrs. Sotherton that neither her daughter nor Scrooge was bothered, because it bothered *her*. She was of a mind that, in order for a fire to stop burning, the fuel must be removed, and all smoking embers doused! It was time to do so, one way, or another.

"Well," replied Priscilla, "I don't see what I could possibly say that you have not said, and if she is determined to believe that she and Scrooge have a future together, would I not reinforce that, by approaching her to discuss it?"

"I do not see that as an inevitable outcome," insisted Mrs. Sotherton. "I think it all depends upon your approach. Could you not simply ask her what leads her believe such a thing?"

"But then she would ask, 'What thing?', and we would be back where we began. She could skirt my questions by being vague, as she was with you, and I would make no headway, whatsoever."

Mrs. Sotherton was in no humor to be put off. "My Dear, I am only asking you to make the attempt. Could you not? If anyone can talk to her, perhaps it is you."

Priscilla was not at all convinced, but as a favor to Mrs. Sotherton, she would call on Mrs. Purdy and see if any good could come from the conversation.

CHAPTER SIXTEEN

His Esteem Is Gladly Received

Tobias Blythe did return to the Purdy residence the following afternoon, according to Mrs. Purdy's spontaneous invitation. Each had an expectation of carrying on in the ease of their acquaintance of two years previously, but from the moment he entered the home they were both a bit stiff. It was an unexpected sensation.

Neither even considered that their formality could be due to the fact that they were on the precipice of something beyond friendship. There was no longer a relaxed ease in their conversation, and both sat on the edges of the seats, trying to think of a subject to discuss, but it was no use. Small talk had become impossible and they were in new territory, the terrain with which they were both unfamiliar. Mr. Blythe knew he must do something. Anything. Once again, his brain did not keep pace with his tongue.

"Mrs. Purdy," he managed, "do you mind being a widow?"

Oh, dear. What sort of question is that? I have no right to ask about such a delicate matter. He had asked it, however, and she seemed prepared to answer, after blinking several times as if to be certain she had heard correctly.

"I am resigned to it, Mr. Blythe, but, in truth, I much prefer being a married woman." *Dear me, why did I say that to him? I was not particularly happy when I was married, but I enjoyed the status and having someone "there," even though I felt alone most of the time.*

"I see," he replied. "I, myself, have never entered into the married state, but I imagine it is a pleasant thing, if one is blessed with an enjoyable partner."

Without thinking, Mrs. Purdy replied, "Yes, I imagine it would be." She did not realize that she had admitted to not knowing what it would be like to have an enjoyable husband.

"I have often wished for a wife with whom I could easily share joys and sorrows," remarked Blythe, in a wistful tone of voice. "Yet, I have to assume that being paired with the wrong partner would be worse than the loneliness of being by one's self, do you not agree?" Mrs. Purdy heartily agreed, but she was unwilling to admit outright that she agreed because loneliness had been such a large part of her marriage.

Mr. Blythe was gaining courage with each exchange. "Mrs. Purdy, we have known each other for several years now, and I have always found you to be a very pleasant companion. In fact, I do not know if you are aware of it, but there were times when you rescued me from the Purgatory of yet another dull and disappointing social gathering. You would speak to me and show an interest in what I had to say. For that reason, you have always been a sort of angel to me. A special angel of mercy."

She placed her fingers on her chest. "I, Mr. Blythe? I did not know it, but I am pleased to hear you say so because, for my part, there were gatherings where you were the only person who spoke to me the entire night." She could not believe what she was divulging about herself, but he seemed unperturbed by the admission. She was spared embarrassment by the fact that he had said as much with regard to himself, so they were on equal footing.

It was time for Mr. Blythe to implement his original plan, or, rather, his original hope. "Mrs. Purdy, would you . . . do you think you could . . . that is, I would very much like to . . . to escort you to various events. Would you be amenable to accompanying me?"

Her heart leapt as she allowed that she would definitely enjoy that. Her response produced a daring in him he could never have foreseen.

"I mean to say, Mrs. Purdy, I realize this is quite sudden, but I would like our time spent together to be more than simply companionship. I would like to court you, with marriage as the desired end." *Ulp.* Blythe's Adam's apple bobbed like a float on a fishing line. *Well, the cat's out of the bag now, so I might as well keep going!*

"Would that be acceptable to you?" He wiped his forehead with his handkerchief, and she stopped breathing, praying her heart would not cease altogether. It had happened too quickly, but neither of them was going to hesitate with regard to this Heaven-sent opportunity.

"Yes, Mr. Blythe," replied Mrs. Purdy, once she caught her breath. I would like that very much, and I look forward to spending a great deal of time with you." She let out a little whinny and a very small, nearly indiscernible snort.

The following day, Priscilla Wilkins paid her obligatory call on Mrs. Purdy. She was doing so under duress, at the prodding of Mrs. Sotherton, who was not a woman to refuse. She had been awake most of the night, tossing about as she envisioned hundreds of possible ways to address the rumour with Mrs. Purdy, but none of them made sense, or were too outlandish to even consider.

How could she ask, "Did you plant the gossip about being betrothed to Mr. Scrooge?" Or, "Why haven't you told people you are not marrying him?" If she asked anything at all, Mrs. Purdy was likely to quibble, and they would get nowhere. Oh, this was too much! Why did she ever let Mrs. Sotherton push her into such a task. She knew why. Because no one said "No," to Mrs. Sotherton, that's why.

Mrs. Purdy greeted Priscilla Wilkins as if she were genuinely pleased to see her. Priscilla had always liked Honora well enough, although she could understand why others found her company difficult. It was because of the snorts and braying that were often interspersed with her laughter. No, the two of them had never been great friends, but Mrs. Purdy's demeanor today suggested otherwise.

Priscilla had never seen Honora looking better, and there was a gaiety about her that gave her a more youthful appearance. She had always given the impression of being a bit dull about her person, but she now emanated a sort of glow – a very attractive subtle radiance.

"Mrs. Wilkins, how good it is to see you!" Mrs. Purdy offered her a chair and ordered tea. It was surprising how Mrs. Purdy's cheerful attitude managed to change the atmosphere of the room. The last time Priscilla visited she had felt a heaviness in the air – almost as if the walls were closing in on a very sad life – but that was certainly not the case today.

Priscilla assumed these changes were because Mrs. Purdy had finally convinced herself that she and Scrooge were to marry, and she was giddy in that belief. *So, it has actually gone this far.* Priscilla was dismayed by the realization and she could see no way out for the poor woman. It was too, too bad. Well, there was nothing for it but to have a cup of tea. It would serve no purpose to even attempt to talk sense with someone who had lost contact with all reason, as Honora Purdy surely must have done.

The two sipped a very good light Darjeeling while chatting about the weather and several common household issues, and within a few minutes Priscilla realized she was actually enjoying the visit. She detected no lunacy in Mrs. Purdy. In fact, she seemed more rational than ever.

"Mrs. Wilkins; how are you and Mr. Wilkins faring?" asked Honora. "Does he still spend much time in Town, and is he still in contact with all of our old acquaintances?"

It was the opportunity she needed, so Priscilla replied, "Yes, he is, and, as you may recall, he is always bringing home all of the tittle-tattle he picks up here and there. Not long ago he even heard that you and Ebenezer Scrooge were betrothed." Priscilla gazed into her teacup, trying to give the impression that the remark was offhanded and meant nothing.

Honora looked perplexed. "Is that so? Well, I suspect someone simply got the wrong information because that is certainly not true." She flipped her serviette, settled it back on her lap, and added, "Oh, he's a perfectly nice man, and I will admit to you that at one time I thought him a very good catch, but we are definitely not suited, nor are we betrothed."

After all Priscilla had heard about her vagueness, and how she had fanned the fires of gossip concerning herself and Scrooge, Honora was being surprisingly direct with what Priscilla knew to be an honest answer. She must ask, "Were you aware of the gossip?"

"Oh, yes. I knew, but there is really no way to stop such a thing is there? No matter what you say, it gets interpreted in a way that suits those who are spreading it. One simply tries to ignore it all and carry on."

"Well, Mrs. Purdy, I must say you are taking it very well. I'm not certain I would be as gracious, were my name being bandied about."

Honora smiled and said, "I have good reason to be gracious. I will tell you a secret, and it is not gossip." She smiled and announced, "I *am* soon to be betrothed, but not to Ebenezer Scrooge. No, it is Tobias Blythe whom I plan to marry! He is a wonderful man. We have discussed it and he has as good as made me an offer, but I would prefer that you not say anything quite yet, even to Mr. Wilkins, since it is not settled. It will be shortly, I am convinced, and then the entire world may know!"

Mrs. Purdy lifter her cup to her mouth, shook her head in wonder, replaced the cup without drinking and said, "It is rather humorous when you think of it. Mr. Scrooge and myself!" She gave a quick snort and wondered aloud, "How do you suppose such stories ever come about in the first place?"

Tobias Blythe and Honora Purdy decided to marry in a very private ceremony since neither wished to encourage further gossip before the wedding. The recent untruth of Honora's being betrothed to Ebenezer Scrooge had been quite enough, and the sooner they could put that debacle behind them, the better. If anyone wanted to jabber on about them after they married, well, let them!

They were wed within weeks and, although it was a short courtship, Tobias and Honora had been acquainted for a number of years. To their great delight they now found, in each other, the acceptance and companionship both had desired for so long. They had not yet, however, discovered the deep love that was beginning to bud between them. It would be in full bloom by Christmas.

THE CURIOSITY OF SCROOGE

CHAPTER SEVENTEEN

A Visit to the Countryside

Scrooge's mind was as busy as the railway wheels that rumbled toward the village where Mr. Brownlow and Oliver resided. He knew his chances of succeeding were, as the adage said, "a long shot," but he was determined to visit Brownlow and at least speak to Oliver Twist about his earlier life.

Brownlow had been as good as his word, and he had issued an invitation to Scrooge. Thereafter the two of them exchanged letters, finally settling on a date for Scrooge to visit. His stay was to span two or three days, during which time Scrooge hoped not only to question Oliver, but also to become better acquainted with Brownlow, who had made a very favorable impression on him.

Outside the rail car's window, the landscape flaunted its spring renewal with colorful bloom. New greenery and fragile blossoms emphasized the ancient splendor of bucolic England, but its calm beauty failed to ease the niggling anxiety Scrooge was feeling. An annoying doubt made him question his current hunt for details concerning Peter Langstone's death so many years earlier. No, he did not have Rebecca Langstone's permission to inquire into the matter, but surely, she would not object.

A small portion of Scrooge's brain was questioning the integrity of his plan, but the majority of his mind overruled his doubts and justified his actions. He was, after all, only pursuing the truth, wasn't he? He was doing the right thing. He was doing it for her!

The Brownlow cottage was at the end of a country lane just outside the village, and it presented a welcoming façade. The setting was rustic but charming, with its stone walls, thatched roof that had been sculpted around paned glass windows, and its tall chimneys. The house was surrounded by a wall over which cascaded abundant vines and colorful flowers. The bees were busily gathering nectar to be transformed into lovely honey inside the hives behind the cottage. Beyond the house lay a green sprawling landscape that was producing new crops and hosting fat livestock.

Mrs. Bedwin, the housekeeper, greeted Scrooge at the door, bid him enter, and did her best to get him settled. His case was taken upstairs to his room and he was allowed to refresh himself before being ushered to the garden where Brownlow sat with a book in his lap. He was not reading because he had, instead, drifted into a comfortable nap which ended when he heard them talking. Seeing them, he set aside his book, stood, and greeted his guest.

"Ah, you have arrived," said Brownlow warmly. "I hope you had a pleasant journey. He gestured to a chair and bid Scrooge to join him while Mrs. Bedwin left to prepare tea.

Scrooge could see how some might prefer this setting to a noisily crowded, dirty London, but as a businessman he required, and perhaps preferred, the constant activity. Even so, he could imagine re-visiting Brownlow from time to time to enjoy his company and his pastoral situation.

"I am sorry that Oliver is not here to greet you, but he has gone to visit his aunt who lives not a mile away. I am certain he will return in time for tea."

Oliver did return in time, and the afternoon was thereafter spent pleasantly enjoying Mrs. Bedwin's delicious tea and buns, viewing the garden and discussing mutually satisfying topics such as books and various investments that were bringing good returns. Oliver was silently attentive to the discussions of economics, but he did join in with appropriate and knowledgeable remarks concerning books that he, and they, had read.

Oliver was a quick learner and always enjoyed conversations about new ideas. Brownlow had not neglected his education and he knew the boy would put it to good use as an adult. Why, he was already nearly there, and Brownlow was not at all concerned about his future. He was persuaded that Oliver would always behave honorably and would be a success at any chosen vocation.

The next morning, Scrooge, Brownlow and Oliver strolled into the village where they explored several shops and halls, gaily greeting neighbors who were also out and about. They then wandered to the parsonage, where Scrooge was introduced to Oliver's Aunt Rose and her husband, Harry Maylie, the local parson. Residing with them was Harry's mother, Mrs. Maylie. A doctor, Mr. Losberne, who had moved from London to the village to remain near his close friends, also joined the gathering since he did not want to miss being introduced to Mr. Scrooge.

As they entered the vicarage, Scrooge was immediately struck by the sense of harmony that permeated the home. Mr. and Mrs. Maylie were all friendliness and adept at hosting social calls, whether planned or unplanned. The conversation was lively, and Scrooge found that he was relishing his visit to this small village, and to these people, very much. For the time-being he even forgot the other unpleasant purpose of his trip.

Scrooge revisited that objective later in the evening following dinner at Mr. Brownlow's, but it was not he who introduced the subject.

"Mr. Scrooge," said Brownlow after clearing his throat. "I believe you mentioned that you would like to hear more of Oliver's story. Is that still your desire?"

Scrooge folded his serviette and replied, "Yes, it is. I have a specific reason for wanting to know, and I am happy to share that reason with you both if you are willing to guarantee your secrecy on the topic."

Both Brownlow and Oliver were surprised, but they readily gave their steadfast oaths to keep the matter among themselves. Scrooge was unsure of where to begin, so he relayed the simple truth as he knew it.

"You see gentlemen, I have a friend whose son went missing from a London park ten years ago, when he was but six years old. He was with his nanny, and she turned her back for a few moments to give someone a direction. When she turned back around, he was gone. He could not be located and his pitiable body was recovered from the Thames perhaps three weeks later."

There. His desire to learn what happened had overruled his doubts and disallowed Marley's troublesome interference!

Brownlow and Oliver were appalled with the account, and neither could think of what to say until Oliver asked, "And how can I help, Mr. Scrooge?"

"If I understood you correctly, Oliver, you were forced into a life with villains which, I assume, would place you in a situation of knowing something about such things in London." As the thought occurred to him, Scrooge asked, "May I enquire as to what year this was?"

"Of course. It was circa 1838 that I was a captive of that fiend Fagin and his dishonorable band." He gave a slight involuntary shudder as he recalled the depravity and the evil he had witnessed, not only with Fagin, but in his entire life until he was rescued by Mr. Brownlow.

Scrooge did not expect to be given a quick solution to his problem, and he did not want to distress Oliver, but he was disappointed that Oliver's experience in London's netherworld was after Peter Langstone's death. Oliver surely knew nothing that would help Scrooge in his pursuit of the truth, but Scrooge would ask him two further questions since he seemed so willing to assist.

"Oliver, when you were in the clutches of this Fagin and his band, did you ever witness such a thing as outright abduction of a young child? And was murder a common means of dealing with difficulties?"

Oliver thought for a moment as if he were making up his mind whether to be forthright or to mitigate the truth. Finally, he responded by saying, "I was 'inducted' into the group through deception since I was alone and unprotected, so no act of kidnap was required to bring me into the 'fold.' However, they did kidnap me later, after I had made an escape, since they feared I might alert the authorities. So, I know Fagin's group was capable of kidnap, but I never knew them to kill anyone, other than one instance where a depraved member of the group killed a woman whom we all knew. That was around the time that the 'family' was disbanded."

Before allowing a response, Oliver added, "I'm certain you realize too, Mr. Scrooge, that this was only one of many such gangs in the whole of London, so the chances of my knowing of your friend's son are very slight." It was as Scrooge feared. Still, he would ask one more question.

"Do you have current knowledge of anyone who was in Fagin's group in 1836?" It was a simple question, and he expected it to be answered in the negative.

Oliver stared at the ceiling for a moment before looking back at Scrooge and replying, "There were several whom I can recall, but each met with a wretched end. I am sorry, because I would very much like to help you."

Both Scrooge and Brownlow assured Oliver that they knew he had done his best and that it was appreciated. Then, just as Brownlow refilled Scrooge's cup, Oliver cried, "Wait! There was one fellow who did not meet the end that his lifestyle deserved. In fact, he chose to renounce crime, and he left London."

Oliver looked at Brownlow for anything further that he might remember and was rewarded when Brownlow said, "Yes, my dear boy, you are correct. It was . . . Charley, I believe." He scratched his upper lip with his index finger before they cried in unison, "Charley Bates!" In fact, Charley had called on them once, as he was preparing to leave Town.

Brownlow explained, "He knew where we resided because he asked the owner of the book stall where he and the Artful Dodger robbed me when you, Oliver, were arrested for their crime. If memory serves, Charley said he regretted the part he played in what you had suffered and that he had turned from a life of crime."

"Yes, that is correct," cried Oliver. "He was going . . . north, to his family? In Northamptonshire, I believe . . . to work in agriculture. He said he wanted to become a grazier. At least, that was his plan at that time."

It wasn't much, but Scrooge was delighted to have even that one scrap of information. They spoke no more on the subject that night but instead returned to their shared love of books.

Scrooge departed the following morning, and as they bid each other farewell Brownlow shook his hand and apologized. "I'm truly sorry that we could not help you find the truth of your friend's son, but I'm afraid we told you all we know." Oliver could only nod and smile resignedly.

Scrooge again thanked them both for the delightful visit and for their friendship and assistance. He also expressed regret for compelling Oliver to re-live such a distressing situation. The boy's response surprised him, however.

Oliver insisted, "Oh no, Mr. Scrooge. You did not distress me. I grant you it was a very unpleasant time, but I have no wish to forget it, at least not in its entirety. I hope, instead, to somehow make use of what I learned of good and evil and perhaps find a way to employ that knowledge for the benefit of others."

The boy's statement showed a great deal of maturity, not to mention an unselfish and forgiving nature. Scrooge admired him for it, as did Mr. Brownlow, who smiled and puffed out his chest a bit, looking as proud as a peacock.

On the trip back to London Scrooge mulled things over as he considered all sorts of questions. What exactly was he so bent on solving? Rebecca knew her son was gone, and she knew someone was responsible. What more did she need to know? It had been ten years now, and she had reached a sort of peace, so why was it important that she know who kidnapped him, or who ended his life?

Was it imperative that Rebecca know why, how or by whom he was killed? Would she be able to endure a criminal court case if someone were actually charged? At what point would the solving of the crime become unbearable? Or, would it? Hadn't she hinted at the fact that not knowing had made things more difficult? Perhaps, but then again, perhaps not. He was unsure because he had no clear recollection of her needs in that regard.

The meeting with Mr. Brownlow and Oliver only increased Scrooge's own need to discover more about Peter Langstone's death, even though Marley had specifically warned him against doing so without Rebecca's cooperation. Scrooge had once again talked himself into setting Marley's notions aside in order to satisfy his own purposes.

Of all of the current challenges Scrooge was facing, this was the most important to him because it had long been in his mind, and it concerned his dear Rebecca Langstone. He would, however, need assistance. Once again, he would turn to Constable Norris, but this time it would be in a confidential capacity.

Constable Rollo Norris could be counted on to be discreet, and he had always managed to get the job done, no matter the obstacles. His methods were occasionally unorthodox, but he and Scrooge were an effective team, for the most part. This time Scrooge would accept no one else. It must be Norris.

CHAPTER EIGHTEEN

An Impulsive Action

Scrooge and Rebecca did not vary their lives during the few weeks of what Scrooge would later refer to as "Honora's Folly." They continued to be seen together at various gatherings, thinking that might even stifle the talk of a betrothal between Mrs. Purdy and Scrooge, but it did not. In some instances, its effect was the opposite since gossips turned their energies to deciphering what it could mean, and what on earth could Scrooge be thinking, being seen with another woman. Never mind that it was the same woman he had been seen with now for nearly two years!

Once, while attending a play together, Scrooge and Mrs. Langstone were chatting with Dick and Priscilla Wilkins and Lucy and Edwin Carter, when a Mrs. Popper and her friend, Miss Dodd, approached them. Without giving a polite greeting to anyone, Mrs. Popper looked down her nose at Scrooge, glanced slyly at Mrs. Langstone and declared, "I wonder at your being here together, but then perhaps I have misjudged you, and you are not the upright persons I have always taken you to be."

Forestalling any response, the two ladies turned and glided away, secure in the fact that they had done their moral duty. They were, at that moment, planning how they could repeat what they had seen and said, to others who were temporarily loyal to Honora Purdy and had her poor interests at heart. They failed to see the astonished glances shared by everyone in Scrooge's group, and they certainly did not hear the laughter that promptly erupted.

Throughout "Honora's Folly" Scrooge and Mrs. Langstone seemed to be growing closer – not only in their hearts, but in the possibility of marrying. He had not yet proposed, but it was definitely on his mind. Unfortunately, of late that desire had been pushed into a small corner of his mind to make way for the investigation into Peter's death. He thought on the investigation often. He was not altogether obsessed, but he had become fixed on his need to discover the truth.

At times Scrooge seemed diverted, and Mrs. Langstone wondered about his uneasiness. Conversations were occasionally cut short, or he seemed to be occupying another sphere of existence. More than once Mrs. Langstone worried that he might be overworked, or that the rumour regarding Mrs. Purdy had actually affected his well-being.

One evening, after Scrooge and Mrs. Langstone had attended a musicale, they returned to her home where she was serving him coffee. It was a happy ritual of sipping coffee and conversing after an evening out, prior to his returning to his own home.

"My Dear," said she, to get his attention as she held out the cup for him to take. Rather than respond, he continued to stare into the distance as if he had not heard her. She tried again by asking a direct question.

"Ebenezer. Would you care for some coffee? I have added cream, as you generally prefer." He continued to stare until she repeated, "Ebenezer!" He blinked, looked at her and smiled, then accepted the cup.

"I apologize, my Dear. I was gathering wool. Please forgive me."

"Of course." She compressed her lips before she said, "Although I do hope you are not working too hard and that these recent events with Mr. Martin and Honora Purdy have not been too demanding. Perhaps you are overtired and you are in need of some rest."

"No, Rebecca, they have not been too demanding. I have you, and that is all I need." He had been imagining Peter Langstone playing in these rooms, and as far as her being all he needed, that was not entirely true because he had developed a need to learn things where Peter was concerned. It was almost as if he had been acquainted with the child in life, and he had convinced himself it was she who needed to learn the facts surrounding his disappearance and death, and that he was doing it for her.

Later that night Marley appeared just before Scrooge fell into a deep sleep. Instead of his usual greeting however, Scrooge felt a decided slap on his thigh. When he was finally awake enough to realize it was Marley, he wondered how in the world a ghost had managed such a thing.

"Scrooge," said Marley sternly, "I see you are up to your old tricks of ignoring sound warnings. You are treading a hazardous path without questioning your destination, and you need to check yourself before it is too late." Marley paused, then continued as if teaching a child.

"You are still bull-headed, Scrooge, the way you were in business before your spirit was renewed. Now that you are a new man, you need to be led by the Spirit in all areas of your life."

Marley waved a transparent hand. "Oh, you have done well in loving mankind, and you have made the welfare of others your true 'business,' but in a few areas you are still like a dog with a bone, because once you sink your teeth into it you won't let go. Until you walk more in faith and less in your own wisdom and your own desires, you will bring on trouble, and that trouble will affect others as well as yourself.

'I suggest you examine your motives as if they were someone else's. It is the best way to apply sound judgment to yourself because we can always see what is amiss with someone else's thinking."

At first Scrooge did not understand Marley but then realized he must be chastising Scrooge for his determination concerning Peter Langstone. He opened his mouth to reply, but before he could do so, Marley vanished. He simply was no longer there. No mist. No fading. Not even a good-bye. Marley had departed, and there would be no discussion.

Scrooge knew Marley's manner of leaving was an indication that no debate would change his message. Still, he refused to believe that Marley's inflexibility was due to the seriousness and absolute truth of his message.

As is often the case when one's prized plans are questioned, Scrooge was immovable. As far as he was concerned, Marley had interfered too many times to count, and he did not understand that Scrooge needed to finish his investigation or wonder about it for the rest of his life. He could not marry Rebecca if he dropped the matter now, because he would believe he had let her down. He could actually do what no one else had done with regard to her son, and he needed to do it.

Scrooge gave his pillow two or three vigorous punches and muttered something about "spirits who no longer understand anything having to do with the human heart."

Scrooge was ill at ease when he finally slept, which was no doubt one reason he began to dream. He was not exactly riding the night mare, but his dream was definitely unsettling.

Scrooge and Rebecca were in the midst of a small wedding in a country church, but it was unclear if the wedding was their own, even though they were standing in front of the altar. The setting itself was vague, yet Rebecca's young son was standing next to her, holding her hand. She bent down to kiss him before he turned and walked toward the door, all the while looking back over his shoulder, smiling and waving good-bye to them both. Rebecca stood immobile and displayed no emotion other than a pure love that emanated from her heart, but Scrooge was weeping violently.

Scrooge awoke in a sweat. He wished Marley would return to interpret the dream for him, but he knew his old friend had departed for possibly a very long time, and it would do no good to demand that he reappear.

Scrooge had long desired to marry Rebecca Langstone but had not pursued it for various reasons, not the least of which was their pleasant companionship that seemed to satisfy them both for the time being. He did not realize that Mrs. Langstone was beginning to question if he would ever ask her to become his wife, but his current difficulties were surprisingly driving him to finalize their partnership. He needed that stability. He wanted to be with Rebecca because he truly loved her. For those reasons, and a thousand others, he found himself in her withdrawing room one evening, trying to find a way to say what was in his heart.

"My dearest Rebecca," he began, but he could not continue.

"Yes, Ebenezer?"

"Ahem. I need to reaffirm how much you mean to me. I count on your devotion and constancy each day. I only hope you can say the same about me, for I fear I do not always show you how much I care for you. Truth be told, I can be a very obstinate and headstrong man." He made that particular admission but would not divulge his quest regarding Peter. Not just yet. Not until he had something solid to share with her. If he discovered nothing, she need never know of his attempts.

Rebecca smiled. "I know you care. There is no question of that, but has there been something on your mind of late? You have seemed so far away at times. Perhaps there is something you would like to discuss? We have never been unable to speak our minds to each other, and we have always spoken the truth."

Scrooge's heart was beating much too fast, and there was no way of slowing it down but to do the thing that needed doing. He hadn't meant to mimic how a much younger man would behave, but he jumped from his chair and suddenly found himself on one knee before her, holding her hands in his.

"Rebecca, my love. You do realize I want to marry you, do you not? Will you please do me the honor of saying 'yes,' now? Surely, we know each other's hearts, and we are certainly old enough to know our own. Mine is asking for you to spend the rest of your life with me, and I only pray I can make you as happy as I know you will make me."

Rebecca hadn't expected a formal proposal just then, but she had no desire to refuse. Scrooge was everything a man should be, and he made her happier than she thought she could ever be again. They had weathered some storms, but she knew that life brought difficulties. The key was to weather them together. She would not even consider refusing him.

"Yes, Ebenezer, yes. I will marry you. I cannot think of one thing that would bring me more joy." He leapt up, pulled her to her feet and gathered her into his arms to kiss her with a promise of wonderful things to come.

In that instant it occurred to him that he had not given her a ring. He stepped back while still holding her arms and said, "Rebecca, I didn't think to give you a ring for our betrothal, and I admit I don't know what is proper at this stage of life. Would you like to have a ring? I will do whatever you choose." He could picture her wearing a beautiful ring, *his* ring, that declared to the world that she had chosen him, but he would do her bidding in this instance.

"I will think on that Ebenezer," she replied. "Meanwhile, let us enjoy the delight of this moment. We can decide details and dates during the weeks to come, do you not think?"

He agreed, and the two of them talked until very late, happily planning their life together as if they were in their youth. It was decided that they would not announce their betrothal yet but would enjoy the intimate secret between themselves for the time being. They were happily unaware of the anguish that lay just ahead.

THE CURIOSITY OF SCROOGE

CHAPTER NINETEEN

Forging Ahead

R ollo Norris and Scrooge met for luncheon at the George and Vulture, where they could speak without fear of anyone overhearing them or caring if they did happen to pick up on a sentence or two.

Scrooge did not want his search for the truth regarding Peter Langtone's death to become common knowledge, not only because he was unsure that he could succeed, but because he did not want to cause Rebecca consternation. If she were to be made aware of his plan, she would either forbid it or accept it for his sake, but she would still be apprehensive. Each day it would be in her thoughts, and she would no doubt be uneasy regarding its outcome. He did not wish that for her since she had suffered enough.

For all his intellect and business acumen, Scrooge often failed to apply sound analysis to his own behavior. He failed to see the possibility that solving Peter's death could force his beloved Rebecca to unnecessarily revisit and relive a terribly painful time in her life that she had finally managed to surmount, and it would be his doing. Worse, it would actually be his wrongdoing.

Scrooge was already seated at the George and Vulture when Rollo arrived, and he had arranged for their food. Norris knew there was something interesting afoot because being involved with Scrooge was never dull, but first he must ask about another unrelated topic.

"Mr. Scrooge, there is talk around the station that Constable Lynch took credit for the arrest of Henry Martin, but it is being 'suggested' that he did nothing to earn such accolades. Do you know anything about such a thing?" Scrooge not only knew, he was present at the time of Martin's arrest. Lynch was not.

Scrooge was relaxed in the friendship that had long been established with the constable, and he used Norris's Christian name. "I do know, Rollo, and I am willing to tell you if you will keep my name out of anything you may repeat." Norris nodded his promise, and Scrooge continued.

"You will notice I did not ask you not to repeat the content of what I am about to tell you, and that is because I trust you to tell only those to whom it should be made known. I believe you will also keep it to yourself until the proper time." Scrooge took a sip of punch that had just been placed before them and waited until the server was gone. He had more to say on the subject.

"I will be blunt. That lazy no-good Lynch had nothing whatsoever to do with the success of the venture. It was Stagg, the officer onto whose shoulders Lynch dumped the entire matter, who brought it about. He's a good man to have in the police.

Lynch was nowhere to be seen, of course. Even Fred and I did some of Lynch's detective work before he threw everything onto Stagg."

Scrooge gave a derisive chuckle when he added, "And *then*, Lynch had the impudence to write his report of success and turn it in to the Inspector, who was so impressed he made a visit to me to say how proud he was of Lynch. I seriously doubt that poor Constable Stagg was even mentioned in the report, even though it was he who brought about the desired end to the matter."

Norris leaned back and said, "I suspected as much. Most of us are aware of Lynch's habits, and we stay out of his way because he is always looking for someone else to do his work while he seizes the credit, or to take the blame when something goes amiss.

"Rest assured that I will honor this information and will only repeat it if need be. Even then, I will only inform the appropriate people." He took a drink and said, "However, if there is an argument about the truth of the report, I may have to quote you. Is that acceptable?"

Scrooge thought for a moment and said, "It is, my good man, it is." Then he said, "But here is why I wanted to see you," and he related the story of Peter Langstone.

Norris was unaware of Rebecca Langstone's son's disappearance and death, and he listened intently as Scrooge gave him the few details he knew. When Scrooge mentioned his visit to Oliver Twist, Norris reckoned that he knew where Scrooge was headed, but he would wait until he had heard the entirety of Scrooge's discourse.

"So, Rollo, we have come to my intent in speaking to you regarding all of this. In fact, I need your help in discovering the truth of what really happened to little Peter. You have connections I do not have, and you are acquainted with the nuances of criminal discovery, so I know you are the man to help me, if you are willing to do so."

Rollo rubbed the back of his neck and considered the matter. He was unsure of the soundness of the plan and said, "Mr. Scrooge, I have two questions for you. First, why do you want to dig up the dead? And second, what does Mrs. Langstone think about your doing this?"

Since Scrooge had been justifying his curiosity to himself for some time now – years, in fact – he was ready with a reply. "She is not aware of my search, but wouldn't any mother want to know the truth of her child's demise? She was forced to come to grips with his death without knowing any facts, and she has lived with that vacuum for years. I want to help her settle this thing once and for all in her mind, and I must say I even want to do it for Peter himself. He deserves more than a grave that testifies of a death that does not include the how and the why of it. Do you not agree?"

Norris was uncertain and said so, but he could see some merit to Scrooge's argument, and he would be helping a friend rather than making a judgment on the morality of the thing. Scrooge could work that out with Rebecca Langstone however he saw fit. After all, Norris was a policeman, not a clergyman. He took a deep breath and forged ahead.

"As I see it," began Norris, "There are several avenues we might pursue. There is Fagin's gang itself, although I'm not certain what we could find there that would be helpful. I am presuming that most anything we needed to know about Fagin we could learn from Oliver Twist. There are also, hopefully, police records of Fagin's boys and what happened to them when the gang was disbanded. As far as Peter, we would do well to speak with the policeman who dealt with the body and knows how it was discovered." He continued to think aloud.

"There are two things I believe we could glean from those sources. One is, of course, the details surrounding the discovery of the body and any investigation that followed. The other is to discover the whereabouts of Charley Bates in order to interview him for any possible clues about Peter's death since he may have been in Fagin's 'family' at that time. I realize it is highly unlikely that it was Fagin's group who kidnapped Peter, but we need to at least try, since it is the only clue we have." Then, if that door closes, I think we may be at the end of it."

Scrooge was nodding, but Norris would not allow even a fragment of false hope. "Mr. Scrooge, you must force yourself to grasp the fact that it is doubtful that we can uncover enough information to satisfy you. Are you willing to proceed, having that understanding?" Scrooge believed he was, although that belief had not yet been tested. And so, they did proceed.

CHAPTER TWENTY

Private Assistance

Constable Norris could have consulted the City of London police registers, but he was convinced he might do well to first ask his fellow officers for the names of any constables who were employed as such in 1836. He would do that before searching what might prove to be lengthy and ambiguous records.

It had been ten years since Peter Langstone's death, so Norris knew it was likely that whoever dealt with the case was no longer a policeman. That was confirmed when he asked for the names of any current officers who were in uniform in 1836. There were three, and the first two could not recollect the incident, but the third, a Constable Booth, recalled the event even though he had not been connected to it.

According to Booth, the officer who handled the incident was Owen Clarke, who left the force with the rank of Sergeant in 1844. Of course! Norris had forgotten the man, but he had known him and liked him because he was honest and reliable.

He obtained Clark's direction, and it seemed prudent to include Scrooge in the visit rather than attempt to recount the conversation to him at a later date.

The former Sergeant Clarke was at home and was happy to welcome his visitors. Norris had often reported to Sergeant Clarke when he was on the force, and they had a mutual respect for each other. Norris opened the conversation.

"Sergeant, we have come to pick your brain regarding a certain incident that occurred in, we believe, the autumn of 1836. I'm sorry we don't have the exact date, but you may recall it, at any rate. It was the case of an affluent family's six-year-old boy, Peter Langstone, who was abducted from his nanny while on an outing, and his body was recovered from the Thames three weeks later." Norris knew it was unlikely that Clarke would remember, but it did no harm to enquire.

Without hesitating, Clarke replied. "Oh, yes. I remember that case. It was sad. Very sad. I was the one to tell the parents, and I thought we might lose them both right there on the spot. Lovely people they were, and that's the truth. They were so kind because they felt sorry for me for having to bring them the news. *Me*! When all the while their hearts were breaking." Scrooge swallowed hard and forced himself to listen.

Norris asked how the body was found, and Clarke had a clear memory of the entire case. It seemed to have made a permanent impression on his brain, much like the new daguerreotypes one heard about these days. He easily recalled the details.

"Some mudlarks found him during low water at Wapping when they were looking for bits to sell, and the Marine Police took control of the body. They advised us because the family had posted notices on boards near the Royal Exchange and in shop windows around Town, so they asked if we could identify the body. Rather than put the parents through it, I went, armed with a portrait miniature of him, but it was difficult to tell for certain because of the condition of his flesh." Scrooge was very nearly ill by this time, but he managed to control his stomach as the Sergeant continued.

"Several things convinced me that it was Peter. First was the fact that the body was missing the two front teeth and one on the lower front right. His parents had been particularly specific about that when they reported him missing. He also had dark hair and was the right size. The nanny was recording his height as he grew, marking each year on a door jamb in the nursery. She had made the last mark a few weeks earlier, so I measured it and then compared it to the body. There was no doubt in my mind that we had found our missing boy, but I took no pleasure in declaring it so." There was more, so he continued without anyone asking anything.

"The body appeared to have a head wound, but I don't think the police doctor decided if it came before or after death, and there was no way to know if it was the cause." Not knowing the relationship between Scrooge and Mrs. Langstone, Clarke did not realize how brutal his words were. It was better that way because he spoke the God's truth without concern for injuring anyone.

"As you can well imagine, we had no clues and no idea of who or where to question anyone. We did look into our recent records for anything that might tie the body to an occurrence in Town, but nothing came of our search. If I recall correctly, the Coroner's Officer did not order an inquest, nor was a post-mortem conducted, even though it was most surely foul play, in my opinion."

The three of them sat for a moment, no one knowing what to say. Eventually Clarke broke the silence by offering to re-search the records of the crime, or any nearby events about that time, but neither Norris nor Scrooge believed that would be profitable. Scrooge did have an idea, but he wanted to speak to Norris about it before making the suggestion to Clarke.

Scrooge and Norris thanked the Sergeant as they departed and began to walk toward a street where they could hail a cab. Norris was considering what Clarke had said when Scrooge interrupted his thoughts.

"You know, I believe I recognize in Clarke a capable and honest man."

"I agree," said Norris, adding, "I worked with him several times and always found him to be honest in analysis and accurate in his reports. He also told the truth when testifying, even when it did not present him in the most favorable light, unlike some I could name."

"That certainly does speak to the man's character, which is exactly what I was hoping. You see, I have an idea." Scrooge stopped, which required Norris to do the same, and they faced each other.

"Rollo, what say you to my hiring Clarke privately to investigate this thing, and to locate Charley Bates?" Before Norris could answer, Scrooge explained. "Neither you nor I have the time required to locate him, but I believe Bates is our only hope of getting to the truth of the matter, even if that hope is as thin as a spider's web."

Norris thought a moment before he responded. "If I were you, and I were seeking the answers you seek, I would hire him if he will accept the task." Scrooge nodded. Norris's words were all he needed to settle his mind, and he would make Clarke an offer in the next day or two.

Clarke was surprised to find Scrooge on his stoop, but he invited him in, partly because he had been favorably impressed with Scrooge and partly because he was curious as to what brought about this second visit.

"I beg your pardon for this intrusion, but since our earlier conversation I have been thinking, and I have a proposition to present to you." Clarke was intrigued and bid him to continue. Scrooge did not quibble.

"Now that you know what I am seeking, which is the truth of Peter Langstone's death, and considering the fact that you already know a great deal about it, I am wondering if you would be willing to investigate further as a private individual. I would pay you whatever you believe is a fair salary, of course."

Clarke raised his eyebrows at the unexpected suggestion. Such a thing had not occurred to him, but it was the sort of thing he could do well, and he missed the activity of being a policeman.

"Well, Mr. Scrooge, there are several things we would need to establish before I could agree. First and foremost, how do you expect me to discover the truth of Peter's death? You must have some idea of what it is you want me to do, or you would not be sitting here now."

"You are correct, Clarke. There are two people who may have some information. One was a gang leader, Fagin, who I understand went to the gallows in 1839; and Charley Bates, a boy who was in Fagin's 'family' until its demise in that same year. Obviously, you cannot speak to Fagin, but perhaps someone who knew him learned something about Peter before Fagin was executed. My contacts say that Bates gave up his life of crime and may be living somewhere in Northamptionshire, working in agriculture. As to age, I believe he is in his early twenties. My hope is, of course, that he might have known Peter. I should add that I realize it is unlikely that this particular gang is the one we are looking for, if it was, in fact, a group that was responsible for Peter's death, rather than one person, acting alone."

The name "Fagin" was vaguely family to Clarke, but he couldn't place him. Setting that aside, he asked, "Mr. Scrooge, it is none of my business, but why are you on this quest? What do you plan to do with any knowledge you may gain?"

What *did* Scrooge plan to do with it? It was difficult to say, although he had begun by thinking he was doing it for Rebecca. Now he was uncertain. He knew only that it was something he was bound to pursue, even though he doubted anyone would ever come to trial over the matter. So, he simply said, "I hope I will know that when and if I discover the truth. I may share it with Mrs. Langstone, but I do not know at this point." That reminded him of something else he needed to make certain that Clarke understood.

"Mrs. Langstone does not know about my search, so I ask that you not speak with her. Off hand, I cannot think of a reason why you would need to, but if it should come to that, I must insist that you consult with me first." Clarke had not asked how Scrooge knew Mrs. Langstone, and he would not do so now, nor would Scrooge enlightenment him.

"Well, Mr. Scrooge, I must say I am intrigued by this puzzle, and I believe I would like to try my hand at setting the pieces in place. As far as payment, I will let you know my fees when I have settled on an approach, although I will be requiring certain expenses in addition to payment for my time and efforts. Once we agree on amounts, we can shake hands on it unless you would prefer a contract in pen and ink." Scrooge agreed that a handshake would suffice since he believed Norris's reports about Clarke's honor.

CHAPTER TWENTY-ONE

An Assault at the Pub

There were several reasons why Rollo Norris was no longer attentive to Martha Cratchit. Uppermost was the fact that he suspected Martha preferred Homer's absolute devotion to his own unclear intentions. Then, last Christmas, Rollo was introduced to Fred's wife's sister, Flora, and was immediately taken with her beauty, her musical aptitude, and her child-like interest in everything within view. Flora became Rollo's fascination for a time, but she was a step above him socially, and he refused to attempt to cross that line. He knew his station in life and would never compromise his happiness by trying to be something other than what he was. He needn't have been concerned about such a thing however, because destiny was about to intervene.

The fracas began inside a working-class tavern, but it had already spilled into the street by the time the constables were alerted and made their way to the scene. As was usually the case, it began simply enough.

"'Ere," barked a man waiting for his pint. He had just been elbowed aside by a thirsty drinker who attempted to squeeze in ahead of him. "Don' be pushin' yer way int' the queue! You'll get yer bub in due time!"

"'Oo's pushin?" the crowder retorted. That ain't pushin – *this* is!" and he gave a hefty heave-ho that landed the man on his back on a nearby table. Cheap ale splattered in all directions as the men who had paid good copper for their drinks leapt up and out of the way, cursing everything but the Queen, herself.

By then the two instigators of the scrap were rolling around on the floor, locked in tandem, trading blows and making it nearly impossible to separate them. Other drinkers made feeble attempts to grab at the shirt of first one, then the other, before giving up and leaving them to their disagreement. After all, everyone was entitled to stand up for himself, whether right, or wrong, wasn't he?

Since it was unclear who was right or wrong, most of the drinkers soon began to choose sides. Not that they cared or even had a definite opinion, but because it was an opportunity to take a meaningless stand and back it up with a few good wallops. Many intended punches missed their marks, coming from those who were unquestionably sozzled and could not stand without swaying like canvas in a high wind.

One such punch, however, actually made decisive contact with the jaw of a particularly unbalanced lushy – a stout man whose numbed brain made him as dangerous as a misguided slingshot. He flew out of the open doorway at exactly the same moment a young woman named Lily was passing by, toting her basket of vegetables for the cook of the house where she was employed. They were meant for tonight's dinner.

Upon impact, both of Lily's feet were lifted off the ground and her lovely vegetables flew above her head, scattering everywhere. The collision left Lily face down on the stone, with the oversized pugilist sitting on the back of her shins. His head wobbled as he enquired, "Oi! What's 'appened 'ere?"

Pedestrians tried to help, but when they pulled him up and away from her, he realized he had not yet won the fight, and began to swing at anyone within the reach of his arms. He did not notice the squashed cabbages and carrots under his feet as he stomped unsteadily, destroying once for all a goodly portion of the evening's dinner. All Lily could do was watch him as he removed any hope she had of recovering her purchases.

A few men who had given up the battle noticed the wreckage he had caused and ventured outside to bring him under control. He was having none of it, however, and within half a minute the entire scuffle had moved to the street where it involved innocent pedestrians as they were pushed out of the way or even knocked down. The constables finally arrived and attempted to restore order, but it was not an easy task.

In Metropolitan London Sir Robert Peel's policing principles included the rule that officers should use physical force only when all other efforts, including persuasion and warning, had been exhausted.

Although the City of London was a separate police entity, some of its officers recognized the value of Peel's principles and attempted, on occasion, to put them into effect. The incident in question, however, was one of the times when there would be no "persuasion," although a few loud threats were articulated, along with the sound of one or two wooden truncheons making contact with a few hard heads.

A kindly woman was attempting to help Lily to her feet, and she had made it half-way up just before two men trying to best each other knocked them both down again. Neither one noticed the women, but Rollo Norris did as he collared one of the miscreants, and he determined to come to Lili's aid as soon as the situation was under control. Unfortunately, it would take several more minutes.

Meanwhile, Lily remained sitting. It seemed the safest thing to do. The right side of her face had deep abrasions where she had landed on the stones, and she was destined for a blackened eye by evening. Besides that, large sections of her body and legs were bruised and scraped, and she would soon be stiff and sore. Her straw basket was in tatters and the vegetables unrecognizable. It was unlike her to be faint-hearted, but when she saw the misfortune that had befallen Cook's vegetables and realized she had been injured, Lily's eyes welled with tears. They spilled down her cheeks, streaking with the blood from her injuries, and she began to sob.

Before Lily knew it, a constable was bent over her. He placed his hands on her heaving shoulders and gently helped her up. Once she was on her feet he continued to support her arm, should she faint or lose her balance. He couldn't help but notice that she was very pretty, even with a face that was scratched and puffed from crying; a bonnet that was half-way off her head, and hair that was no longer obeying the dictates of its pins.

"Here, Miss. You're alright now," said Norris, soothingly. He produced a clean handkerchief and handed it to her. She wiped her eyes and blew her nose, then thanked him, but she had the presence of mind not to return it without offering to wash it first. When he realized that would mean he would see her again, he agreed. "Don't you worry about giving it back to me just now," he said. "I can get it from you another time."

Lily gave a small, grateful smile. After all, she would rather not have to wipe her eyes and nose on her sleeves! Having realigned her bonnet as best she could and retrieved the bits of what remained of her basket, Lily set aside her own pitiful state because she realized she had bigger problems.

Lily was terrified of having to return home empty-handed. She dreaded facing Cook, who was going to be without many of the ingredients for dinner. In her alarm Lily once again began to weep, allowing her imagination to race to the worst possible conclusion.

In between sobs and gulps she cried, "I don' know what I'm gonna do, I don't! I've gone and ruined their dinner 'n Cook will 'ave to blame me. She won't want to, but she'll 'ave to tell the truth, an' wot will 'appen to me then? I'll lose my situation!" How would she ever find a better place of employment, or better employers? That last thought set her off with more moans and whimpers, which was not her usual reaction to trouble.

In the end, several constables managed to narrow the guilty down to the two men who initially started the row with their shoves, and the one who blundered into Lily, causing her injury and splintering her hamper and its contents. The miscreants were herded away to lock-up, to eventually face a magistrate, leaving Rollo to see Lily safely home. Initially, she resisted his offer since she did not want him to witness her getting the sack, but she finally relented when he said, "I will explain what happened, and we'll make certain they understand you weren't to blame."

Lily led Rollo to the house, which he recognized as the home of Fred and Catherine Symons, but he refrained from saying so as Lily pointed him to the back stairs and guided him into the kitchen.

The moment they entered they were met by a very cross cook who placed her hands ominously on her ample hips and demanded, "Just where do you think you've been, my girl?

And where are my vegetables? I've been waiting near an hour and I can't finish the Missus' dinner without them!"

The words had no sooner left her mouth when she saw the constable and noticed that Lily looked as if she had fallen off a wagon and been dragged at least a mile. The appalling truth then dawned on her, and although she couldn't believe it of this particular girl, she blurted, "You're not tellin' me she's been *arrested*!" Her hands flew to her face and she cried, "What's she *done*?"

Rollo might have chuckled had Lily not, at that very moment, let out a heartbreaking wail. "I've done nothin', Cook, I swear, but I got run into and there's nuthin' left o' my basket, nor your vegetables. They're in bits 'n pieces by the pub, but honest, it wasn't my doing!" She tugged at Rollo's sleeve and begged him, "*Tell* her! You tell 'er what's happened. She'll believe *you*!"

Rollo did tell Cook, who tutted and clicked her tongue throughout the entire heartbreaking account, feeling ever so sorry for "the poor little thing." She sent for the doctor, patted Lily on the shoulder and clucked, "Now, don't you worry, Luv. I'll tell Missus what's happened and I'm certain she will make allowances for this meal. Meanwhile, you get cleaned up and I'll give the constable a cup of tea before I send him on his way."

Lily was already finding it a little painful to get around, but she did as she was told, turning back around before going upstairs.

"Thank you for helping me, Constable. I'll get your kerchief washed and I hope it won't be stained."

He was still standing, so he nodded and said, "You are welcome, Lily. My name is Rollo Norris, and I will be back to see how you are. You can give me the handkerchief then, if you please." Both of them smiled, albeit she did so with some effort because of the wounds on her face. Then she slowly worked her way up the stairs while Cook poured Rollo a nice cup of tea.

CHAPTER TWENTY-TWO

Her Testimony Is Required

Norris appeared in Court on Monday morning, when the three troublemakers' cases would be heard. He decided not to bring Lily as a possible witness since he assumed that the men would own up to their misconduct. That proved to be the case with the two who had started the uproar, but the man who had so forcefully collided with Lily had other ideas.

Lily's assailant gave his name as Hoyt Huckstep, but he did not entirely resemble the man of the previous Saturday evening. He was still very disheveled, but his ale-induced aggression had been replaced by a more sobered sluggishness, which is often the calling card that drink leaves behind when it departs the body.

When called, Rollo recited the charges. "Mr. Huckstep was disturbing the peace and committed an assault, Your Worship. He caused moderate injury and property damage to a young pedestrian when he crashed out of the public house and onto the street." As additional evidence, Norris stated, "Huckstep is, as you see, a large man, and his victim weighs little over seven stone."

Huckstep was horrified at the charges. "I never!" he insisted. "There ain't no way I'd ever 'arm a body smaller'n me. I ain't no bludger, 'n that's the God's truth. Why, it wudn' be a fair scrap!" He looked at the magistrate and pleaded. "It jus' in't my nature to do such a thing to another 'ooman being. I'm a peace-lovin' individual wot's always tryin' to 'elp, not 'arm, me fellow man. No, Sir! I never did such a thing!" He continued wagging his head and repeated, "I never would do, specially to a little fella!"

Norris was thereby forced to offer to deliver the victim to court, and the magistrate continued the matter until after luncheon.

"You want me to *what*?" squealed Lily. "I musn't be seen anywhere with my face the way it is, much less talk at people in public, in court!" It was true that Lily's injuries had bloomed in the intervening day, leaving dried red abrasions on her puffy cheek and a blackened eye that suggested an awful beating. As a witness she would be perfect because, as a victim, she was pathetic.

Between Rollo and Cook, Lily was convinced it was her civic duty to testify in Court. The compelling argument came from Cook when she asked a question that touched Lily's soft heart. "Do you want this man to do this to someone else on another day? He's less likely to, you know, if he's held to answer for what he did to you."

So, Lily donned a bonnet that hid her injuries to some extent, took the Constable's arm, and let him lead her into a place she never in her wildest dreams ever imagined she would set foot – a real, live courtroom, of all things!

The clerk had just reconvened and Mr. Huckstep's case was called. There he stood, so certain that he was being maligned, and steadfast in his readiness to defend his honor against these trumped-up charges.

Before bringing Lily into the courtroom, Norris convinced her to remove her hat, which allowed her injuries to be indisputably displayed. She was mortified, but she had come to trust Norris to the extent that she removed it. Then, her innate courage rose within her and she somehow managed to hold her head high and march into the courtroom on the Constable's arm. All eyes were on her, but most especially the two in Hoyt Huckstep's head.

Huckstep's expression turned from self-preservation to astonishment. He gasped, blinked and rubbed his eyes with both fists. *Dear Lord, it's a helpless little lass, and a proper bit of frock, she is.* She had indeed "copped a mouse" on her right eye, and she had severe scratches on her cheek. It looked as if she were walking a little stiffly, too, so she must be bruised all over. He suddenly knew without a doubt that he was responsible. The realization hit him in the chest like the ball from a cannon, and he began to speak without thinking.

"Oh, Miss . . . dear girl. I didn't mean to 'arm you. I din't even know you was there, I swear! S'truth, I can't even 'member the fight they say I was in!" Having said so, he hoped against hope that not remembering would somehow mitigate his guilt, but it did no such thing. In fact, it worked the opposite. For the first time in years he saw himself as he truly was. He was a wastrel and a lushington. The realization could work for his betterment, or it could increase the speed of his race to ruination, but that was yet to be seen.

Lily was called as a witness and was sworn by the clerk, her hand visibly shaking as she took the Holy Scriptures. The prosecutor leaned in toward her and peered over his spectacles before pointing at Huckstep and asking, "Is this the man who caused these injuries to you, and is he the one who also ruined the goods you were carrying home to your mistress?" Lily tried to lick her lips and swallow, although it was difficult since her mouth was so dry, but she gathered enough courage to answer. Her testimony came out in a timid little squeak, and she looked at the magistrate as she replied, "Yes, your Highness, he looks jus' like him, he truly does." He smiled but did not correct her misuse of the royal title. She was then released, since no one else had any questions.

There. She had stood in front of all of these people, looking like she, herself, belonged in goal, and even so had spoken the truth, but she was not victorious. She was thoroughly fatigued. In addition, she pitied Huckstep and prayed for the Lord's mercy as the magistrate declared him guilty.

The magistrate then prepared to pronounce sentence, and Norris grasped Lily's small shoulders to usher her from the courtroom as quickly as possible. Mr. Huckstep bellowed after her, his eyes watery, "I'm sorry Miss. I'm so sorry." He raised his voice even more and shouted, "*Please forgive me!*" It was unfortunate that he had no way of knowing that she already had.

Before Norris and Lily worked their way to the door of the courtroom, and as the magistrate began to actually pronounce sentence, a commotion erupted from every corner of the room regarding Huckstep's punishment.

Observers and those accused of various crimes began shouting their own reactions to what they had just seen and heard. Some considered the outcome to be Huckstep's just deserts while others cried out against what was, to them, an obvious miscarriage of justice. The man was repentant, was he not? Because of the clamour, Lily did not hear the sentence as it was delivered, which was precisely what Rollo was hoping.

Lily had made an impression on Rollo from the time he saw her after she had been knocked down on the sidewalk; bruised, bleeding and bawling like a baby. She was definitely no baby, though. Not Lily. She had shown herself to be strong and willing to do what was required of her, even when she was unschooled in the thing, such as testifying in court, or afraid. Yet, with all that, she was kindhearted, and she did not hold a grudge against her attacker. Instead, she felt sorry for him!

Rollo began to take notice of Lily's virtues after they departed the courtroom. He had expected her to be cheerful and relieved that the hearing was completed, so when he asked why she looked so sad, she replied, "It's that poor man – Mr. Huckstep. I can't get him outta my mind." Rollo tried to reason with her, to remind her that it was Huckstep who had injured her, not the other way 'round, but all she said was, "But did you hear the things he said to me? He was truly sorry, and that makes *me* sorry for *him*!"

Rollo was surprised by the fact that he admired Lily for her sentiments, and he could only shake his head as she spoke. Every day he came into contact with women of all walks of life, but he had never before met anyone like Lily. Yes, he had been fond of some, but he tended to regard those few like fine paintings. They were handsome, but they didn't have the spark of life that shined from within Lily.

Lily was spunky and yet tender-hearted even though she did not have an easy life. Her nature was pleasing, and it kept her from being spoilt or demanding, which somehow engendered a desire in him to take care of her. Naturally he did not think these things through, but the ideas were beginning to form in his mind just the same – even if they were only rattling around in a bit of a jumble.

Lily, on the other hand, hadn't given Rollo much thought at all other than to be grateful to him for his help and his understanding. She could not have described him in terms of height or hair color, and she had no opinion at all regarding his character. Rollo suspected that she was not particularly impressed by him, and of course that provoked all the more interest from him. He was set on becoming better acquainted, and he would take whatever she might eventually give in terms of affection, even if it meant only friendship. He would choose her fealty as a friend over the fickle declarations of love from many he had met.

It was with that truth, although as yet only an undefined tingle in his brain, that Rollo decided to see Lily as often as possible. He would not ask for the return of his handkerchief today. Instead, he would return for it at a later date, but very soon.

CHAPTER TWENTY-THREE

The Private Investigation

Owen Clarke was as good as his word. He and Scrooge had agreed on the venture and how and what he was to be paid. So, with a handshake he at once became a confidential detective. He was pleased, since quitting the police had not brought with it a pension. Upon leaving the force, Clark was given a few parting pounds, which was not normal practice, but his performance on the job had been stellar, and he was rewarded for his work, at least to some extent.

Newgate Prison would be Clarke's first stop since it was where Fagin spent his last days before his execution. Even though there was only a slim chance that it had been Fagin's group who abducted and killed Peter, there was no other possibility at this point. He only hoped the prison's records were in order, or that someone would recall the people he needed to see. It would be even better if those he wished to interview were still employed at the prison. It had been only seven years, so there might be someone around who remembered or had actually spoken to this Fagin. In fact, Clarke himself had heard the name while he was still on the force, but he had not had any direct dealings with the man, that he knew of.

The search was extremely wearisome. Records were nonexistent for many prison wardens and gaolers, which meant the only way to find someone who had spent time with Fagin prior to his execution was to ask the current warders.

Clarke spoke with several men and received shakes of the head or rude answers until he asked one final turnkey, Old Plunkett, who actually recalled Fagin and the terrible time he had given everyone prior to his death. Most of Plunkett's teeth were missing and he slurred his words as if he had been tippling from the bottle in his pocket, so he was difficult to understand. Nevertheless, Clarke did gather that Fagin had been raving mad at the end and "grew so terrible" that his two attendants kept watch together, rather than be alone with him.

Since it was the easiest means of communicating, Plunkett was able to literally point Clarke to one of Fagin's attendants whom he spotted several yards away. The man affirmed that Fagin has said little to any of them that made sense and nothing concerning the death of a small boy whom they may have kidnapped. He confirmed that Fagin had been delirious and at one time cried to someone who existed only in his mind, "Saw his head off!" That did not seem to apply to Peter Langstone, considering how he had died.

One of the attendants knew a guard, Eli Deedle, who had been with Fagin as he was marched to the gallows, and he took Clarke down some dark and filthy passages to speak to him. Deetle confirmed that he was with Fagin just prior to his execution, and Clarke asked if Fagin had mentioned the name Charley Bates. It was no doubt owing to Fagin's terrible end that Deedle recalled such details, but he said, "'E talked about 'is 'boys' and I think 'e did mumble sump'n 'bout Charley bein' a good boy and that it was 'well done,' but 'e did't say nothin' more. 'E were ravin' awright." Although it was slightly more than Clarke had expected, it was still no help at all.

While Clarke was at Newgate, Scrooge spoke with his friend Dick Wilkins, who was an expert at ferreting out information from his associates. Without telling Wilkins the reason, Scrooge asked that he "nose around" the Royal Exchange to see where in Northamptonshire the most, or the best, wool was produced. Wilkins assumed it was a business matter and agreed to get to it as soon as possible. He had no idea he was being asked to assist in possibly naming the murderer of Mrs. Langstone's son.

Naturally Wilkins was successful, although there was no way of knowing if his succeeding at his task would lead to anything meaningful for Scrooge.

"Well, old friend," said Wilkins, "I can tell you that I spoke with a number of investors and tradesmen. Although they did not all agree on where the most and best wool is produced in Northamptonshire these days, the name of the town 'Kettering' popped up the most often. Evidently it was once known for its prolific wool production, but it is dropping off a bit as other industries take hold. I can't guarantee anything about the wool itself, but it continues to have a reputation in the trade."

Scrooge had thought as much since, as a businessman, he made it his concerns to know such things, but he was pleased to have his belief confirmed. He would be happy to pay Barnes's expenses to travel North, even for such a slim chance of discovering a piece of the truth.

Clarke decided to examine local Police Court records for any entries that may have mentioned Charley Bates. Had the boy been arrested, the records might show a place of abode or possibly mentioned family members. Even a witness list for his crimes could provide valuable information. Clarke, a former police officer, would have an easy enough time gaining access to the archives since he still knew many of the men at the gaol and the Magistrates' Court.

The arrest and Magistrate records for eight to ten years earlier were stored in a dusty out-of-the-way area, but Clarke was undaunted since he was well-acquainted with the disorder and the eerie atmosphere that seemed to accompany such spaces. Once or twice it occurred to him that he was on a fool's errand since all of his and Scrooge's efforts were being poured into Fagin and his gang, when it was highly unlikely that they were the ones responsible. Still, it was all they had, so he would pursue whatever notions or leads he could discover.

Clarke knew that Fagin was hanged in 1839 and that his "boys" were generally fairly young, because boys of that age were more agile, more easily controlled and ate less. They could also act as snakesmen and work their ways into homes through small areas, then let the others in through the doors. Given what he had, Clarke decided to search the record from 1835 through 1840, which was a bit beyond the time Bates told Brownlow and Oliver that he was moving north.

The search was arduous. Poor lighting and undecipherable handwriting took a great deal of time and patience, but Clarke was determined to be thorough, and it took three days. After searching his chosen six years of records, the only conclusion he could draw was that Bates had never been arrested, at least not under that name. At any rate, arrested or not, the police and court records offered nothing that would contribute to the search. Clarke had no way of knowing, but Bates had never been arrested because he was the Dodger's sidekick and more a shadow than a substance in terms of criminal behavior.

On a whim, Clarke re-visited his old station to ask Constable Booth if he had ever had contact with Fagin's boys, and shouldn't have been surprised that the officer knew who they were. In fact, several officers had an idea of who they were and kept an eye out for their misdeeds.

Booth had had words with two of Fagin's boys on one occasion when they tipped over a fruit stall, either to steal some fruit or, more likely, as a diversion to pick someone's pocket. They claimed it was an accident, and he could not prove otherwise, so he gave them a stern warning. However, he and another officer did not let go of the boys' collars until the boys gave them their names.

Booth was unable to recall the names they chose, which were no doubt quickly devised aliases, but when he asked if they lived in London, one of them, the one who smiled and chuckled as if he were having the time of his life, replied that he was from "up North," where his father's family worked the farms. Booth recollected, "He responded quickly and with apparent candor, so I suspected that bit of his information was true." It was enough to suggest that Clarke was perhaps on the right track.

Clarke invited Scrooge to meet with him at Clark's home, where they could converse privately about his efforts, which had resulted in very little real information.

"Let's see what we have then, at this point," suggested Scrooge. It was his enterprise, but it was definitely Clarke's investigation since he was the man with the expertise. Scrooge would participate in the discussion, but it would be Clarke who would guide it. He began.

"Mr. Scrooge, we have not established any proof of anything at this point, but there are two or three things we must consider. Firstly, we have nothing to tie this Fagin to the death of Peter. That does not, however, mean it did not happen within his ranks, with or without his knowledge. Since his boys are the only group about which we have any information, we have no choice but to proceed along those lines. There is an extremely remote possibility that Fagin's group will lead us to the death of Peter." Scrooge nodded. He was aware that it would be nearly impossible to reach a satisfactory conclusion to the thing they had begun.

"Secondly," continued Clarke, "We have Charley Bates calling on Brownlow and Oliver. During that visit he apologizes to Oliver and announces that he is going to Northamptonshire to become a grazier." He smiled and said, "And here we can begin to put two and two together! A street boy, a pickpocket no doubt, once told Constable Booth that his father's family was from 'up North,' where they worked the farms. I suspect that boy was Bates since the remark agrees with what Bates told Brownlow and Oliver.

"Thirdly, we know that Bates was in Fagin's 'family' at least while Oliver was there, which was most likely sometime between 1837 and 1839. Bates was older than Oliver and may have been a pickpocket for a few years prior to that. If so, it is probable that he knew Peter if it was Fagin's band who kidnapped him."

Clarke sighed and admitted, "But as you can see, there are so many "ifs" that I fear you must prepare yourself for disappointment."

Scrooge knew that was the case. He also knew that any prudent person would not waste more time on this. This entire endeavor could well be a pointless task and he could only imagine what Marley would then have to say about it. But . . . he could not bring himself to give up the chase! There was still one piece of information that Scrooge had not shared with Clarke.

"Owen, an associate of mine tells me that Kettering in Northamptonshire is known for its wool production and, as you know, wool requires graziers. Kettering itself is most likely too large for farmers to reside, but there must be hamlets nearby, where Bates may have settled."

Clarke agreed that they had most likely arrived at their best bet for finding Bates, and he agreed to travel north to the area of Kettering and do his best to locate him. It was also agreed that, should he find him, Clark would either return to London and inform Scrooge, or he would inform Scrooge by mail and wait for him in Kettering. It was important to Scrooge that he be in attendance should any interview with Bates take place.

CHAPTER TWENTY-FOUR

Her Heart Is Softened

Constable Rollo Norris returned to the Symons' kitchen as often as possible. He was always greeted heartily by Cook, who made tea and served him her latest sweets. She made no pretense of not liking him, and she continually sang his praises to Lily, although she could generate little reaction from the girl. It wasn't that Lily disliked the officer. She enjoyed his company very much, but she was unlike other girls.

Lily was not seeking a man who would rescue her from domestic service by putting a ring on her finger only to then expect her to perform even more domestic service, but without pay. Her reasoning did not include the element of "being in love" however, and that was because she had never experienced such a thing. She didn't miss it because it was not a part of her thinking. She believed such love existed, but it had nothing to do with her.

Cook, who had never been married (although she used the title of "Missus" since that was what cooks often did) had the heart of a young maiden when it came to romance. For that reason, she could not understand Lily's disinterest in Constable Norris. Wasn't he everything a young woman might want? He was handsome; he earned a good wage; he was very sociable; and, most importantly, he had been paying his sincere respects to Lily on a regular basis throughout the spring months. Could that little slip of a girl not see it? How could she not think of him as a possible suitable mate? What was wrong with her? More than once Cook had thought, *If I were eighteen again, I would not let that man get one foot out the door without reaching some sort of understanding before he could turn the key!*

There was no way of knowing how much longer Rollo Norris would continue to pay his respects to Lily without giving up the chase altogether. He had thought he could settle on her friendship, if that were all she had to offer, but if that be the case, he would certainly not be stopping at the Symons house quite so often. He did, however, enjoy Cook's scones, biscuits and tarts, so that would always be an effective incentive to call and say hello.

Lily was, contrary to all appearances, a very passionate girl. Her beliefs and her sensitivities ran deep, but where a suitor was concerned, those particular passions had not been awakened. It would take more than sharing a cup of tea and passing a plate of crumpets to someone to open her eyes to possibilities that currently lay dormant within her heart.

Lily's route to and from the greengrocer and the fruiterer continued to take her by the pub where she had been so roughly knocked down by Hoyt Huckstep. That particular spot seemed marked for upsetting occurrences because today Lily was privy to another scene, and although it did not touch her physically and did not damage the items in her new basket, it did prick her soul which, in itself, came as quite a surprise.

Lily was daydreaming about how Cook was teaching her to prepare meals and had even remarked that Lily was a "natural" when it came to matching seasonings to various foods. Cook also said that Lily had an eye for making dishes attractive. Lily's enjoyable recollections of those compliments were suddenly interrupted by the sounds of a man and woman talking, but it was not a normal dialogue. Instead, they spoke as if there were an intimacy to their relationship.

Lily did not have the experience nor the vocabulary to put words to what she was hearing, but anyone else would have instantly recognized the words for the lust they conveyed. She did, however, recognize the man as Rollo Norris, and he was in the company of a rather tawdry woman who was leaning her body against his. The two of them were a distance down the street, and they did not notice Lily since they were totally occupied with each other.

The woman let out a coarse laugh. "Ah, now, Rollo, don' be playin' coy with me! We've known each other a long time, in't that right? So you jus' be yourself 'n lemme give ya a big kiss – right 'ere in fron' o' everbody. I've fancied you from the start, ya know!" Rollo's arm was around her waist as he guided her toward a passage where they turned and disappeared from view, her suggestions becoming bawdier as her voice grew less distinct and eventually dissolved in the distance.

Lily was horrified. In shock, her eyes dilated from green to black. She stood immobile, resembling Lot's wife who had turned into a pillar of salt after looking in the wrong direction. Lily did not know what to think or what to do. Yes, she did know what to think, and what her mind was imagining was unthinkable. As to what to do, she ran home as swiftly as her long legs could carry her, losing only one small apple in the commotion.

Lily charged through the kitchen door, slammed her basket on the table and plopped into a seat, breathing as if she had been holding her breath for several minutes. She did not realize she had been crying until Cook asked her what was wrong and what on earth had brought her to so many tears.

"Oh, Cook," cried Lily, having left all of her self-control at the scene of Rollo and that woman. "I've jus' seen Rollo, 'n he's with some awful woman. She was fallin' all over him and he had his arm around her! The things she was sayin' were awful, Cook! Terrible things, they were, 'n he jus' let her go on and then he took her down an alley." Here she burst into tears again and felt an awful ache in her chest. Cook was not stupid, and she used the incident to point Lily in what she considered to be the proper direction.

"Now, Lily," purred Cook. "Why are you upset? You do not care for the man, so what does it matter what he does with another woman? It's nothing to you, is it?"

Lily dabbed her eyes. Through the hiccups one gets from sobbing, she said, "N-n-no, I suppose it isn't, but it was like he sorta s-s-stabbed me in the heart, an' I dunno what it is I'm h-h-howling about!"

"I think I know," said Cook. "Could it be that you care for this policeman more than you thought you did? Or, at least differently than you thought?"

Lily was horrified by the idea. "No! I don't care a whit for him in that way! Love and marriage is a trap, an 'I'm not about to be caught. I've got my own ideas about life and bein' on my own, an' that hasn't changed."

"But your feelings for him have," said Cook wisely. She knew Lily was not yet prepared to admit anything to her, much less to herself so, like coffee in the pot, Cook would let things percolate a bit. Lily would figure it out at some point, hopefully before Rollo lost interest altogether. Meanwhile, Cook would tempt him with her cooking to keep him coming back!

Rollo could smell freshly baked cake as he approached the kitchen door. He was confident that, once inside, Cook would place a large piece in front of him and pour him a strong cup of freshly brewed tea. Yes, he was being overindulged. He knew it, and he enjoyed it. Neither he nor Cook would apologize for what had become for them a very pleasant ritual.

Lily had dashed up the servants' staircase the minute Rollo entered the kitchen because she was experiencing a number of emotions with which she was not familiar. Not the least of them was jealousy, although she did not recognize it since she had never felt it before, but it was extremely unpleasant. She was also vastly disappointed in the man she had come to think of as her policemen friend.

Rollo swallowed a chunk of cake, took a sip of tea and asked, "Where is Lily today? I thought to see her."

Cook was not one to tell tales, but she could not resist the opportunity, and she would present it in her own way, with her own end in mind. She knew what she was doing, and she knew how to do it.

"She does not want to see you."

Rollo stared at her blankly. "I don't understand. Whyever not?"

"Because she has discovered that you are not the gentleman that she thought you were."

Rollo sat up straight. "How so? What could I possibly have done to make her think I am anything other than who she has come to know?"

Cook heaved a big sigh and let it hang in the air for a moment, keeping Rollo just a bit uncomfortable. "She saw you with another woman and it was not the sort of thing a girl such as Lily should see, or hear, particularly from someone she has come to respect and admire." She included the word "admire" on purpose.

Rollo frowned and shook his head. "I have no idea what she could have seen or heard that would make her think less of me. Did she say what it was?"

"She did. It seems you were with a less than desirable woman who was clinging to you like cat hair on wool trousers, and things were being said that no one should hear in private, much less in public."

Cook pursed her lips in disapproval and delivered the final blow. "Then . . . the two of you slipped down an alley and disappeared, for who knows what purpose." She looked at him without smiling and awaited his response. It was not what she expected.

"What?" he cried. Then he did the most extraordinary thing. He broke into an explosive laugh. When he saw the expression on Cook's face, he laughed even harder, until he thought of poor, sweet Lily, which quickly silenced him.

"Cook, is Lily in the house?" She nodded, and Rollo asked, "Would you please see if she is willing to come here for a moment?" Cook did so, and ten minutes later Lily appeared in the kitchen, her eyes red from weeping, which raised his hopes. It was all Rollo could do to keep from gathering her into his arms.

Instead, he asked her to sit across from him while he explained, with Cook overseeing the entire exchange, of course.

"Lily, I can't deny what you saw yesterday, but I can deny what you believe was taking place. That woman and I are not, and never have been, lovers. Her name is Etta and she is what you would call 'an unfortunate woman.' I have known her for two or three years now because I have had to place her under arrest on several occasions, which is precisely what I was doing when you saw me. She was, as is her habit, full of gin, hence her vulgar behavior."

Both Lily and Cook were extremely relieved, and they believed Rollo, which was just as well since it was, in fact, the truth. Without realizing it, both women began to smile, which allowed Rollo to give a small relieved chuckle, and soon they were all sharing tea and cake and a very relaxed conversation. Things between Lily and Rollo had definitely turned a corner, and they would never be the same.

CHAPTER TWENTY-FIVE

A Hamlet in Northamptionshire

T he railway had not been laid as far as Kettering, so Owen Clarke traveled by rail as far as possible, then proceeded by hired carriage the remainder of the way. He was, of course, being paid for his time and expenses, but he was beginning to believe that he was taking unfair advantage of Ebenezer Scrooge by accepting payment for what he knew was a losing proposition.

Had Clarke been one to make a wager he would have bet against Scrooge. That was why he had attempted at every opportunity to make Scrooge aware of how unlikely it was that they would solve the mystery of Peter's death. And that was another thing . . . what was Scrooge planning to do with the information, if he *did* discover anything? It was almost as if Scrooge himself did not know. Ah, well, Clarke sat back and resigned himself to profiting from another man's folly, as improper as that seemed to be.

Clarke's first stop was the postal office in Kettering. His assumption that the postmaster would receive the mail for surrounding hamlets proved to be accurate, and the postmaster was willing to share information when Clarke stated who he was and the purpose of his visit.

"Bates, you say? Charley Bates? Oh, yes. The family lives in a hamlet not a few miles from here. Decent enough folks. Yes, I knew him because I saw him often, right here in this very office."

"You *knew* him?"

"Aye. Dead now, isn't he? Died about three years ago. Suffered for long months before he was taken, poor soul."

On the one hand Clarke was disappointed to have come this far only to be told that the object of his search was dead and buried, but on the other hand it was so final that now Scrooge would have to accept an end to the matter. Still, Clarke might as well learn the details of his death, now that he was here. Any good detective would do so.

"You say he suffered? How so? I would think he was too young to have a wasting disease."

"Too young? Nah, not that old fellow. The man was sixty-some, if a day."

"But . . . how can that be? The man I'm seeking is in his twenties."

"Ah. Then you must mean Young Charley, his great nephew. He lives in the hamlet with the rest of his people. I can give you their direction."

Clarke thanked the man, scribbled a brief note which he then posted to Scrooge, and returned to the inn where he would await Scrooge's arrival.

Scrooge and Clarke hired a pony and trap to make the trip to the hamlet where the Bates family lived. Each was in a state of agitation over the ending of this search, on way or the other, and its possible effect on Scrooge, and on anyone else who might be drawn into the thing, for that matter.

The cart clattered along amid grazing land with its graziers and their flocks. There was something calming about the scene, with its peaceful movements of sheep and their bleating. Dogs barked occasionally, sometimes nipping at the ewes' legs to keep them in order. It was quite a change from the commotion of London.

Once they arrived at the hamlet the men requested the driver to wait for them since they did not expect to be long. They were correct in that assumption because, as they dismounted from the cart, Charley wandered in from a nearby field. Although they did not yet know his identity, he knew theirs because Charley immediately recognized Clarke as a policeman. He had always said he could "smell a blue bottle through a brick wall!" and his instincts told him that here was one invading his world after all these years.

Bates' immediate reaction was to run, but he stood his ground. Enough time had passed that he knew he was out of harm's way but seeing a policeman had catapulted him back to the streets of London where officers had power over him, a mere child. But he was a man now, so he approached Clarke and Scrooge even though his stomach was churning. Using a similar "nose" from his many years as a policeman, Clarke also knew they had found Charley Bates.

"Charley Bates?" asked Clarke.

"Could be," replied Charley.

"Let's assume you are then, and I'll tell you why we're here."
He stepped a few feet closer to Bates. "I'm Mr. Clarke and I was
once a policeman, but no longer. This is Mr. Scrooge, and he
and I would like to ask you some questions about something
that happened in London ten years ago. It's naught to do with
you however, so you are under no suspicion for any crime. We
are hoping you can help us find out the truth in another matter."
He did not add that he had little to no hope that Bates knew
anything, since saying so would only promote Bates' silence.

Bates had relaxed somewhat but was still wary. He continued
to hold his tongue.

"Do you recall where you were ten years ago?" That was too
far-reaching, so Clarke asked again. "Were you with Fagin then?"

So, they truly know who I am. His thoughts reeled. *What can
they do to me if I don't cooperate?* His mind recalled all of the
capers he and the Artful Dodger had managed, but something
about these two led him to answer them. Carefully, mind you.

"P'rhaps I was. It's a long time now, and my mem'ry in't
so good."

Clarke was in no mood to coax, so he replied with authority.
"We know you were, so there's no use pretending otherwise.
As I said, we are not here to make trouble for you, nor are we
accusing you of anything. We are attempting to find answers
about the son of a friend of Mr. Scrooge. Unfortunately, the incident in question occurred years ago, and you are the only person
who may be able to help us." Bates' character had matured
enough through the years that the word "help" did the trick, and
he agreed to at least listen, but not to "snitch."

It was Scrooge's turn to explain. "Charley, my friend had a
son, Peter, who was kidnapped when he was six years old, in
1836. He disappeared for three weeks and then his body was
found in the Thames. This poor woman has not known the truth

of her son's disappearance for all of these years, and we are hoping you can help us solve the thing. If you know anything at all, we beg you to tell us."

Scrooge's use of the word, "beg" handed Bates a certain amount of power, and since his basic nature was to be on easy terms with others, he thought a moment before slowly nodding his head. He motioned for them to follow him to a low rock wall, where they all sat. Scrooge's heart was slamming against his chest, as well as in his ears, and he felt lightheaded. Was he finally to learn some of the facts he had been seeking since he first knew of Rebecca's son? He sat, gladly, and tried to steady himself.

CHAPTER TWENTY-SIX

Evil Sadly Recalled

Bates began. "I don't know ever'thin' firsthand like, but I do know about the boy 'cuz I 'member him."

It was almost unbelievable that after such a long time Scrooge was about to hear the truth. To keep from toppling over altogether, he placed his forearms on his thighs and bent down as if he were merely listening to what Bates was saying. Bates continued.

"I dunno how the boy got there, but when me 'n the Dodger got back one evenin' he were there, locked in the other room. We knew better'n to ask a lot of questions."

Scrooge had to know, "Was he mistreated?" He failed to realize that he and Bates would not necessarily agree on the meaning of the word.

"Nae, he weren't particularly mistreated. Nobody beat him bad or starved him, least not any more'n the rest of us, but he were jus' too young 'n he come from a fam'ly wot treated him a lot better'n they was treatin' him." With more sympathy than he realized, Bates explained, "He were soft-like, poor little mite. He said his name was Peter, but we called him 'Crybaby' cuz they said it were easier 'n better not to be usin' his real name, y' see."

Bates looked off in the distance where sheep were grazing and remarked, "Such a beautiful boy, an' he had a gentle spirit too, y' know? Kinda like a little fairy. Sweet, he was. He was too young though and was so afraid. My heart went out to him 'n I tried to protect him, but they wouldn't allow any special treatment. Oh, no. Not them!" Bates shifted his weight.

"The evenin' they first brought him in they took his clothes, to sell, and they put him in rags. He was hungry but they kept him locked away from the rest of us until the next day 'n they didn't feed him. They wanted him to know who was boss. Boss! As if a baby needs a boss. He needed his family! The rest of us didn't have mothers nor fathers, but he did, 'n that's where he belonged." Bates was obviously troubled by the vivid memories, and he took a moment before he continued.

"We felt sorry for Crybaby. He wouldn't talk much. He jus' cried or buried his head in a pile of rags most o' the time unless me or Sikes' friend Nancy sat next to him 'n held him kinda' close. The Dodger 'n me wuz gonna take him out one day 'n give him up to the 'blue bottles' 'n say we found him, which would'a been the truth. We hadn't yet cooked up a story to tell Fagin when we come back without him, but we was working on that angle of it." He took a deep breath and blew it out through partially closed lips.

"We thought to make like he was gonna be our pet, 'n let him run with us. Then we'd figure a way to get him home, but he couldn't help with that cuz' he was too little to know the way back to where he lived. After he was gone Nancy saw a poster 'bout a missin' boy that sounded like him, but it was too late then, wasn't it?"

Scrooge was horrified, but he was unable to stop the narrative. He dreaded hearing it but would in no way turn from it now. He had to know.

Clarke then asked the question that was at the heart of the matter. "What happened to Peter?"

"Now there's the part where I dunno other'n what I was tol', but it were the Dodger what tol' me, 'n I know he spoke the truth." There was no reason not to tell these men what he knew, particularly if it could help someone finally settle it in his or her mind.

"The baby kep' on cryin' 'n couldn't get straight, 'n finally one night Bill Sikes blew up, grabbed 'im 'n dragged him out o' the place. Fagin tried to calm Sikes down, but he'd lost his patience with the boy 'n didn't pay no attention to Fagin. The rest of us jus' sat there 'cause there weren't nuthin' we could do, much as we wanted to. We'd got sorta attached to the babe an' wanted to protect him, but we was helpless, too. I think Nancy might'a yelled somethin' at Sikes, but I don' remember what.

"I think it's cuz he cared for Crybaby that the Dodger followed them, 'n when he come back he looked pretty well 'batty-fanged' like. He was upset 'n couldn't talk much, so he waved me off when I asked what happened. It wasn't 'til the next day, when we was out 'n about, that he tol' me."

Bates paused and said, "I don' remember all o' the details, but the Dodger said they headed to the River 'n he knew then that Sikes was gonna drown 'im. The poor little thing kept fallin' an' Sikes jus' kept yankin' him along, bangin' 'im up 'n scrapin' his legs. The Dodger said Crybaby wasn't cryin' then though, that he was quiet the whole time. He didn't even yell out when he got hurt, leastways not more'n a little 'Ow' like when he fell 'n scraped himself." Scrooge wanted to weep but held it back with great effort.

"They got t' the Bridge and Dodger was trying to figure quick what he could do to save the boy when Crybaby fell again 'n Sikes yanked him up an' spun him 'round the other way. When he did, he accidentally slammed Crybaby's head against a bridge pole 'n it topped 'im, that quick!" he said, snapping his fingers. "He jus' lay there, 'cause it were all over for him. Then Sikes tossed him into the River as if he weren't nuthin' but a sack o' rubbish."

Bates stared into the distance a moment, then looked down and lowered his voice as he said, "The Dodger was bothered 'bout it for a long time 'cause he couldn't somehow rescue 'im. He wouldn't talk 'bout it though, an' once I caught him wipin' his eyes 'n blowing his nose after I mentioned the babe. That weren't like him, but this was more'n what we was used to. It were a cruel death of an innocent, not jus' a handkerchief or a watch slipped outta someone's pocket, 'n it hit Dodger hard. It hit both of us hard. Nancy, too."

Bates glared at them and raised his voice. "I say now, 'n I'll never change my mind; I curse Sikes and Fagin's horrid black hearts, dead and buried as they both are. I know they're in a tormentin' Hell 'n I hope they blaze red-hot forever! What they did to us was nuthin', but what they did to little Crybaby was . . ." Bates stopped, and neither Scrooge nor Clarke asked him to finish his sentence. After a moment, Scrooge did ask, "And you never told anyone?"

"Course not. We was that sorry, but we wasn't daft. We was afraid o' Sikes if he knew the Dodger had been a witness." He pulled a face and said, "Oh, there was times when the Dodger considered telling Sikes what he knew, so's to have sump'in' to hold over him, but we both knew Sikes. It would have worked against us both, and Sikes would never 'a trusted us again. He might'a got rid o' us too, jus' to keep our mouths shut."

Up to this point Bates had been answering the questions, but he had one of his own. He made a small frown and quietly asked, "'Oo was he, Mr. Scrooge? 'Oo was Crybaby? You know his family 'n what they're like. I figure they must be nice, cuz he were sweet like, 'n he missed 'em so."

It was difficult for Scrooge to reply because he could barely speak to the question, but after swallowing twice, he managed.

"They were good people, son." The word "son" just slipped out, although it seemed acceptable, considering the conversation and the pain both Scrooge and Bates were feeling. Scrooge continued.

"His mother is still alive, but his father died several years ago." For some reason he did not want to tell Bates that Mr. Langstone had essentially died of a broken heart, so he explained his death by saying, "He was a bit older than she."

Then he thought of one more thing he should tell Bates. "Peter's mother helps support a house where street children can go for shelter, food and a certain amount of education. You might be interested to know that because of her generosity the home has been renamed 'Peter's House.'"

Bates smiled and nodded before he said, "I reckon it can't be big 'nuff to help 'em all, but I guess somthin' is better'n nuthin. At least some little good come of Crybaby's life if some street orphans are 'elped because of it." He purposely did not say that they were helped because of his death.

The name "Bill Sikes" was familiar to Clarke and he asked, "What happened to Sikes?" Bates gave a sardonic smile and said, "He got wot was comin' to him, 'n fair enough. Hanged himself by accident, didn't he?" Then Clark remembered the case and the names Oliver Twist, Fagin and the rest of them fell into place. Why hadn't he put Fagin and Twist together? Well, it still wouldn't have solved anything because there would have been no way to tie them to Peter Langstone. Only Charley Bates had been able to do that.

CHAPTER TWENTY-SEVEN

A Few Loose Ends

As an ex-policeman Clarke was curious about any loose ends and wanted to discover as much as possible about Bates. Scrooge's curiosity was played out, and he seemed a bit green about the gills, so he opted to sit for several moments before catching up with Clarke and Bates as they wandered about the farm. It was the first time Bates had carried on a true conversation with an officer of the law, and he was surprised at the ease with which he could speak to Clarke.

Bates told of becoming one of Fagin's "boys" after losing his parents when he was fairly young. He did not know what happened to them because they had simply disappeared, leaving him to "griddle" on the streets for some time before being taken in by Fagin. He could recall very little about his mother and father other than that his father's people were from Kettering in Northamptonshire. He could not explain why he had remembered that particular fact, but later figured that the recollection had been Providence saving him, in the end.

Both Scrooge and Clarke were curious as to what had turned Charley from his life in London to the life he now led. In truth, when Sikes murdered Nancy before accidentally hanging himself, Bates saw his own life for what it was. Bates even discerned the Dodger's lack of empathy for his victims. The Dodger's arrest and deportation convinced Bates that the criminal lifestyle was generally unprofitable.

In addition, Bates had a naturally cheerful approach to life, with an uncomplicated need to enjoy each day with his fellow man. One could not do that if people were nothing more than potential "marks" by which to enrich oneself. He attempted to explain it to the man from London.

"Ever'body thot I got turned 'round 'cuz o' Sikes killin' poor Nancy, 'n that was so, but there were more to it. I also got turned around 'cuz I knew he'd killed another one, too, din't I? Poor Little Crybaby. Helpless, he was. I didn't wanna be nuthin' like any of em, 'n I didn't wanna pay the price, neither. Even the Dodger got caught for some petty "dippin'" an' got sent to Australia. So, instead, I come to Daisyville, din' I? He laughed at the slang word for the countryside.

It hadn't been easy. Having left London, Bates slowly made his way north, working at hard labor and barely staying alive until he located his father's kith. They gladly welcomed him and put him straight to work. After a few years he was allowed to learn the skill of grazing sheep, and he now had dreams of becoming the best and "merriest young grazier in all Northamptonshire."

At the end, Bates was not what Scrooge and Clarke had expected. He was essentially a cheery fellow who, at one time, exercised his good humor wickedly. In those days, he found amusement at every turn, mostly in the discomfort or victimization of others, particularly if he had been the author of their misfortune. Even seeing someone else, such as Oliver Twist, blamed for his own crimes could keep him laughing for hours. Peter Langstone had been the exception that exposed a more sympathetic and thoughtful side to Bates.

In the ensuing years, having parted from Fagin and the others, Bates had faced the hardships of bending his back to maintain an honest living and had thereby acquired a certain amount of virtue, as well as hearty muscle. He no longer took pride in inflicting injury, be it physical or mental, and had, in fact, developed an active, if not extreme, conscience. His nature had been tamed, thanks to backbreaking toil, small pay and the constant recollection of just how evil an ungodly man's heart could be.

Once again at home in London, Scrooge attempted to return to his normal routine. He had satisfied his curiosity but was now weighed down with profound guilt. It was the last thing he had expected to feel, but there it was. Scrooge had gone behind Rebecca's back to discover what happened to her son, and he expected to be elated. He had even expected to present the truth to her as a splendid gift, but that was absolutely not the case. Knowing the horrid details of Peter's death had not brought about the liberation he expected. Not at all. Instead, he felt the weight of it in his stomach, tight as a knot, and he did not know what to do with it. He was not led to tell her anything. In fact, now he wanted to protect her from the truth, which meant he must bear the weight of it alone.

CHAPTER TWENTY-EIGHT

A New Customer

Homer Probert had always loved Martha Cratchit. From the time her father introduced them when Homer was a new clerk at the counting house, Homer knew that she should eventually be his. That belief was shaken, however, when Martha met Rollo Norris, who was immediately captivated by her beauty. Norris began paying his attentions to her, which she seemed to welcome.

It was a dismal time for Homer and there was little he could do other than continue to present himself to her as a possible suitor as often as possible. Martha was never discourteous to either man, which was owing to the fact that she preferred neither over the other. She found them both to be of good character and diverting in their conversation and activities. When she was in the company of one, she thought him charming. When she was with the other, she thought the same of him.

Both men were handsome. Homer was a Welshman; tall, dark and mysterious. Rollo was English; tall, blonde and in uniform.

Both men could fight, having been schooled in the art of fisticuffs. Both men could carry on meaningful conversations with persons of all ages and crafts. Both men cared for Martha, but Rollo came to realize early on that he and Martha were not entirely suited. Their interests and their ideas were too often dissimilar.

Rollo's life as a policeman demanded a certain temperament in a woman. Martha was a bit too refined. His wife would not be required to be a part of his work, but she would be required to understand it. Rollo needed someone who was somewhat less genteel, who would come by an understanding of the policeman's lot more naturally.

It was true, too, that another reason Rollo realized he was not resolute about Martha was the fact that he continued to have a bit of a roving eye. Homer did not. So it was that, at some point in time, Rollo conceded that Homer was the suitable man for Martha, and Rollo gradually disappeared from her life, at least as a suitor.

Martha Cratchit's employer, Lucy Carter, was gladly spending less time at the millinery shop since her marriage to Edwin Carter, which meant that much of the shop management fell to Martha, who was more than capable. Mrs. Carter continued to oversee the books, but she rarely found any item that required correction or further training where Martha was concerned. Mrs. Carter had the utmost confidence in the young woman because she was good with figures and purchasing supplies, and her poise and charm worked wonders on their patrons. She was also the best designer Mrs. Carter had ever employed, or known, for that matter. Her sense of color, fabric and structure were superb, and she possessed an innate talent for matching the bonnet to the person. Customers left the shop delighted with their purchases and pleased with the regard by which they had been pampered.

Martha thoroughly enjoyed her work. Patrons who entered the shop could immediately sense the order and appeal of the place. Naturally they made referrals to their friends when their bonnets were so flattering, and they certainly mentioned the marvelous Martha, who was so charming and talented. Each day Martha received a number of compliments, but she was not conceited, nor did she believe she was superior to anyone else in any respect.

Martha always thanked patrons for their kind remarks and never thought more of herself than she should, which was wise, since she was not perfect, even though Homer thought her to be. That was due to the fact that he had never made her cry, nor seen her stomp her foot in frustration.

In the middle of a particularly hectic day an attractive woman in her middle age stepped in the door of the shop. She was exquisitely groomed, perhaps upper middle class, and she carried herself with a great deal of composure. She was self-assured but did not patronize. With characteristic ease, Martha smiled at her, excused herself for a moment from her current customer, and offered the woman a chair. She explained that she would be a few more moments and then she could attend to her. Meanwhile, she was welcome to peruse the items on display. Within five minutes Martha had completed the bonnet fitting and waved at her assistant, Rose, to complete the financial arrangements and also see to another woman who had just come through the door.

After making a sincere apology, Martha asked, "Now then, thank you for waiting. How may I assist you?"

"I am looking for a bonnet that is not too fussy. It must be fairly stiff with some ribbon, but no bows other than under the chin. I want the brim and crown piece to be two pieces. It may host a few flowers around the back rim, but they must not be overdone. I also require several lace caps and headdresses to wear at home."

Martha examined the woman's face, noted its shape and the placement of the eyes, nose and mouth, and brought her some samples with which to try various accouterments. Against her customer's directions, she quickly draped a wide ribbon loosely under her chin and drew it toward the back to show how a bow off to the side her face might look, and both were stunned at the becoming effect.

"My dear, you have changed my appearance within seconds! I have never had a bonnet with such a bow, and I see now that I have been deprived! Yes, I will take this if you show me how you would apply the trim."

Martha did so, and both were very pleased with the results.

"I will complete the bonnet and deliver it to you two days from now, if that will be acceptable. That will be Thursday morning, most likely at 10:00 o'clock, if that suits your schedule. We will of course try it on you before you decide whether or not to keep it."

The woman agreed, and Martha asked for her name and direction.

"The name is Miriam Probert." She watched intently as Martha surely recognized her surname, and then gave Martha her direction. Martha did not show any recognition, nor did she blink an eye. It was not her place to ask certain questions that might be impertinent or a bit too personal.

The women bid each other a cordial "au revoir" before Mrs. Probert nodded and gracefully swept out of the shop. Her nod meant more than good-bye, however. It was a nod of appreci- ation and approval. Her trip to meet Martha had yielded much more than she expected because she not only approved of her son's choice, she came away with a bonnet that was far beyond her expectations. She had never had such a fitting, nor purchased such a fetching bonnet! In addition, she had never been so competently treated and with such affability.

If Martha promised a delivery on a certain date, she would ensure that she fulfilled it, even if it meant she got no sleep the previous night. The Cratchit home had often been the scene of hats, ribbon, flowers and lace scattered over one of the tables in a late-night flurry of millinery. It was so in this case, and it was exacerbated by Martha's uneasiness in dealing with the woman she suspected was Homer's mother. Did she know who Martha was? Was this all a ruse? A trick to expose Martha as being unworthy of her son?

It was all too much, and when Martha explained her concerns to her parents, rather than steady her nerves they seemed to join in her unease. Not that they believed she could in any way disappoint Mrs. Probert. Never! It was simply that they knew how important Homer was to their dear Martha and they could not bear to see her disappointed. Surely Mrs. Probert would see her worthiness. Surely, she would welcome her as a daughter. Pray God, she would.

Martha appeared at the Probert home on time, on Thursday. Although she was a bit anxious, she was proud of the hat she was delivering and hoped Mrs. Probert would think it was a splendid bonnet. Martha had added very little in the way of ornaments because she believed it was better to err by putting too little rather than too much. She could always add more if Mrs. Probert wished it.

"Ah, here is Martha and my new bonnet, right on time," greeted Mrs. Probert when Martha entered her parlor. "Please sit down and let's see what you have." When Martha took it out of the hatbox Mrs. Probert clapped her hands and cried, "Oh, my. Just look at what you have created. It is perfect! How talented you are!" She then sat at a chair that had been placed before a mirror and allowed Martha to place the bonnet on her head. It truly was splendid. Martha also produced several lace caps and head-dresses from which Mrs. Probert selected three she particularly liked. Naturally she requested that a shop's account be opened since she planned to frequent it often.

When their business was concluded, Mrs. Probert said, "Now, my dear, please sit back down – over here. I have ordered tea for us and we can have a pleasant visit. You do have time, I hope." Martha did have time since Mrs. Carter was tending the shop that day, and she was both pleased and surprisingly calm at the prospect of chatting with Homer's mother. It was still not clear whether she knew who Martha was.

When the tea and pastries arrived, Mrs. Probert poured and asked Martha about the shop. The questions were simple enough: did she enjoy her work; were the customers pleasant on the whole; and what other creative endeavors did Martha pursue, such as painting or music. Martha suspected that Mrs. Probert disapproved of a woman working until she admitted to Martha, "I would like to have had such a shop, but I married, instead." She then added, "I do not believe my son would necessarily have a problem with a wife using her talents to make a few pounds, as long as he and the home were uppermost, and as long as there were no children." Then she smiled at Martha and asked, "How do you feel about such things?"

Oh, dear. She must know who I am, but why not simply say so? Why this pretense? Perhaps she is not Homer's mother. She could be his aunt, or no relation whatsoever. Probert is not a particularly uncommon name, after all. Martha thought a moment before setting her teacup in the saucer she was holding on her lap. She had been taught to be honest, but to speak honestly without offending or insulting, if possible.

"I am undecided about such things at this point in my life, but that is likely due to the fact that I manage a millinery shop, and I do enjoy my vocation. My mother, on the other hand, has lived her life solely for my father and her children, and her life has been vastly fulfilling." She must truthfully add, "I admire her very much."

Mrs. Probert smiled, and they finished their tea while speaking of other topics. It was a very pleasant time during which the women seemed to make up their minds about each other.

CHAPTER TWENTY-NINE

Insights Are Shared

Ebenezer Scrooge could be a creature of habit, particularly when it came to luncheon, so if someone desired to speak with him at that time of day, one's best bet was to go to the George and Vulture. If he was there, one could sit down with him and share some meat pies or sausages. Since Norris definitely wanted to discuss something with Scrooge, that is precisely where he went.

Once settled with a pint sitting before him, Rollo and Scrooge fell into a relaxed conversation, recalling their recent adventures. Naturally Rollo asked if Scrooge had been successful in his quest for someone who knew about Peter Langstone, and Scrooge answered honestly, although he did not give details even though he knew Rollo could be trusted not to repeat whatever was said.

"We were, Rollo. We were. It was quite an undertaking, but Clarke was up to it and we found Charley Bates in the end. It turns out he actually knew Peter, and one of his fellow pickpockets observed what happened to him. I must tell you that I found

THE CURIOSITY OF SCROOGE

the truth upsetting, and although I suppose it could have been even worse, it is not something I care to repeat." Norris understood and did not pry. He had heard and seen enough brutality that he did not need to hear more.

"Here is one bit of information you may find interesting," said Norris. "It seems our old friend Henry Martin, Jr. is now in Bedlam. When he was first questioned by the police, he admitted he was attempting to avenge his father for your sins against him, but right off Stagg informed them that it was not so, since his father had never invested with you." He took a drink and continued.

"As they asked further questions, Martin's answers became more and more bizarre. It turns out he has been hearing voices for some time, and one in particular speaks to him about his father and those who wronged him. It was that particular voice that told him why he should pursue you, and instructed him in what to do, and how. I believe you were the first of four men whom he meant to put to death for his father's failures in life because he had a hand-written list of intended victims in a pocket."

Scrooge mused, "It makes me wonder how many people have been harmed who did nothing wrong. They may have been the victims of gossip, or misunderstandings, but they became victims, nevertheless."

"Oh, that happens, alright. I've seen it more than once and all of the apologies in the universe can't make it right, once it's done." Scrooge had a new appreciation for Norris' statement, having himself almost become one of those innocent victims. It also occurred to him that Martin, who was now an inmate in Bedlam, was not the only one to hear a voice, since Scrooge not only did so on occasion, he could also see the host! The difference, of course, was that the voice Martin heard was one that led him to do evil.

Norris admitted to Scrooge that he had some doubt as to the true insanity of Martin and suspected it may be a ruse to avoid prison, although Bedlam was not any better, in so many ways. Their "treatments" for insanity could often be undeniably inhumane. Rollo continued with his suspicions.

"That 'voice' Martin heard was no doubt an echo of his own father's, recited by him to his son many times. I believe it is likely that the senior Mr. Martin did not want to admit his own failures, so, if you will excuse me for saying so, he used the name of a man known to be treacherous in business in those days. The funny thing is, during that time, a time when you admit to being so ruthless, you took the time to give a stranger a warning, and the one who heeded your words avoided loss."

Scrooge looked at Norris in appreciation and said, "Thank you, Rollo, for that. It is good to be reminded that even in my darkest years I still had a spark of decency, on occasion." His smile was ironic.

Norris nodded. He had one last thing to say. "Stagg tells me that Martin has been asking to see you, although Stagg did not know why. Martin has not recanted his story, nor has he said anything about wanting to apologize to you. I said I would pass his request on to you, but that I doubted anything could come of such a meeting, and Stagg agreed."

Scrooge could see no good reason to meet with Martin either, and said so. In truth, his natural curiosity about things had been greatly diminished in the last week or so, and since Martin gave no specific reason for wanting to speak with Scrooge, he gave Norris his answer. "It could serve no purpose that I can see, and I will give it some thought, but unless I believe it would do either of us any good, the answer is 'No.' I am certain you will tell me if you have more information," and Norris nodded.

Marley's ears, such as they were, must have been burning while Scrooge and Norris talked that afternoon because he made an appearance just as Scrooge slid one foot into his bed. Scrooge should not have been surprised to see him since he tended to materialize either before or after Scrooge experienced a disruption of some sorts. "Disruption" was a kind word for what Scrooge had brought on by discovering the details of Peter Langstone's death. Marley tended to visit either to warn, or to scorn, and Scrooge prepared himself for a dressing-down.

Marley was shaking his head, but it was, surprisingly, not in derision. In fact, Scrooge felt more understanding emanate from Marley, than scorn. It was as if Marley were thinking, *There is a storm ahead, old friend.*

Scrooge hung his head as a child would when being scolded. He could think of nothing to say, so Marley began, but it was not about Scrooge's insistence on investigating Peter's death.

Scrooge, you and Rollo Norris discussed Henry Martin, Jr. today and I wish to expand your thinking a bit. Take Henry Martin, Sr. for instance. He had a bad run and committed suicide. Another man, James Stanbury, also suffered losses, but he began again, starting from scratch, and he succeeded. Compare the two. Why were the ends of these two men so dissimilar when their circumstances were so alike?" He did not wait for an answer.

"They were different mainly because of the influences they heeded. One was reduced to despair, and the other found hope. The Senior Mr. Martin fell into many temptations by listening to the wrong ideas, or 'voices,' throughout his lifetime, and it caught up with him because in the end he hadn't the strength, nor the virtue, to overcome hardship. Man is, after all, a spirit inside, and he has the freedom to make all sorts of choices, but he also reaps whatever he sows in this world.

"Some call it conscience, others believe it is good or bad luck, but the fact is, there are influences that are either good, or evil." Marley took a moment to heft one shoulder in order to shift what little remained of his original chains.

"Regardless of what occurs, if we are of sound mind, we are each responsible for the state of our souls. We choose how we respond, even when it is terribly difficult. Have you never considered that many murderers truly repent of their sins and thereby partake of a Divine afterlife, whereas their victims may have died in a state of depravity and gone on to a very different and woeful fate?

"Lest you say I have no compassion for those whose minds are not sound, I will say that perhaps they are not to be blamed for their lunacy, but insanity does not erase culpability. Had Martin's aim been better by a few inches, you would be dead, and he would have been responsible for it. Being insane would not have changed the fact that he was the one who killed you. The difference, in a court of law, would be that his state of mind may require a more compassionate sentence than that of being hanged as a reprobate criminal."

Scrooge knew from the conversation that he was not going to get away without accounting for his own selfish curiosity regarding facts he did not need to know about Peter Langstone. He knew Marley would have ample to say, but for some reason he was no longer feeling submissive, so his back was already up when Marley approached the subject.

"There is also the matter of your disregard of possible repercussions when you insisted on going you own way, alone, to satisfy your curiosity regarding young Peter. The choice should have been Rebecca's, not yours."

191

Scrooge crossed his arms petulantly and said, "You know I did it for altruistic reasons, to help the woman I love, and I will not countenance being derided for such motivation!" There. He had stood up to the fellow – or whatever Marley was – and it pleased him to have done so. Never mind that he knew he had been wrong and was now burdened with all of the terrible knowledge he had gained and could not share with Rebecca. Never mind that Marley had been right. There was something inside Scrooge that raged against being corrected when he already felt such overwhelming shame, so he stiffened his neck and waited. Let Marley say whatever he liked! But Marley said nothing, for he was gone.

CHAPTER THIRTY

Human Counsel

S crooge had not seen Rebecca since his return from the north the previous week. He always had a good excuse, and she was certainly understanding, but the truth was that he was afraid to go near her. He knew too much and wanted to protect her from what he knew. It was as if he feared the truth might somehow seep out of him and become visible to her. Yet he yearned for her company. He wanted to simply touch her face, her hair, and hold her hand, but he was fairly certain that he would be unable to do so without thinking of all he knew about Peter, and she might somehow read his mind!

Tonight, however, they were going to the theatre and there was no getting out of it. He desperately wanted to see her and was ready to test himself in her company. He prayed he would be able to carry on a conversation with the same tone he had used before meeting Charley Bates. Of course, he could. He simply needed to exercise some fortitude and behave like a grown man. It wasn't as if Rebecca would be scrutinizing his behavior, since she did not even know he had made a trip north, much less the reason for it. Just realizing that should have helped him to relax, but it only increased his guilt. He was keeping secrets, and they concerned *her*!

The play was a comedy presented by Fanny Kelly's acting students at the New Royalty Theatre. Both had been looking forward to the evening with anticipation, having heard all sorts of reviews regarding the theatre's productions. Some critics loved the melodramas, some hated them, and it was the same with the comedies. Scrooge hoped to achieve some relief by laughing again with Rebecca, and he prayed it would be a turning point that would allow them to return to the easy familiarity they once enjoyed.

The play was well-received by the audience, but it was a failure for Scrooge and Rebecca. He could not keep his mind on the thing, and he often stared into space, not hearing Rebecca when she spoke to him. He failed to laugh when others laughed, and he clapped only when he eventually recognized the sound of applause coming from those around him. By the end of the evening the two of them were very nearly strangers.

Rebecca knew something was terribly amiss, but she had no way of discovering what it was because when she asked Scrooge he waved away her concerns and blamed his inattentiveness on a preoccupation with business. She knew that to have been the case in more than one instance, but this was something more, and she was frightened.

Scrooge felt like a man outside himself, observing his own behavior. He realized how unfairly he was behaving toward Rebecca, but he seemed to have no control over the man he was observing.

The question clearly was whether or not to share his information with Rebecca. The lovely Rebecca, who had weathered such tragedy so many years ago and, as Marley said, proceeded with hope to once again participate in life and all the joys it had to offer. Would telling her destroy all of that? Would she have to begin once again from the point of abject despair? He did not know, and his indecision over his secret was becoming a growing problem between them.

Scrooge knew he must talk with someone, and the best person, since Marley was no longer speaking to him, was Colin Gifford, the Rector of St. Michael's Parish Church. He knew Rebecca would not appreciate his spreading the truth around the Town of London, but he did not need to give details.

The Rector and Scrooge were good friends, so their greeting was cheerful.

"My dear Scrooge! How good it is to see you when I am not in the pulpit and we can actually visit. What brings you here, my friend? Are you ready to be outdone in a game of chess?"

"No, Colin, I am here for counsel, and you are by far one of the best to give it. Besides that, I can be honest with you about myself, for you know me well, and yet you somehow still manage to care for me."

"Ah," said the Rector. "Then sit, please, and let's talk it out."

Where to start. Should he begin by saying how selfish he was? How unforgivably curious? What did he want from Colin, anyway? Was he seeking absolution, or did he simply need someone to say he was not the Devil incarnate, for he felt as though he were. How could anyone absolve him when he couldn't even absolve himself? He must begin somewhere.

"Colin, are you aware of the fact that Mrs. Langstone's six-year-old son disappeared in 1836 while on an outing with his nanny, and his body was found in the Thames three weeks later?"

"Yes, Ebenezer, I am. In fact, she happened to literally wander into the Church several months later, almost in a daze. She did not know why she was here, or why she chose this particular church, but we talked, and I like to think it helped her."

"It did help her because she told me of the incident not long after we met. I did not realize that it was you who spoke to her, though." Scrooge settled back and continued.

"Over two years ago I imagined how wonderful it would be to decipher the truth of Peter's death because it seemed to me that she was even now weighed down with the mystery of it all. Without going into detail, I will admit to you that I pursued the matter and have recently discovered, through a witness of sorts, what actually occurred." He held up his hand to let Gifford know that he had more to say.

"I should tell you that I was warned not to pursue the matter without consulting her first. I admit to you that I disregarded the warning and am now ruing that reckless decision. I am not only sorry, but I no longer want to share the truth of the matter with Mrs. Langstone because of the damage reliving it could do. I do not know how to proceed. I am not using profanity when I say I am literally 'damned if I do, and damned if I don't.'"

"Hmmmm." The Rector sat back and twiddled his thumbs for a moment. "Let me see if I understand your concerns. I believe I have three questions from what you told me."

Using his fingers, he ticked off three points. He held up the index finger of his left hand held it with his right index finger. "What were you trying to achieve by learning the truth?" Next, he ticked off the middle finger of his left hand and said, "What did you plan to do with the information you might find?" Lastly, he ticked off his fourth finger and asked, "What should you do now? I think it is imperative that you be perfectly honest in your answers, no matter how distressing it may be for you. To do otherwise will get nothing solved."

Scrooge slowly nodded. He knew his friend was right, and it was time to be honest with himself. He was embarrassed by how he had responded to Marley, and he was sorry for his neglect of Rebecca. He had managed to ferret out the truth about Peter, so he'd best get busy and seek the truth about himself.

"I believe I first wanted to know for altruistic reasons. I was so shocked by the tragedy that all I could think was how she must have suffered. I wanted to be able to give her answers. I suppose I wanted to be her champion. I wanted to be a miracle worker in her eyes, to do what no one else could do, and to answer her questions about what happened so many years ago. Then, I couldn't seem to let go of the idea. It became an obsession with me that grew stronger with each step I took." He chewed the inside of his lip and managed to keep going.

"As to your second question, or rather, *my* second question that I hoped to have answered when I came here, I believe I meant to give Mrs. Langstone a gift of the truth about what happened to Peter. For some reason I was proceeding on the assumption that she would want to know, but she already knew enough. She knew he died and perhaps to know more would serve no good purpose. It wasn't until I actually had those answers that I realized what a powerful weapon they were, and that it was not a weapon I wanted to use against her!

"With regard to what to do now. I have no idea, but I need to stand on solid ground. I need to allow both of us to be comfortable and put this thing to rest. Right now, that means I must somehow put it out of my own mind, or find a corner in my brain where I can store it, so that I can carry on normally with her, because I am not doing so now, and I am certain my behavior is troubling her."

The Rector held his breath, then made a suggestion. "You say you need a place to stand. Alright, let's give you one. The second half of Proverbs 11:13 says that 'a man of understanding holdeth his peace.' In other words, sometimes it is wise to keep things to yourself. Do you think you can do that? I'm not certain you have much choice at this point."

Scrooge agreed. He could see no other alternative, and it helped to have Holy Scripture back up the idea.

"There is something else," said the Rector. "The one thing I do know about all of this is that our gracious Lord can bring good out of any situation, no matter how impossible that may seem. Scrooge gave a nod that showed more hope than expection."

As Scrooge left, he said, "I know I do not need to caution you to keep this information to yourself," and the Rector patted his friend's back as he walked toward the door. "Of course, my friend. Clergy-penitent privilege, you know!"

CHAPTER THIRTY-ONE

An Afternoon in the Park

Since spring was just beginning to turn to early summer, Scrooge and Rebecca decided to stroll through Hyde Park. It was a lovely day. The sky resembled a watercolor painting overhanging an expanse of green grass that seemed to go on forever. The couple meandered through gardens and under spreading trees, eventually reaching the Serpentine, where they enjoyed the swans and other fowl. It was wonderful how their conversations had returned to normal, and Scrooge seemed less distracted, which reassured Rebecca. They found a bench and sat down.

The setting reminded Rebecca that her son had been abducted from such a peaceful setting and she remarked so to Scrooge. It was only a bit of information, with no tone of grief in her voice, and Scrooge responded without thinking.

"Yes, they find childr . . ." When he realized what he had begun to say, he stopped short, leaving the sentence hanging in the warm summer air.

"What were you about to say, Ebenezer?"

"Oh, nothing. Certainly nothing we need dwell on today. This is a pleasant outing, let's keep it that way." His words became tangled between the burden he was carrying about Peter and the fact that he simply meant she might not wish to talk of unpleasant things, but Rebecca inferred that to talk about Peter would be unpleasant.

"What could possibly be unpleasant?"

"It just occurred to me that you might not want to talk about Peter because it might distress you."

"Oh, no. You and I have spoken of my son many times and I have not been distressed. Why would I be now?" Rebecca was studying him as if he were a specimen in a zoo, and she said what was on her mind.

"Ebenezer, you have been acting strangely since you came back from your trip. Perhaps we should discuss whatever it is that is bothering you. I like to think I am a good listener."

"You are a good listener, surely, but let's not discuss it now. It's a fine day and we should be walking about!" He slapped his legs as if he were preparing to stand, when she stopped him by placing her hand on his arm.

"No, my dear. This has gone on for weeks now and we need to settle whatever it is that is upsetting you." He did not reply and looked, instead, at the swans, rather than face her.

It was suddenly too much. He had been dodging questions and mistreating Rebecca with his avoidance, and it must stop, here and now. There was nothing for it but to admit something, which would be a huge relief, but there was no way on God's earth he was going to tell her the entire truth. He would rather his head be displayed on a spike at the Bridge, which would be fitting – traitor that he was! It was too bad that particular practice ended long ago, because he would gladly request it for himself.

What could Scrooge say but, "I have discovered some things about Peter because I thought you wanted to know what actually happened to him."

She was bewildered. "I do not recall ever saying anything that would lead you to believe I wanted to know more about Peter's death. That is because I doubt that I could quell my imagination once I heard them." Then she asked the obvious question.

"Are you saying that you know what happened to my son?" Scrooge lifted his hand slightly and took a breath as if to reply, but he was not about to reveal sordid details to her. Instead, he closed his eyes, exhaled and let his hand fall back onto his thigh.

"Yes," said Rebecca, wearily. "I can see that you do. You know it all – every heartbreaking detail. You have discovered the truth and that has stood between us for the past weeks, I am certain of it." Scrooge was not above begging at that moment.

"Please, Rebecca, let me explain myself." He had no idea how he could do so without giving details, but he would die trying. He was spared having to try since she spoke before he could utter a sound.

"I cannot comprehend why you have done this. You have overstepped your privileges, and you have made us adversaries." Rebecca managed to sit still, her back straight.

"Why did you not ask me prior to embarking on this enterprise of yours? Wouldn't that have been the best approach? Contrary to what you no doubt made yourself believe, you have totally ignored my needs, in this matter." She slapped her lap and repeated, with more emphasis, "Totally!"

Rebecca was not yet finished, and Scrooge could only sit and listen. "By learning something you were not even certain you could or should ever share with me, did that not essentially make you a liar, and place me in the position of being lied to?

How can I trust you in the future? It appears to me that we are left with no middle course."

Scrooge had never heard her expound in such a manner and with so little restraint, and he did not know what to do. As it turned out, he did not have to do anything further because Rebecca suddenly stood and said, "Please take me home." He knew she would brook no argument.

Rebecca spent the next twenty-four hours dividing her time and energies between sobbing in her bed and walking the floor, railing against Scrooge's investigation into hers and her son's tragic history. She wanted to accept what he had done, but it was impossible because she felt so violated. The pain was too intense, no matter how much she cared for him. In the end, she could see no way to overcome her sense of having been horribly betrayed.

The following morning, Rebecca penned a letter to Scrooge.

Dear Ebenezer,

I must speak to you by means of a written letter because I cannot bear to do so in person. If I were to attempt to do so I would be more apt to respond to your emotions than to express my own. Yet, I must express them in order for you to comprehend the damage you have done to our deep and what I once believed was a lasting attachment.

I am not attempting to injure you in any way, but you have a right to know the simple truth of what is in my heart.

I have never been so disappointed in anyone as I am now, with you. I have asked myself over and again what you were hoping to accomplish, and I am unable to invoke a sound reply. Were you simply curious? Could this terrible situation have come about from merely a thoughtless and selfish motive? That would not be the behavior of the Ebenezer Scrooge I know and loved.

I cannot understand why you took on such an endeavor without consulting me. You have discovered a terrible secret that concerns me and a loved one, and it is something I am certain I do not want to hear. I do not wish to add new revelations to all of the imaginations I finally managed to put behind me. Yet, you cannot forget what you have learned, and I cannot overlook the fact that you hold such a terrible secret. If I attempted to force you to keep that knowledge to yourself, my demands would also create discord between us as you tried to guard your tongue, lest you slip and say something amiss.

You have placed me in an untenable position. I cannot re-live Peter's death. It would be more than I could bear. Yet, naturally, I want to know anything that concerns him, particularly since his death was so tragic. I am torn, and I can see no remedy for us, other than to avoid each other's company.

You and I are now cruelly separated. Our minds, our very souls, are no longer in concert. That has been unmistakable in your recent avoidance of certain subjects and in your unexplainable, sometimes even cold actions toward me. The "truth" you discovered is a barrier that has stood firmly planted between us since you learned it, and neither of us can budge such a weighty impediment.

There is no agreeable way to solve this situation, and I am heartily sorry for it. It has cost us dearly in terms of any possible future we may have had. I even question that I once believed your judgment was absolutely sound.

I am deeply grieved because I find I must say good-bye – finally and irrevocably. It is one of the most difficult things I have ever had to do, but it must be done. Thank you for having loved me and I pray you may remember me with kindness.

May God bless you and keep you in all your days.

Rebecca

With the letter still in his grip, Scrooge's hand fell to his side as he stared straight ahead, seeing nothing. He was shattered and knew it had been his own doing. Not only had he destroyed his own expectations, he had also shredded Rebecca's hopes and dreams – foolish, foolish man that he was.

Why hadn't he heeded Marley's warnings? He ignored them because he had hopes of accomplishing so much by solving the mystery. He had been short-sighted and had not fully considered all of the possible consequences. Destroying his bond with Rebecca had not been in his plan, and now it was too late. Her letter was clear. She wanted nothing to do with him. He could not discern if she was angry or sorrowful, or both, but it mattered not. She was no longer his, and there was no help for it.

CHAPTER THIRTY-TWO

Secret Aspirations

Martha Cratchit could have chosen any man she wanted, but she adored Homer. No other man could measure up to him because he was all she had ever dreamed a man should be. That was particularly so because they had never had a genuine quarrel, so she had never thought him a tyrant or a thoughtless bully. He was neither, in fact, and she was not likely to ever think of him as such since both of them were generally cheerful and optimistic, easily deferring to the other when a small disagreement occurred.

It was difficult to offend Martha because she would not "take" offense. She simply refused it. It was a convenient trait to have since she worked in trade and was required to deal with people most of the time, some of them determined to be dissatisfied. More than once a customer had abused Martha only to run head-long into Martha's charm and grace in the end. Like Homer, she was determined to do the best job she could, to please her employer.

As to that, Martha was not yet aware of it, but Homer was uncertain about remaining a clerk for his entire life. Martha's father, Bob Cratchit, and Homer both worked for Scrooge and Symons, and both were amply rewarded for their proficiency, but Homer wanted to do more. He wanted adventure and something beyond what most men at that time desired. Hadn't he read Meriwether Lewis's tale of the expedition of Lewis and Clark in North America? Hadn't it caught his imagination and made him wish he could be on such a trek as that?

Homer knew things were different in America now, but he had a nagging need to travel there. It was an impractical idea because it would mean leaving his family, his position and Martha, unless she would agree to go with him, which he doubted very much. She was too close to her family and she ran a successful business that she was hoping to buy. That might change, however, if they married.

Besides all of his fancies about America, Homer desperately wanted to marry Martha, even if it meant he remained perched on his stool in the counting house forever! So, he called at the Cratchit home one evening and asked to speak with Bob Cratchit privately.

Naturally everyone in the household knew what was going on, so the younger girls and their brothers tittered behind a closed door, although the boys did more poking and shoving each other than tittering. Martha and her mother waited quietly in the kitchen, not saying much at all. Neither of them was apprehensive, for they knew how much Bob Cratchit thought of Homer, which is why they were so taken aback by what next occurred.

Cratchit threw open the door and charged through it, furious, while Homer trudged behind, crestfallen. Mrs. Cratchit and Martha were stunned and watched in horror as Cratchit cried,

"Do you know what this man has done?" They had thought so, but evidently it was not what they had hoped.

"He has asked for my eldest daughter's hand in marriage, *that* is what he has done." He ignored the upset women who stood by, helpless and beside themselves with disappointment. They were terrified of what awful things they must be about to hear.

"Yes! He has had the audacity to think we would want him to marry our Martha!" Mrs. Cratchit let out a tiny squeak and promptly covered her mouth with her hands. Then Cratchit smiled and said, "And he is right. We would be *delighted* to have him in the family. They have my permission to wed, and with our blessings."

The relief was palpable. Just as Mrs. Cratchit cried, "Oh, Bob, you did give me a start!" the younger children burst through the closed doors, hurrahing and clapping as if their father had just played the best joke ever. Martha was in tears and clinging to Homer, who was smiling proudly.

Cratchit and his good wife had been hoping for Homer's proposal for some time. They did not admit it to anyone other than each other, but they were relieved that Martha had not settled on Rollo Norris. Not that there was anything amiss with Rollo, per se, and he would have done his best to make Martha happy, but the two of them really did live in different worlds. His life was a bit "rough and tumble," whereas Martha was brought up with a finer view of life. She had an understanding of fashion and civility, not the policeman's lot with its daily sordidness.

The family celebrated that night by toasting the happy couple with a nice rum punch, made mostly with water and sugar for the children. Homer seemed to have been part of the family for some time, but now it would be legal. He would be a son *in law,* which pleased the Cratchits very much. They were all aware, too, that Martha had met Homer's mother and liked her very much.

Homer shared with them that Mrs. Probert remarked, "Homer, you have found the very best. I was extremely impressed, and you two will make a beautiful couple."

It was true. They were admired every time he escorted her through Town, because they stood out. Onlookers wondered who they were, but Homer and Martha were unaware of being noticed because they did not think too highly of themselves, so they did not expect it from others. In fact, it was their nature to be kind to people of all classes, and even though they accepted their own station in society, neither of them subscribed to the idea of anyone being "born better" than others. They believed everyone had equal standing before Almighty God.

It was that common philosophy that brought them, one day, to a discussion of Homer's wish to someday see America. "Can you imagine, Martha? A country that is open to all sorts of ideas and adventure, where a man can make something of himself by whatever talents he has been given." His excitement made her a bit uncomfortable, particularly when he admitted, "You know, I can understand why many or our countrymen emigrate."

"Are you saying you want us to emigrate, Homer? I have always been curious about America and would like to see New York, with its shops and millineries, but I would be satisfied with a visit. Truly. I would not wish to leave England forever. This is home. This is where our families live!" She was becoming distressed and asked, "Must we?" It was clear, from that simple question that she would accompany Homer to the moon, if need be, but he would not abuse such loyalty. Those sorts of decisions would be made together, as husband and wife.

"No, my dear," replied Homer in what he hoped was a calming tone of voice rather than one of disappointment. "I am not suggesting we emigrate. We agree on the attraction America has for both of us, but it is only a dream. Do not worry."

The day following Homer's marriage proposal there was more warm punch and rejoicing at the counting house. Cratchit asked for Scrooge and Fred's attention, bid Homer to stand and happily informed them that Homer and Martha were to be wed. Everyone was wishing Homer well, pleased that he had won the very fair maid's hand.

"Congratulations, Homer, my good man," said Fred as Scrooge disappeared into his office. When he returned, he also shook Homer's hand and gave him one of the new folding paper envelopes. "It is not every day a man gets married, my boy, and I hope this will assist you in beginning what we all hope will be a long and happy life together!" Inside the envelope was a cheque for a substantial amount, which Scrooge and Fred declared was well-earned and the least they could do for the groom-to-be. Homer was humbled and said so as he tried to tell them how much he appreciated it.

As they celebrated, Edwin Carter entered the counting House and joined in the festivities. He and Cratchit had become good friends so he was aware of how much the Cratchits thought of Homer. Carter thought well of Homer too, having relied on him with several of the ventures he had undertaken through the offices of Scrooge and Symons.

"Oh, that's fine, Homer. That's fine! I know you will be very happy. Please accept my congratulations!" They shook hands and without thinking Homer asked, "Mr. Carter, was it very difficult to invest, in America?"

Carter did not realize the seriousness of Homer's question and replied that brains and a strong constitution could turn a small sum of dollars into a goodly return, *if* one were not reckless. Homer nodded, thanked him and returned to his stool, where his brain rebelled against the work he must complete. So, he ruminated instead.

I would have to resign my position here, and they would be required to fill it, so I could not expect to return to things as they are now. Martha might think me mad and try to talk me out of the idea, but Carter managed to make his way in America. I am definitely not reckless, either. Surely, I have brains and brawn enough, and with Martha beside me . . . Martha. Ah, well. There's the rub. So, enough pretending! There is a contract in front of me that wants completing.

CHAPTER THIRTY-THREE

A Prodigious Proposition

With their parents' agreement, Homer and Martha decided to marry in April of 1847. Both liked the idea of a spring wedding and the new beginning it symbolized. Waiting until then would give them ample time to decide on a home and to make necessary plans regarding the wedding itself.

On a day when both Lucy Carter and Martha were working in the shop, Lucy asked if Martha and Homer would like to call at the Carter home that evening. Martha was certain Homer would be glad to do so, and they set a time.

That evening the four of them were seated in the parlor, conversing on various subjects when Edwin Carter cleared his throat and said there was something they wished to discuss, and that he and Lucy had a proposition for them.

"We know you plan to marry in April, and we are extremely pleased. Our pleasure will, however, be increased if you will consider what we are about to propose. Please do not decline until you have thought it over thoroughly and discussed it with family, friends, and whomever."

Homer and Martha were taken by surprise but interested. "What is it, Mr. Carter?" asked Homer. Lucy was smiling.

"I don't know how Martha feels about it, but I am aware that you, Homer, would like very much to go to America." Homer looked surprised and Carter said, "No, you haven't said so, but you have given hints without realizing it." He took his wife's hand and said, "Lucy and I have discussed it, and it is our wish that you both accompany us to America in November."

Homer could barely keep from leaping from his chair with a whoop, and Martha gasped audibly.

"We have been speaking of making the trip for some time, but we have only just this week solidified our intentions. We plan to spend time in New York, but we will also be required to travel a bit. Not as far as your Lewis and Clark my boy, but most likely into Pennsylvania and possibly Ohio. We may even end up farther west than that, on a riverboat! We'll see." Both Homer and Martha were staring wide-eyed in amazement.

"That is why I had not yet said anything to you, Martha," explained Lucy. "We were not yet certain where we were going, exactly. We still aren't, truth be told, or even precisely how long we might be gone."

To America! With the Carters! Homer needed no further details, he was prepared to pack his trunks that night or leave his belongings behind altogether, but Martha required a bit more convincing, and it showed in her countenance. Lucy discerned the astonishment and fear on her face and explained further.

"We are not emigrating, mind you, but we will most likely be gone at least a year. Edwin has holdings which he needs to see to. There is also the prospect of acquiring more."

"And I would be delighted to employ you Homer, to help me oversee them," finished Edwin. "I know your abilities so you would be very helpful to me, and you could learn so much."

"You and I would be companions Martha," added Lucy. "I plan to sell the shop, and I wish to give you a large dividend for all of your hard work and the success you brought to the business."

Martha could not speak, and Homer *would* not because he knew he would be overly enthusiastic and that would surely frighten Martha completely off of the idea. Finally, he promised that they would think about it and thoroughly discuss it with each other and their families. Meanwhile, if they had any questions they would ask the Carters.

"When would you need to know our decision?" asked Homer.

Mr. Carter thought a moment and replied, "We will not be leaving for a few months, but if you could tell us within a week, that would be best. It would leave us enough time to finalize our plans and dispatch the rest of the necessary paperwork."

Lucy added, "There will also be passages to book." Then she thought of an additional detail.

"Unfortunately, your wedding would need to take place quite a bit earlier, perhaps in November, before sailing. I believe the current term is, 'honeymoon,' is it not? You could spend your honeymoon on a trip to America."

Homer and Martha's heads were spinning when they finally bid the Carters goodnight. They thanked them profusely for the offer and decided to walk.

As they made their way to the Cratchits' house, Homer kept silent because he knew his enthusiasm would overwhelm Martha, and she kept silent lest her caution dampen the fire that had been ignited in his imagination. She did, however, smile as she thought, *New York! America! With the Carters!!*

After five minutes of silence, they could stand it no longer and both began to jabber like magpies. Among the things they recalled was the fact that, with Homer's gift from "Scrooge and Symons," and her bit from the sale of the shop, they might have enough for a small stake in the American economy, under Mr. Carter's tutelage, of course. And she could learn so much about American fashion and the business of women's clothing in New York under the guidance of Lucy Carter! Just imagine, their first trip as a married couple would be aboard a steamship crossing the Atlantic!

Finally, they hailed a cab and rode back to the Cratchits' in a daze. The Cratchits would be told of the offer tonight and Homer would tell his mother and father tomorrow. Neither Homer nor Martha was likely to sleep a wink before morning, and it was the same for Mr. and Mrs. Cratchit, unfortunately.

By morning the exhausted Cratchits were beside themselves. As far as they were concerned, both Homer and Martha were as good as on that ship and who knew when, if ever, they would see them again. What if they decided to remain in New York? What if they became Americans? What if they never again set foot in dear old Camden Town?

It was entirely possible that Bob Cratchit and his good wife could have grandchildren they would never meet! The whole idea was terrible and it near broke their hearts to even think on it. Yet they would never try to stop them from going because they recognized it for the singular opportunity it truly was.

Carter, a naturally exuberant man, bounded into the counting house the next day, to see Cratchit. Because of the strong friendship they had forged during the past year, Cratchit trusted Carter.

He also trusted Lucy. Hadn't she taken extraordinary care of their Martha during the years Martha was in her employ? Hadn't she allowed Martha to nearly run the shop after she married Carter? She was a good woman and she was certainly reliable, but oh, my, to take the children all the way to North America!

"Bob, I can see you need reassuring this afternoon," said Carter

"Ah, yes, my friend, I suppose I do, but it's naught to do with you or your wife. It's only me looking at missing our Martha, and Homer here." Homer was trying not to pay attention, so he looked up, smiled, and returned to his figures.

"I am glad you don't hold the offer against me because we were hoping it would be a trip that would benefit them for the rest of their lives."

"There is little doubt as to that," admitted Cratchit with a pained smile. "It could be the making of them. Please do not conclude that we don't want them to go, because we do. We just don't want them to be gone!" They both laughed at the absolute truth of what sounded like an absurd statement.

Of the four parents, Homer's father was the most vocal in favoring the idea. He had been a Navy man himself, and he realized the value of travel and learning to make one's way in a foreign setting. His time with the Royal Navy spanned the years of relative peace following the Napoleonic Wars, but there had been plenty of adventure, nonetheless.

For Mr. Probert, being separated from family for a time was not a terrible thing, but that was because he was the one who had been experiencing new people, places and customs. His wife, on the other hand, could attest to the loneliness and worry of those left behind, although she had never burdened her husband with that particular point of view.

It was true that the Cratchits had every confidence in the Carters and trusted them as much, or more, than they would trust anyone else, and their oversight of the "children" would make it bearable to wave good-bye in November. On one occasion, when Mrs. Cratchit and Lucy Carter were chatting, Mrs. Cratchit made it a point to tell Lucy that she was pleased that Martha would be in good hands, and that she knew Lucy would take good care of her.

"It's good to have another woman around, particularly when one is newly wed, and she will have you – like a mother." Mrs. Cratchit laughed lightly, realizing that may have been an insult, and quickly added, "I realize you are not nearly old enough to be her mother, but you are someone she admires, and she will listen to your guidance. That reassures me a great deal."

It wasn't long after the Carters advertised the shop as being for sale that they were offered more than they dared hoped for, which meant that their gift to Martha would be quite substantial. The higher sale price was due to a competition between two potential buyers who both wished to own the well-known shop that was so successful. Lucy Carter hoped the millinery would continue to prosper in spite of the fact that one of the main reasons for its success would be leaving England, with her!

CHAPTER THIRTY-FOUR

The Bitter Summer Months

The absolute breach between Scrooge and Rebecca was now apparent to anyone who was paying attention. There was no contact between the two, which was a sure sign that the courtship was over. Only those close to them suspected the extent to which they were both suffering, but they could not entice either of them to speak of it, so no one knew the actual cause of the estrangement.

Naturally there was no way for the two to avoid each other altogether because they shared the same society. When they did meet, they were at least cordial, and one would think they were nothing more than passing acquaintances.

The situation could be difficult for their intimate friends, however, because speaking to one might seem to be an affront to the other. It was as if they must choose one over the other, so people tended to split their attentions evenly between Scrooge and Rebecca or, as the summer wore on, to avoid them both when at a gathering.

The awkwardness of the situation became particularly evident one evening in July when Dick and Priscilla Wilkins hosted a musicale. They had invited a number of acquaintances as well as dear friends, so naturally both Scrooge and Mrs. Langstone were included. Neither felt comfortable declining the invitation, but neither were they looking forward to the soiree.

As luck would have it, both Scrooge and Mrs. Langstone arrived at the entry at the same moment. They were stiffly cordial to each other and Scrooge allowed her to enter first, following closely behind, which made it appear as if they were together.

Priscilla spotted them just as they entered the door and drew her own wishful conclusions. *They are reconciled!* She cried, "Ah. Here they are, and side by side, as it should be!" Horrified, neither said anything. Instead, their expressions were those of caged wild animals and Priscilla realized she had blundered badly. She quickly took Mrs. Langstone's hand to welcome her while Scrooge used the opportunity to slip away to join some male friends.

When it became obvious that Scrooge and Mrs. Langstone were no longer speaking, much less courting, others began paying their attentions to them both. Mr. Harris, a musician and arranger of musicales, paid particular consideration to the lovely and talented Mrs. Langstone. He used the excuse of wanting to arrange for her to play piano at some of his venues, but his hopes were for much more than that. He would drop hints as to his intentions, and she would deflect them by appearing not to hear, or not to understand his meaning.

While Mrs. Langstone was being wooed by several men, widows and older spinsters implored their friends to introduce them to the fascinating Mr. Scrooge. Naturally they were in hopes of making a favorable and lasting impression. Unfortunately, it was the worst impressions that tended to last the longest. Miss Agnes Willard, a spinster in her thirties, was one of those.

Miss Willard was pretty, but she was unattractive to men. That was due to several things. For one, her hair refused to submit to a combing. No matter how her maid tried, Miss Willard usually looked as if she had just come in from a windstorm. She also had no sense of physical distance from others and would plant her short body too close to the person with whom she was conversing. Her habit of doing so meant their noses were either three inches apart, or hers was near to touching the top button on a man's coat. Attempting a conversation with her could be extremely exasperating.

One dance with Miss Willard was enough for most men to decide against her. She talked incessantly but had no wit, and she often left men's shoes scuffed from the soles of her own as she stepped lively all over their feet! Only one time was Scrooge trapped into a dance with her, and he vowed such a thing would never again come about. He was true to his word and Miss Willard was left to forever savor their introduction and her one dance with the venerable Mr. Scrooge.

The attention being paid to both Mrs. Langstone and Scrooge did not minimize their loneliness. Both managed to carry on with their lives, but they were empty without the other, and there was no way to overcome the break. The difficulties were insurmountable. Scrooge had covertly discovered unspeakable secrets that Mrs. Langstone could not abide, and in order to reject them and his actions, she had rejected him.

Throughout the summer Scrooge did a great deal of soul-searching. He realized he was indeed bull-headed, which could make him a "bull in a china shop" in social situations, particularly romance. He was simply no good at it because he did not know what succeeded and what didn't. He was also prideful. It was his bullheadedness that had resisted Marley's advice because he wanted to prove something to himself and to Rebecca, but it was his pride that had driven him – pride and self-regard that he had sought to satisfy rather than consider Rebecca's needs and vulnerabilities.

By the end of August Scrooge and Mrs. Langstone's closest friends and relatives had had enough, and they were determined to do something about the terrible rift between the two. Never mind that they did not know what could possibly have caused it. That was irrelevant.

Fred's wife Catherine Symons invited her sister Flora, Priscilla Wilkins and Rebecca's mother, Mrs. Sotherton, to tea for the express purpose of devising some sort of plan to reunite Scrooge and Mrs. Langstone. The first order of business was to at least attempt to determine the problem, although that could prove very difficult since no one really knew anything.

Catherine began by saying, "I know they are both human and therefore prone to make mistakes, but I cannot imagine either one of them doing anything so horrid that the other would cut him or her off completely. It is not in their natures, and they esteemed each other far too highly to do anything that would be beyond forgiveness."

"Well," interjected Mrs. Sotherton, "I did ask Rebecca what had occurred between them and all she would say was that what Scrooge meant as a caring gesture she saw as a betrayal. Beyond that, she refused to make any further statements, and she asked me not to bring it up again. I have obeyed her wishes of course, but it nearly breaks my heart to simply sit by and watch them do this to each other, regardless of the cause. All I can say is, it must have been of vital significance to have separated them so completely."

Priscilla echoed Mrs. Sotherton's comments by adding, "And asking them yields nothing in the way of information because they are both as tight-lipped as a letter sealed with wax."

Catherine concluded, "It seems that we will not be able to detect the problem, but perhaps we can still devise a solution amongst ourselves." She then offered more tea and pastries around the group.

"Well," said Priscilla, swallowing a bite, "Inviting them to the same function and trapping them in the same room does not work because I have tried, and failed. All I managed to do was create an extremely awkward and very embarrassing situation, for which I had to apologize to each of them. Separately, of course."

Flora said that perhaps having one of them write a letter to the other would help, but Mrs. Sotherton shook her head and disclosed, "I have already suggested that to Rebecca, and she admitted that she had done so and that the letter said everything that needed to be said. She then asked me to please leave it be, and I have obliged, until today that is. Today I have joined with other loving meddlers to see what on earth can be done to straighten out this unholy mess, for that is what it certainly is!"

"I admit it does seem hopeless," remarked Catherine, which led Flora to say one more thing.

"They still care for each other or they wouldn't be so distant." The others looked at her without understanding. "Yes," said Flora. "It's true. If one no longer cares for another he or she does not try to avoid the other as if he or she is carrying the plague. It's when one *does* care that one finds the other's presence upsetting, even intolerable." She smiled before finishing with, "Well, they certainly are not comfortable in each other's presence, so perhaps we still have enough left of their emotions with which we can work a miracle."

"I believe a miracle is the only thing that can help," remarked Catherine, and the others smiled sadly and nodded.

Catherine had served a nice tea, and the group enjoyed it while continuing to discuss the issue at hand. Unfortunately, by the time the teapot had been emptied for the second time and most of the pastries eaten, any possible miracle had failed to materialize. So, they came away without a plan, but they did establish themselves as a militia of sorts that would keep watch over Scrooge and Mrs. Langstone and take action on their behalf whenever and wherever possible. They would operate in concert and keep each other informed of anything that was noteworthy and any new ideas that might occur to one of them. Should an opportunity arise that might be used to bring Scrooge and Rebecca together, the militia would mobilize!

CHAPTER THIRTY-FIVE

An Apparition Appears

Autumn was in the air, and it had been some time since Marley visited Scrooge. Unlike before, Marley continued to stay away even when Scrooge tried to rally him. Such a request on Scrooge's part had worked in the past, but no longer. It was almost as if Marley were refusing to speak to his old friend simply because he had not done the spirit's bidding. Surely, he would not be so exacting as to believe Scrooge should be his puppet, obeying only his will and not thinking for himself.

It was a difficult thing to admit, but Scrooge knew that, had he heeded Marley's advice, his life would not be in its current state of total disarray. *Perhaps my old friend is gone for good. If that is the case, I have driven two of the most important figures from my life. It is true I still have my family and other friends, but I cannot share everything with any of them, as with Marley. He seems to know the absolute truth about me and my motives, but he never rejects me. At least, he never has before, certainly not to this extent.*

Those thoughts reminded Scrooge that during the past year he had begun to wonder more about just who, or what, Marley was. To be honest, Marley in life had possessed a good head for business, but he was not nearly so "wise," nor as compassionate as this apparition, and Scrooge was not convinced that death could have improved him to quite that extent. Perhaps, if he ever did return, Scrooge would ask him outright to explain his true identity.

Rebecca spent many nights walking her floor, and it was wearing on her. Tonight however, she was finally not only tired, she was truly sleepy, and she expected to actually get some rest. The past months had taken their toll, and her life was no longer the one she had enjoyed prior to her separation from Ebenezer. She missed him profoundly, but she could see no way around the situation he had created. She blamed him, but she did not hate him. She loved him even though she could not abide what he had done, nor live with him since he now harbored such intimate dark knowledge. Scrooge had not exactly committed outright treachery, but the absolute trust and faith she had in him was gone forever.

Rebecca put out her lamp and crawled into bed. She was praying for a proper night's rest, but as she passed from wakefulness into sleep, she began to dream. A man's voice was calling her name. "Re-be--c-ca." She could see no one, but she answered, nevertheless.

"Yes?" Instantly a misty configuration gathered near her bedroom door and floated toward her bedside. For some reason she was not afraid, even though the apparition was somewhat eerie. Suddenly, she woke, but the apparition remained, which convinced her that she was still dreaming, but dreaming that she was awake! The thought made her smile just before the apparition spoke again.

"Rebecca, you are carrying a heavy load." Curious, she sat part-way up as he continued. "It is true that Ebenezer has a propensity to be bull-headed, but that is not always an evil thing. It is one of his characteristics that makes him constant in his affections and steady in his endeavors." She did not speak, but she was not required to since the visitor could evidently respond to her thoughts, which at that moment were, *I have been betrayed. I can never put faith in him again.*

"Yes, my dear, you have been deeply hurt, but pain, in itself, is not a sound reason to choose misery over joy. Wounds can be forgiven and thereby healed – even forgotten. Misery, on the other hand, attaches itself to one's soul, like a leech that draws on one's very life force."

If you are suggesting that I subject myself to a re-telling of my child's final three weeks, I do not believe I am capable of doing so. Nor do I believe that even Ebenezer would wish it. I am unable to re-establish any sort of communication or closeness with him, knowing that he is carrying dreadful facts about my son that he dares not share with me.

"You must speak to him." *No! It is not possible. I cannot! Please go away, whatever you are!* But he did not go away. Instead, he carried on.

"Listen to me carefully. Ebenezer will not attempt to tell you anything you do not wish to hear, but you are to ask for one piece of information from him. If you do as you are told, the two of you may at least find some peace with each other." The mist twirled slightly before speaking again.

"Here is what you are to do. You are to ask Ebenezer to tell you one, and only one thing about Peter's death that he might want you to know. Remember now. He may tell you one thing and nothing more!"

Such an idea! We are finding it very difficult to be in each other's company, much less to speak to each other!

There was no response, and when she looked about the room, the image was quickly dissipating. Still unafraid, she turned over and quickly fell into a sound and restful sleep for the first time in weeks.

Mrs. Langstone had considered the specter's suggestion and the following morning she felt a peace that allowed her to pen a short note.

> *Dear Ebenezer,*
>
> *Would you please do me the honor of calling on me this afternoon, if possible. I will be at home all day.*
>
> *Yours Sincerely,*
> *Rebecca*

Scrooge was filled with both elation and dread as he stood at Rebecca's front door. She had not said the purpose of the call, so he could only imagine, which meant his mind was flitting from one idea to another, keeping him in nervous suspense.

Rebecca greeted him cordially, but the closeness they had enjoyed had not returned. After they both sat, she explained her reason for the visit.

"You will no doubt find this difficult to believe Ebenezer, but I had some sort of 'visitation' last night. Whoever it was could read my thoughts and spoke to me in a man's voice – very authoritatively, I might add." She smiled and said, "I am certain you think I was being fanciful, or you will say I was dreaming, but I do not believe either to have been the case." She clasped her hands in her lap and said, "You may call me mad if you like, but his advice seemed sound to me. Do you mind if we proceed with our visit on that basis?"

So, this is where you've been, Marley, you old scoundrel, and all the while I've been imploring you to come to me!

"Of course, I do not mind. I am indeed curious as to what your visitor had to say, real or imagined."

Rebecca was somewhat surprised that he did not try to make a logical argument against the incident but seemed, instead, to be agreeable to hearing her out – even interested.

"He instructed me to ask you something, and since we have little to lose, I am obeying his directives.

Oh, dear. Well, I'm in for it now.

"Ebenezer, I want you to tell me one thing that you found out about Peter's final three weeks – only one thing, mind you, and absolutely nothing more."

Scrooge was dumbfounded. Surely it was Marley who had made the suggestion, which meant it was possible for Scrooge to do it, but he must think for a moment. He stood up and walked several feet without saying anything. He knew so much, enough that it had been weighing him down, and now she was actually requesting that he share only one small piece of it with her. So much information was running through his mind that he could not reduce it to a simple statement. Rebecca remained quiet while he paced until he stood facing the fireplace, leaning with his hands on the mantle. Finally, he turned around and knew exactly what to say. It was the truth, too, because Sikes' actual plan had been to drown the boy. *Tell her!*

"Rebecca, Peter died instantly, by accident."

Rebecca was agape. As she stared at him her eyes welled with huge tears that slowly made their way down her cheeks before she began to weep. Then she let go of the anguish she had harbored for ten years and allowed herself to sob uncontrollably.

Scrooge knew he no longer had the right, but he could not bear to see her in such a state, sitting there by herself, looking so small and broken. In tears himself, he took her by the arms, raised her from her chair and gathered her to his heart. There he held her while she released the longstanding pain into his shoulder.

After several minutes Rebecca stood back, wiped her eyes and gently blew her nose. She motioned to him, and they both sat.

He began to apologize for everything, but she stopped him before he could say anything more than, "Rebecca, I am so . . ."

"It's an odd thing, Ebenezer, but I seem to have needed to hear that one particular fact that was buried in all you discovered." She sniffed slightly and shook her head. "I wasn't aware of it, but just to know that his death happened quickly makes such a difference. *Such* a difference." She leaned back and closed her eyes for a moment.

It was evident that Rebecca was spent, and any additional conversation would only tire her further. Scrooge begged her to remain seated and said he would show himself out. He took her hand, bent over it and kissed it as he would do with any lady to whom he wished to pay formal homage. At the door he charged her maid to look after her well, since he was unsure of when or if he would see her again.

CHAPTER THIRTY-SIX

Assistance Is Proposed

M rs. Sotherton had never been one to remain immobile when there was something to be done. For that reason, she invited Catherine Symons to tea since she and her husband Fred were Scrooge's closest relations. Catherine and she were by far the most fitting women to take extreme measures due to their family ties to Rebecca and Scrooge, and they had the attitude for it. They could inform Flora and Priscilla once they were ready to execute the plan.

It had been several days since the "women's militia" met for strategic planning, and they had failed in their mission. Mrs. Sotherton had now waited long enough. She and Catherine would formulate a plan and they would keep trying until they succeeded!

"Now," said Mrs. Sotherton as she handed her guest a glass of sherry. "Do you have any compunction about being a bit aggressive in this instance? After all, we are talking about people we love and whom we wish to be happy. They are not happy now, and we must do something about it!"

Catherine, who was known to be resolute when necessary, agreed wholeheartedly and said she was up to the task, whatever it was. "But what can we do?" she asked. "They are grown people and if they believe we are interfering, we could even damage our own relationships with them."

"Tut-tut, my good woman," said Mrs. Sotherton. "Do not be faint-hearted. Here. Have another drop of sherry. Their happiness may rest with our willingness to risk their crossness with us, even a hostile break for a time, but if we do not at least make the attempt, we know we will not succeed, and things *cannot* continue as they are!"

Catherine agreed because she was truly up to the task, whatever it was.

"Now, my dear," continued Mrs. Sotherton. "I have influence with Rebecca, and you have influence with Ebenezer. We are bound by familial love and they will not cast us off forever, no matter what we do, so long as we do not insult or degrade them, and as long as they know we are speaking out of our affection for them. In addition to those parameters, our approach must be kept within limits."

"Just what are those limits?"

"That we act only for their good."

"Ah." Catherine took another sip.

"Now, here is what I propose. I will speak with my daughter and you will speak with your Uncle Scrooge. All you and I have to decide is what, exactly, we are going to say. We must be firm though, in whatever we say to them. I am Rebecca's mother and that carries a good deal of authority. You are Ebenezer's niece, and he feels a great deal of tenderness for you. We can use our standing with them to say what someone less connected might never be able to get away with saying."

"Do you think Flora's idea of sending a letter is best?"

"No, my dear. We must say it in person. It will be less easily discarded or misunderstood if we speak with them face to face."

Catherine was not shy, so she had no problem with the plan, but they did need to decide what to say, and also to agree to say the same things.

It took a bit more sherry and more discussion before the two women knew how they were going to approach their respective relations, but finally it was settled. They would call on their relatives and *insist* that they be reasonable and do whatever it may take to save the relationship, and that was that!

They then penned notes to Flora and Priscilla to tell them what was about to occur.

Mrs. Sotherton called on her daughter the very next day, which was the same day and time that Catherine was to appear at the counting office. They would be saying nearly the same things, hopefully with success.

After they exchanged greetings, Mrs. Sotherton sat down and looked her daughter in the eye. "Rebecca, I know that things do not stand well with you and Ebenezer. Anyone with one blind eye can see that, and it is time you and he ended this feud, or whatever the disagreement is. You must make up or you will regret it the rest of your life! You must not let him get away!"

Rebecca's response shocked her mother because she merely replied, "Well, I am willing to speak with him if he is willing, and I will do my best, Mother."

At the same time Catherine and her Uncle Scrooge were locked in Scrooge's office, having very nearly the same conversation. However, at the end of her monologue Catherine said, "You will never find another Rebecca Langstone. Not even close. You love her, and Fred and I love her. Please do what you must to save your, and our, relationship with her!"

Scrooge had merely calmly replied, "You are right, and I don't mind giving it a try. I will do my utmost to preserve what we had, for all our sakes."

Later that day Mrs. Langstone called on Catherine and they compared their experiences.

"My dear," cried Mrs. Sotherton. "It was far from what I was expecting. There was no argument; no tears, nor anger. I thought to have a wildcat on my hands, but she acquiesced immediately and promised she would do her best to patch things up!"

"It was the same for me!" exclaimed Catherine. "Not only did Uncle Scrooge not disagree, he was as tame as a lamb. I know he still cares for Rebecca and wants things to be as they were because he assured me that he would talk to her and see how things turned out. He even winked at me when I left!"

Both women were thrilled with their success and gratified that they had been able to give a firm nudge to their loved ones, to reunite them. They also agreed that it could be the miracle Flora had inadvertently predicted. Now all they had to do was wait and see, but they were not above making another strategic move, if necessary. They would keep their eyes and ears open and act accordingly!

Both Scrooge and Rebecca wrote notes asking to meet at Rebecca's home the following morning, and their letters crossed in the post. Because of that, Rebecca received Scrooge's request to call at the same time Scrooge received her invitation. The notes were fortuitous and informed each of them that the other wanted to meet.

When they came face-to-face in the Langstone drawing room the atmosphere was more relaxed than their last meeting. Rebecca had ordered coffee to be served, and she received Scrooge with civility. Miraculously, neither of them seemed upset with the other, and both were anxious to discuss the situation. After Scrooge seated himself in his usual chair, they both spoke at once.

Scrooge began, "Rebecca . . ." just as she said, "You may be . . ." which made them smile. He gestured with one hand for her to continue, and he mimed with the other as if buttoning his lips.

"I imagine we were both going to explain our reasons for wanting to visit, weren't we?" He nodded and agreed. "Yes, we were." Then he allowed her to continue.

"I had an interesting conversation with my mother yesterday, and she was adamant that you and I speak. She had no way of knowing that I had already planned to do so, and I allowed her to believe that she had convinced me." She smiled and said, "Between you and me, I believe it will do her good to think she has won a battle, if not the entire war!"

"Now that *is* interesting since I also had a conversation with a very determined lady yesterday – my niece, Catherine. Yes! Our conversation was of a very similar nature. I believe she was surprised when I failed to argue and simply agreed that her idea to speak with you was a good one. Like you, I had already planned to do so, but I didn't tell her so. Best to let her think she has had her way, you know," and they both laughed before taking a sip of the hot coffee.

It was wonderful to be in each other's company again, both of them relaxed enough to speak without rancor or pain. They could even have moments of silence without suspecting each other of bitter thoughts. How had all of that ill feeling been relinquished? It would certainly be the subject of their conversation although neither dared hope it would result in a return to their former closeness.

"Rebecca, I am so very sorry and ashamed of what I have done. I should have thought the thing through because, had I done so, I would have seen the unsoundness of my plan and the possible distressing effects on you. Please forgive me, if you are able."

"Most certainly, Ebenezer, but as it turns out, there is nothing to forgive. Had you not embarked on your mission of discovery you would not have been able to tell me the one thing I desperately needed to hear. I was unaware that I had been host to a painful hardness in my heart since 1836, but I realized it when it was suddenly gone!"

Rebecca's expression changed to wonderment when she looked out the window and added, reflectively, "And I would not have asked you to tell me one, and only one thing, had not that vision, or apparition, or whatever he was, directed me to do so, because I was too confused to feel anything but rage."

Don't worry, Marley. I won't give you away." A more recent knot in Scrooge's stomach had also disappeared with his realization that Rebecca no longer minded that he knew Peter's entire story. Her lack of concern quelled the torment he felt for knowing it.

"Ebenezer, I wondered how one short statement could make such a difference to me, and I believe it is because I desperately needed to know that Peter's death was not drawn out or torturous. I have evidently been angry about all that concerned him for a very long time. I heaped it all onto you when you discovered the truth, and that stirred the deep ache I had come to accept and live with. But then, because of that truth, you were able to give me a gift I have needed for so long. Good certainly has come out of this, and God bless you for that." Tears were again gathering in her eyes, but she dabbed them with her handkerchief and quickly collected herself.

"I should say one thing, Rebecca. I was uncertain at the outset as to whether or not I should pursue my investigation, and I had been warned against doing so without your permission. I kept at it for the wrong reasons, and I created serious problems for both of us because, once I learned the truth, I couldn't tell you, and it became a wedge between us.

"Perhaps, if you had spoken to me about it first, we would have avoided the agony we have been through, because I doubt very much that I would have agreed to your investigation. Still, we have gained so much through all of this even though it was terribly unpleasant at the time! She looked thoughtful and continued. "I still can't help but wonder just who, or what, my apparition was."

Since Scrooge would not reveal Marley's identity, he could think of nothing more to say other than that he was thankful that they were again friends. He wanted more, but relations between them were fragile and he would not risk additional breakage by imposing his wishes on the situation.

With that, he rose to leave, and she also stood. They were facing each other, and he extended his hand to courteously take hers when she reached up with her left hand and placed her fingertips lightly on his cheek. It was a tender touch, and they could not help but allow their eyes to meet. When they did, he lost all reason and swept her into his arms as she gladly wrapped hers around his neck. Their kiss conveyed all of the apologies and the forgiveness they both needed.

CHAPTER THIRTY-SEVEN

Plans Are Finalized

All was settled and the plans were being implemented. Homer and Martha would marry in November at the Cratchit home and two weeks later set out for New York with the Carters on one of the new trans-Atlantic steamships. They would land in Boston and travel to New York from there.

Leaving in November meant they would not celebrate Christmas in England with their families, but there was no alternative since they must adjust to the shipping company's schedules, rather than their own.

It was an exciting time, and both were anxious to begin their travels, but as November neared, Martha began to have second thoughts. Not only was she dreading having to say good-bye to her family, she wondered if she were indeed strong enough for this sort of undertaking. She had begun to experience fits of what was known as homesickness, and they hadn't yet sailed! She showed occasional signs of melancholy and could not always control her tears. They would appear without warning and cast gloom on the entire undertaking, not only for her, but for Homer and also the Carters. Her uncertainty showed itself in the questions she seemed to continually be asking.

"Homer, are you certain this is the right thing for us to be doing?"

"I am, but I admit I am concerned about you. What can I do, my dear?"

"Nothing. Nor can I. I only pray I can reform before we board the ship, because on occasion I feel as though my heart were being torn in two." With that, she burst into another round of weeping, leaving Homer helpless. Everyone involved had discussed her state, but no one knew quite what to do other than cancel the trip entirely, at least for Homer and Martha.

Tim Cratchit, who was not so tiny these days, loved his eldest sister and would miss her dreadfully, but he wanted her to be happy, and he knew in his heart that she and Homer would regret it the rest of their lives if she prevented them from taking this opportunity. So, he appeared at the millinery one day, thankfully at a time when the shop was not bustling with customers. He had a simple plan of what to say. He hoped it would work.

"Tim! What brings you here?" exclaimed Martha. She was always pleased to see him. He was the most soft-hearted and obliging of them all, and he continued to be the family's pet, even after overcoming his illness.

"I just wanted to talk with you a bit, and tell you how envious I am of your going to America, even if it is only for an extended visit. I also admit I will be envious even more, when you return." Something in what he said struck her. *He is correct. It is only a visit. We are not emigrating, for goodness' sake.* "You are envious, Tim? How so?"

"Well, I would love to see New York and any part of America, for that matter, and you are actually going to do so! Just think, when you return you will know so much more, and you will have experienced a great deal more than the rest of us. You will no longer be the typical English girl of middle class who has had limited exposure to the world. You will be a married woman with much more sophistication." He musn't omit the main thing he wanted to say.

"To be absolutely honest, Sister, I am proud of your pluck. You are very brave to be doing this, but then, you have never let fear keep you from learning new things. That resolve is one reason you are so successful in your vocation."

Martha smiled at her youngest brother. She realized he was saying things he hoped would set her mind at ease, but his words rang true. What was there, after all, to fear that was much more frightening than placing her life in the hands of a strange cab driver, or a railroad locomotive engineer? Or learning a new trade, for that matter. One could find all sorts of things to fear, if one sought them out with that in mind. One could also choose to continue on in spite of any fright that might arise. Besides, she would be with her husband and her dear friends. She would not be alone on this venture.

Martha felt calmer than she had in weeks, and although she would surely still have bouts of uncertainty, she was more determined in their plans, even energized, after listening to Tim.

"Thank you, my dear, dear faithful Brother. I'll be better now. If you have confidence in me, I shall have it too, even when I'm afraid."

Tim was indeed special. He always had been, and she gave him a big hug. As she did so, she realized with a twinge that by the time she returned to England she would most likely have to reach up, to embrace him.

By the end of August things were set right between Scrooge and his beloved Rebecca, and they had reinstated and announced their betrothal. She was finally wearing an exquisite engagement ring of her birthstone surrounded by perfect diamonds. Their relationship had weathered more than one severe storm, but their love for each other had only deepened, and they were anxious to begin their life as a married couple. It was Scrooge who put into words what they had both been thinking.

"My dear, I do not want to be sounding a funeral dirge here, but at our ages do we really want to put off our marriage for months on end? I see no reason to wait longer than it would take to plan the thing, do you?" She agreed, and they settled on the morning of the 19th of September. She and her mother immediately began organizing what was a long-awaited and joyful event for all of those who cared for them.

After Scrooge and Rebecca set a wedding date, he and Fred gave Cratchit and Homer each a sizeable bonus, in celebration. Homer was beginning to feel somewhat well-to-do with both of the recent gifts he received from them, and he said so, which only increased their pleasure in bestowing them.

There was only one hinderance to delay Scrooge and Rebecca's plans. Where were they going to reside? Both had large homes that were well furnished, and neither particularly wanted to move. Should they purchase a new home, where there were no "ghosts" of others to remind them of their pasts? Neither one wanted to forget anyone, nor did they wish the other to do so.

Scrooge did not want to leave his home since it had originally belonged to Marley. Scrooge acquired it after Marley's death, a death which, incidentally, had not kept Marley from revisiting the place! It was also the house wherein he had been visited by those other three spirits who insisted on his reformation, which was of special significance to him.

Rebecca's home held memories for her, too. They did not interfere with her love for, nor her desire to be with Ebenezer, but neither did she wish to lose access to those physical reminders of the past. They were objects she could still touch, even though the people were gone. Nanny had even marked Peter's growth on a door jamb, and Rebecca could not countenance a new owner thoughtlessly painting over those marks. As long as she could view them, it was as if something of her son remained.

It was not long following the announcement of the betrothal between Scrooge and Rebecca that Scrooge received a letter. He was surprised by the contents, but he should not have been since the Rector was aware of some of the difficulties the couple had experienced during the past two years.

The Rector did not know the details, but he knew enough to motivate him to offer any support he could muster, and the letter had clearly been penned with benevolent motives.

My Dear Friend,

I hope you will forgive me if I overstep our friendship, but in this instance, I claim the privilege of Rector. I am inviting you and Mrs. Langstone to join me for a visit, during which we can discuss your upcoming nuptials. I may even offer a bit of Christian counsel, if need be.

I realize you are not a young couple who know little of life, and you are not in need of guidance, but I would be remiss if I did not at least make the offer. Perhaps a short chat would suffice, and my duties as your Rector would be satisfied.

241

*Please reply with your decision. I hope you
will accept my proposal.*

Yours Sincerely,

Colin

Scrooge's initial reaction was to beg off any meeting, but
he would share the offer with Rebecca and let her decide. The
Rector already knew them both intimately, and as he implied
in his letter, they were not "babes in the woods." Scrooge was,
therefore, surprised when Rebecca said she would very much
enjoy a visit with the Rector and was even looking forward to it.

When they all sat down at the appointed day and time, the
Rector naturally did not mention that Scrooge had spoken to him
about their most recent difficulty, but he did ask them if there
was anything either of them wished to address. They both said
no, which was the truth, but then Rebecca admitted there was
one thing they had not managed to solve, which was where they
were to live.

"Is that something you must decide right away?" asked the
Rector.

Neither had thought of it in those terms and they agreed that
they supposed not.

"Then why force yourselves to make a decision at this point?
Sometimes these sorts of things are best left to be worked out
over a period of time. Selling homes and making such big
decisions can go wrong, if rushed. You may want to set a date
at say, six months or so, by which time you hope to have made
a decision and possibly a move, or you may simply revisit the
idea and then put it off for a bit longer. Meanwhile, enjoy your
betrothal and your upcoming wedding and stay in whichever
house you choose, whenever you wish. Use them both!"

It made sense, and they were greatly relieved as they saw agreement on each other's face, but then Rebecca thought of something else, so she mentioned it.

"I fear that we are not always absolutely candid with each other. Scrooge looked surprised, and she quickly added, "Oh, it isn't that we are willfully dishonest, no – never! But sometimes we think we are doing the right thing by not saying what is on our minds, particularly if it could be received as criticism or might plant a seed of fear."

"Ah," said the Rector. "I understand that well." He settled back, ready to tell one of his stories. No one minded when he told a story because they were always interesting and often imparted a truth or a bit of humor, so they both relaxed as he folded his hands on his stomach and began.

"As you know, I am a widower. Julia was the best wife in the world, for me, and we got along very well – at least as far as I was concerned. I was smug in the fact that I took good care of her. It wasn't until she was on her deathbed that she said some things I wish she had said long before, but would I have listened? Perhaps she did try to say them. Who knows?

"She was near the end and began uttering things without knowing she was speaking. One time she said, 'He would never confer.' Then, she opened her eyes but was obviously not seeing anything in the room, including me. 'Why didn't you want to hear me out?' she said. 'So many times. Refused to confer.' It was only one of many things she said during those days, but I particularly remember this because it had a ring of truth to it, and I took it to heart because I was certain she was referring to me.

"It took prayer and serious thought before I realized that she was most likely alluding to the times she would mention a subject that was on her mind, and I would say, 'I'll take care of it,' not realizing that she wanted to discuss it with me. Too often I didn't ask what *she* thought, or allow her to tell me how she would approach the thing, whatever it was. I prided myself on the fact that I managed her problems, but that was apparently something that disappointed her, at least in the way I often went about it.

"You see, by forging ahead, I shut her out. She might want to discuss our garden and I would say, 'Don't you worry about it, my dear, I'll take care of things,' and that was the end of it. My solution of whether to plant roses instead of daisies might not have been what she would have done at all, but I didn't know that, because I was 'taking care of it.' So, many times she must have ended up with roses when what she really wanted were daisies.

"Please don't misunderstand. I do not believe she was an unhappy wife, because it wasn't a big problem, but sometimes it's the invisible piece of lint on your eyelash that causes the most consternation.

How I wish she had simply said, 'Colin I don't want you to fix it, I only want you to listen to me, and together we will come up with a solution that satisfies us both.' I assume she did not do so for fear of hurting me, or she may have been afraid of seeming to be difficult to please, but had I known, I would have made a good effort to meet her halfway, and she would have been happier." He smiled at them both.

"All I'm trying to say to you two is, if you don't share the small things that bother you, they will eventually cause a problem for at least one of you. It's better to patch the first hole in the roof than to wait until the entire thing blows off during a storm."

CHAPTER THIRTY-EIGHT

The Wedding

There were those who expected the Scrooge/Langstone wedding to be a lavish affair due to his wealth and renown and her wealth and social standing, but neither of them was interested in an ostentatious display. Only close friends and relatives would attend, and there would be an informal breakfast following the ceremony that would be officiated by their friend Rector Colin Gifford.

Scrooge spent very little time planning the wedding since he was busy at the counting house. He also believed such things were best left to women, who seemed to have an aptitude for them. Still, his mind did wander occasionally to the fact that soon Rebecca would be his wife, and how much better his life was going to be with her as a constant in it. During one such reverie a thought struck him like a well-aimed bolt of lightning.

Oh, blast! Marley! Surely, he would not dare to visit me when there is another person in the bedroom! Scrooge knew Marley had already visited Rebecca once, but she did not know who he was at the time. At least that experience might lead her to believe her eyes if he did materialize in their bedroom. No matter, Scrooge would still have a great deal of explaining to do since he and Marley had been in contact for almost three years now, with Marley giving him sound advice that Scrooge often ignored.

Then another thought stuck him. If Rebecca were unable to see Marley, but could still hear him, his and Marley's conversations would no longer be private. Would she interject her opinions? Would Marley still be able to read her thoughts the way he did when he visited her, and respond to them? If so, Scrooge would know what she was thinking! Oh, this *was* a proper pickle. *Marley, old friend, I'm relying on you to behave, or find another room in which to show yourself, and only to me!*

The morning of September 19, 1846 finally arrived, and guests were gaily assembling at the home of Mrs. Adelaide Sotherton. The house had been adorned beautifully with flowers, and a breakfast table was heavily laden with an appealing assortment of food and drink.

First to arrive were Fred and Catherine Symons, followed closely by Dick and Priscilla Wilkins. The rest filed in within a half hour, and soon the rooms were filled with greetings and gaiety.

Scrooge wandered among the guests, trying not to become nervous from all of the well-wishers who continually remarked, "Now, don't be nervous!" or, "There is no reason to be upset, you know!" He did know, and he had not been at all jumpy until they started in with their admonishments and suggestions to take deep breaths and not pay attention to the fact that everyone was scrutinizing his every word and move!

Scrooge was dressed in a grey morning coat with a white waistcoat, and darker grey trousers. His boutonniere was a red rose. That particular flower represented love, beauty, passion, courage and respect, all of which were embodied in his relationship with Rebecca.

As a nod to current acceptable practice, Mrs. Langstone, a widow, did not wear a white dress, a veil, or have bridesmaids at her side. Instead, her dress was a soft grey silk with exquisite lace trimming. Lucy Carter and Martha Cratchit had also designed a very becoming matching lace headcover that not only matched her dress perfectly, it also enhanced her loveliness..

Soon Rector Gifford called for everyone's attention and suggested they gather together for the ceremony. As Rebecca approached, Scrooge's heart leapt into his throat at her beauty, and he noticed a glow that seemed to emanate from her face. He wondered if it were something only brides exhibited. Then, before they knew it, the couple was facing the Rector, and the wedding had begun. Rebecca was as steady as the Rock of Gibraltar. Scrooge was like a raft on the rapids.

Both of them gave the appearance of serenity as they began to take their vows, but Scrooge was beside himself. *Dear Lord, don't let me drop the ring. The ring! Where is that confounded th . . . Oh, here. And what if I should s-s-stumble when I repeat my vows?*

"Now, Ebenezer, please take Rebecca's hand in yours." *Uuhh-oooh. I can't catch my breath. Oh, Lord, I can't feel my legs. My knees . . . My knees are buckling!*

"Rebecca, do you take . . ." *Why on earth did we consent to make such a spectacle of ourselves and invite these people to observe me play the buffoon?*

"Ebenezer, repeat after me . . ." *If I falter now, I'll never live it down! Oh, blast it, what did the Rector just ask me to say?*

Scrooge did not falter, however, and neither did Rebecca. They carried the wedding off with aplomb. In fact, they fared much better than the women who were weeping into their handkerchiefs while men patted their arms in what appeared to be attempts to comfort them but were actually endeavors to hush them.

Finally, the vows were said, and Ebenezer and Rebecca were pronounced man and wife. The Rector gave a blessing and Scrooge heaved a huge sigh of relief. He had made it through without creating an unforgettable commotion and was still standing on what had been wobbly knees only moments before. He and his new wife held each other's hands and happily invited their guests to enjoy the lovely breakfast that had been prepared for them.

There were hot rolls and other fancy breads; cold beef, chicken and salmon; ham and eggs; a large variety of vegetables and fresh fruit. Many toasts to the bride and groom were made along with sincere congratulations and best wishes from loving friends and family.

The custom was to have three cakes – the wedding cake, a bride's cake and one for the groom. Scrooge and Rebecca opted for only one English plum wedding cake with elaborate white frosting. Queen Victoria had set the trend of ornate white frosting over the traditional cake several years before, and they liked the appearance.

The Scrooges' cake was large enough to give a piece to each of their guests to take home in a box, but it was not so ornamental as to be ostentatious.

Soon it was time for Mr. and Mrs. Scrooge to depart, but they mingled a bit before leaving. The women showered the new Mrs. Scrooge with their best wishes and once again wept with utter delight.

"Scrooge, old man," cried Dick Wilkins as he slapped him on the back, "you were quite the act up there. Wish I'd done as well at my own wedding. Instead, I was very nearly tongue-tied. Ask Priscilla. And when I did get my voice back, I repeated her vows as well as my own!"

Edwin Carter added, "So glad we could encourage you before the vows, my friend. I see it helped you to stay steady during the ceremony. Sometimes you only need to hear from others who have already been through it." Then they all began to laugh heartily, each for different reasons. They had no idea how far Scrooge had strayed from their advice, particularly since it was likely their well-meant warnings that had brought on so much agitation!

While the men were congratulating Scrooge for harkening to their instructions, Mrs. Sotherton and Catherine Symons had stepped aside to congratulate each other. Although no one knew what had caused the break between Scrooge and Rebecca the previous spring, it was clear to the women that it was their own determination to reunite the two that made today's wedding possible.

"Just think," said Catherine, "had you not devised the plan that we do something to repair this relationship, today's nuptials might never have taken place."

Mrs. Sotherton leaned toward Catherine and lowered her voice, "And if you had not agreed to speak with your Uncle Scrooge and insist that he and she get together and work things out . . ."

Just then they were joined by Flora and Priscilla, who echoed their sentiments and joined in the self-congratulations. Hadn't they, after all, been in on the initial planning?

Finally, Scrooge and Rebecca bid adieu as the guests escorted them to their carriage with cheers and waves. They would leave London directly and be gone for perhaps a month. For some reason the rumour-mongers had put it about that the Scrooges were headed to Scotland following their nuptials. Scrooge and Rebecca gladly allowed that story to spread because it assured them of secrecy, for their destination was, in fact, Italy.

CHAPTER THIRTY-NINE

A Difficult Good-bye

Homer Probert and Martha Cratchit were married in November, in Camden Town. It was a simple affair with only those dearest to them in attendance. Even so, it was a lovely ceremony with the additional excitement of the impending trip to America, although that would not come about for two more weeks. The Scrooges had been gracious enough to offer the Langstone home to them for the interim, which they gratefully accepted.

The only difficulty for the newly married couple had been in having to deal with servants since Martha was accustomed to only day help, and Homer's family employed just two who lived in. But they needn't have worried. At their first glance of the beautiful young couple, the servants were greatly taken with them and made certain that they were overly pampered and very well spoiled until the day they left London.

Homer's impending trip to America had proved to be a definite problem for the men he was leaving behind when Scrooge,
Fred and Cratchit first began to discuss filling his situation. It
would have been best to do so prior to his wedding since he
would not return following his nuptials, but who could possibly
take his place?

Surely there was an adequate clerk somewhere who would
fit the bill, but he would very likely not be the decent and very
efficient young man they had come to rely on and even love.
Their conversations seemed to go in circles because they had
not been able to get beyond that simple fact, from the beginning.

"I know I am biased in this case," said Cratchit, "because
Homer will be my son-in-law, but the truth is, he is remarkable. I have not met many lads who can measure up to him."

"I couldn't agree more," said Fred. "Still, we took a chance
on him, so there must be another who would turn out well, even
if he were not quite top notch at the time of hiring, as Homer
was." They all looked askance, knowing that it was possible,
but certainly not likely.

Scrooge had offered to ask Dick Wilkins if he would keep
his ear to the ground and let them know if he heard of someone
who might be a good choice. They all knew it was a gamble,
no matter whom they hired, as was Homer when he first came
to the counting house. The difference was that they all knew,
during Homer's first week at work, that they had bet on a winner.

"No," agreed, Fred. "It wouldn't be the end of the world if
we hired someone and then had to sack him, but then we would
be right back where we are now, needing someone and having
to start over."

Cratchit must say, "And if he did not prove to be what we
needed, there is no telling what sort of a muddle he may make
of our figures and records in the meantime! I would much prefer

working both mine and Homer's situations for a while rather than have to clean up after someone else's incompetence!"

So, once again they were back at the beginning, with nothing solved. Homer would soon sail, leaving an empty stool in the offices, and they would continue to talk it over and advertise until they found someone who pleased them right from the start. It was a doubtful scheme since they hadn't yet managed to purchase even one advertisement. Perhaps they would place some ads at a later date, once Homer was truly gone. Yes. That was the answer. They would do that. Later.

The Sunday before their departure Rector Gifford ended his sermon with an announcement and a blessing.

"As most of you know, the Carters and the younger Mr. and Mrs. Probert are sailing this week for America. They are, thankfully, not leaving us for good, but it will be an extended trip and I ask you all to join with me as I pray a blessing over them. With that, everyone bowed his or her head, each one imploring God to protect them from whatever it was that particular person feared.

"Our Gracious Lord in Heaven, we beseech You to watch over our loved ones as they make this journey. We ask specifically for Your Divine protection concerning their health and safety, and we also ask you to give them wisdom and minds that are at peace. We know that You are ever with them and they only need turn to you in times of difficulty, which we pray will be few.

"We invoke Psalm 121:8, which says, 'The Lord shall preserve thy going out and thy coming in from this time forth, and even for evermore.' We thank you, Almighty Father, that we can rely on Your promises to preserve those of ours who are going out from among us, and that you will eventually return them safely to us. Amen."

The day of departure was exciting for those leaving and extremely distressing for those who would remain behind. At Paddington Station everyone gathered beside the railway car that would take the travelers to Bristol, from where they would sail to Boston and then travel on to New York. Hearts were breaking as each one tried to memorize the faces and voices he or she would not see again for some time. Letters would, of course, be exchanged, but they were definitely one-sided in terms of communication, and they could not bestow actual hugs and kisses.

Thankfully, Martha was now fully inclined to sail, but she was also experiencing a plethora of emotions. *It would have been so much easier had we never been invited on this trip, but we would have missed the opportunity of a lifetime. Think of it! Within a few weeks we shall be in New York!*

Martha would never have imagined that she, Martha Cratchit of Camden Town, would ever be off on such a trip. And with her husband! They had been married now for almost two weeks, so she was on new ground, no matter which way she turned. She was very thankful that Lucy Carter would be with her to offer advice and keep her steady.

Homer was nearly euphoric. He was actually married to the beautiful and delightful Martha and they were going to America! Two dreams had come true at the same time and he only prayed he was up to both experiences. Thank goodness Edwin Carter was leading the parade, because Homer was somewhat asea – in more ways than one.

Lucy Carter knew she was in good hands with Edwin and was not worried in the least. She was also glad of Martha's company and was happy to take her under her wing. Martha's life had changed drastically in recent weeks, and it was about to change even more with a trip of this magnitude. Hopefully it would all be agreeable. Lucy was, in a word, delighted with everything that was occurring.

Edwin Carter, the only one of the four who had ever made this trip, felt his responsibilities, but he was glad of them. No man had better traveling companions and he would finally be able to show Lucy where he had been all those years when he was working so hard and dreaming only of her. Homer would be invaluable in dealing with business and he would, no doubt, come away with more experience and skills than most men of his age in either America or England. He really was exceptional.

Finally, when it was time to board the railway car, The Cratchits embraced Martha as a group, not wanting to let go, while Mrs. Probert clung tightly to her son. Homer's father stood stoically next to them, controlling his emotions like the good sailor that he was. When the embraces were ended, the men all shook hands with each other and swallowed hard while the women wept openly.

Amid such heartbreaking commotion the four sojourners climbed into their rail carriage. Within days they would be passengers on a ship to America. It was just at that moment that a thought occurred to Scrooge, and he turned to his wife. "Rebecca, my dear, what say you about the possibility of someday making a trip to New York?" She smiled, since the same thought had occurred to her more than once during the past few weeks.

CHAPTER FORTY

The Spirits of 1843

Soon it was December, and since Scrooge and Rebecca would be hosting Christmas Eve this year, they discussed the impending gathering, planning each detail of a party that would surely echo one from long ago.

Scrooge attempted to put into words what the Fezzywigs' Christmas Eve party had meant to him, and what he had learned, even though he seemed to have forgotten it for most of his adult life.

"In terms of giving joy, my dear Rebecca, Old Fezzywig may have topped my list, at least until Christmas Day of 1843, which I should explain to you someday, since I believe it is high time I did.

"As I have said on occasion, my father was a very troubled man whose moods tended to swing between unpleasant at best to cruel at his worst, which meant that my early years were bereft of much enjoyment. The only bright spot during those years was my sister, Fan.

"In fact, I had never experienced such kindness and delight until I was apprenticed to Mr. Fezzywig. How that man bestowed happiness! He was naturally jolly, and he was truly sympathetic toward his fellow man. He never abused his workers and always, always looked to their well-being. I suppose in those days I hoped to emulate him, but that lofty aim was unfortunately quashed by my first big success in business." That said, they moved on to planning decorations and food for their own party.

That night, however, as they prepared for bed, Rebecca recalled what Scrooge had said. "Ebenezer, what was so special about Christmas Day 1843? You mentioned it and said you wanted to tell me something."

"Ah, yes. The joy of that day actually came about because the night before was very disturbing. It is quite a long story, but I will shorten it so that you may understand the basics of what occurred." He sat on her side of the bed facing her as she propped up her pillow so that she was in an upright position. Neither of them was sleepy, at any rate.

"My dear, what I am about to tell you may seem preposterous, and no doubt would be received as such by most people. You, however, have now been privy to a visitation of your own, and I hope that has prepared you for the things to which I have been privy over the past three years – right here, in this very room!"

Rebecca's interest was piqued, and she encouraged him to go on as she gave her pillow another plump-up, then leaned back to listen.

"I hated Christmas and thought it was a sham, you see. If anyone, including my dear nephew Fred, dared say to me, 'Happy Christmas,' I would cry, 'Bah! Humbug!' to his face. I hated most everything and everyone, other than business and any money I could gain thereby. Christmas Eve 1843 was just another night to me, and I sat by the fire eating some gruel when the ghost of my old partner, Jacob Marley, who had been dead those seven years, appeared. Right over there," he said, pointing.

"The specter was weighed down with chains and money boxes and he groaned something terrible. He was a frightful sight and warned me that I was headed in the same direction as he if I did not change my ways. I saw no need to change and said as much, but he forewarned me that I would be visited by three spirits, and he made it clear that I needed to alter my character. I didn't believe him, but the spirits did appear, just as he said they would.

"When the bell tolled one of the clock the 'Ghost of Christmas Past' appeared. I didn't believe any of it, and I spent some moments arguing until it placed its hand on my arm, and we were suddenly at my old boyhood school. I was still in my nightshirt and cap, but I was as warm as a slice of toast right off the fire. I saw myself as a child; my schoolmates; relived my awful loneliness, and I even saw young Fan. Precious, loving sister Fan." They both smiled at the mention of her name.

"I also saw my father and Old Fezzywig's warehouse, where I met Dick Wilkins. I have already told you about Belle, whom I drove away by my growing avarice. I relived all of that before being returned to this bed.

"Then, when the bell tolled two of the clock, the jovial 'Ghost of Christmas Present' appeared and proceeded to show me the Season's joy that others, including Fred, Catherine and the Cratchits were experiencing. I saw, too, the poverty and brokenness of strangers for whom I cared nothing. I was allowed to see and hear many a sad commentary on me and my own life and to learn what people really thought of me. I recall being surprised that it suddenly mattered to me what they thought, for I hadn't cared a whit for decades!

"I was still not quite a believer, but when the bell tolled three of the clock a morose 'Ghost of Christmas Yet to Come' appeared.

It was a terrifying presence, come to show me how things would be after my death. To put it simply, I saw that no one cared, other than how he or she might gain from my demise. I had left a terrible legacy and wasted my life entirely. I was no good to anyone, even to myself."

With a shudder Scrooge said, "Then I was shown my grave and that was all it took. I was absolutely petrified, and I repented on the spot. I begged the Spirit to tell me if things had to end that way, or if I could yet change and make a difference. Suddenly, in the middle of my tirade, I awoke here," pointing to the bed, "and it was Christmas Day – bright and clear and clean.

"I had never experienced a day like that one. The weight of all of my greed and hatred was gone. I was ecstatic, and I wanted to make others happy, too. I truly was a changed man. Not many months after that, I met you, my dear wife, and before long I could not imagine life without you." He took her hand, turned it over and kissed her palm.

Rebecca was listening intently to his narrative and reminded Scrooge that she had not been acquainted with him during those years of his self-described depravity. His name had never arisen in conversation during that time, at least not that she could recall, so she could only imagine the metamorphosis he was describing.

With regard to their very first encounter, she said, "I do recollect meeting you with Fan once, when we were both girls, and I remarked to her at the time that you seemed to be very serious and stern for such a young man.

"Fan said to pay your manner no mind, since that was your 'business face' and had nothing to do with your true character. So, you see, in the years between our first meeting and our next introduction in 1844, I never knew the Scrooge that was so fearsome. I only knew that Fan thought the world of you and believed you to be of excellent character."

THE SPIRITS OF 1843

"I must say," remarked Scrooge, "that I am more than grateful that we were not acquainted during all of those years when I was such a cruel and malicious miser. Having not known me then must make it easier for you to accept me as I am now, without being haunted by a truth that might cause you to trust me less. *Although I have surely given you enough reason to be less than trusting recently!* You certainly know my many shortcomings, but I believe you also know my heart, and you know it very well, indeed. Need I remind you that it belongs to you, totally, with all of its imperfections?"

"You need not, and I accept you entirely," was her reply.

As he climbed into his side of the bed, Scrooge said, "My point in telling you all of this is to admit that I was visited by spirits." He was taking a chance here by adding, "Three of them never returned . . . but . . . Marley did." He didn't dare look at her, but she didn't respond, so he continued, cautiously.

"He has, in fact, returned several times in the ensuing three years and has advised me on many topics. I have ignored him on occasion, much to the chagrin of myself and others, but I hope I am quite a bit wiser now."

Rebecca did not speak, but it was a comfortable silence. Finally, she said, "I believe it must have been the same spirit who visited me. In fact, I'm certain of it. Do you suppose it really was the ghost of Jacob Marley?"

CHAPTER FORTY-ONE

Otherworldly Revelations

It was later that week, in the middle of the night, that Scrooge sensed a presence. Rebecca appeared to be sleeping soundly so he assumed the spirit did not wish to wake her. It did, however, hover near her, smiling, before it moved next to Scrooge and spoke.

"This room is the same as three years ago, is it not? And yet, everything else about your life has changed. In fact, you now have a new 'confidante' who can discuss with you and aid in your decisions as to how to act." He smiled again and said, "I have every confidence in her."

"Does that mean you and I shall not speak again?" asked Scrooge.

"That is most likely."

"Then, before you disappear forever, please tell me who, or what, you are. Given all you have said and done, I tend to believe you're providential. I no longer believe you are Marley, but I do accept the fact that you are a spirit. Are you an angel?"

"I am indeed a ministering spirit and there are more of us than you can imagine. I am part of a very great host. We have assignments, and Marley was mine at one time."

"Why did you present yourself to me as Marley? Surely you could have been yourself. Why the disguise? Why the pretense?"

"Do you think you would have accepted me as I am, and listened to what I had to say? You already had a relationship with Marley, and you tended to listen to him once you were convinced it was he who was actually doing the talking.

"Marley, in fact, has not been here since his death, nor is he residing where you or anyone who knew him in life would expect him to be. Think on it. Had you asked anyone where he would spend his afterlife they would have, to a person, sworn that his soul was damned for his avarice and lack of compassion for his fellow man and that he was surely suffering the flames of Hades."

A tentative glimmer of hope rose in Scrooge's chest. "Are you saying that my old partner did not suffer the fate he, and I, both deserved?"

"I am. You see, Marley's deathbed proved to be his salvation, as it is for many. As he lay there struggling to breathe, I merely explained to him that he had only a few moments in which to choose his eternal destination, and then he would stand before his Maker. I pointed out that it is written, 'It is appointed unto man once to die, but after this the judgment.'

"Marley was not totally ignorant of the Truth, and he chose rightly. He was offered then what you would be offered seven years later. You both were in need of a change of heart, and since it was a spiritual problem, it required spiritual guidance. But there is a bit more to Marley's story, if you are interested." Scrooge was definitely interested and said so.

"During his lifetime I was assigned to Marley, but he did not follow my suggestions because he would not listen to them. His mind and his ears were tuned only to the clink of silver, gold and copper. He did listen to me the one time when, in a dream, he was foretold of Edwin Carter's visit and was told to give Carter a certain amount of money. Carter appeared the next day and requested the exact amount, and since the timing and the amount were exact, Marley loaned him the money, more out of fear than faith.

"Remember, Marley had not, at that point, ever done anything at all by faith, and he saw no need for a Savior because he did not discern between good and evil, only profit and loss. Marley could have changed his life and lived many more years with a different point of view, as did you, but he steadfastly refused until he was only a few breaths away from standing before the Throne.

He was one of those who was admitted to heaven as one saved from a fire. He was redeemed because he repented, but he had no good works to offer. He brought nothing to eternity but himself, his acceptance of Grace, and a faint scent of smoke."

Just then Rebecca turned over and Scrooge watched her for a moment, to confirm that she did not wake. He was unsure of what he would have done had she suddenly opened her eyes. Would she have joined in the conversation? Would she have been aghast? Thankfully she slept on, allowing the spirit to continue.

"When I appeared to you seven years later, I represented myself as Marley in those heavy chains with money boxes attached in order to give you a clear picture of what you were and where you were headed. Also, at that time in your life you were more inclined to listen to the Hell-bound ghost of someone you knew, rather than to a heavenly spirit. It was necessary that you see, in who you thought was Marley, what your lifestyle would bring if you refused redemption. Of course, there were other spirits who assisted, and between the four of us you were convinced. You began a new life then and there, unlike Marley, who required the reality of a deathbed to recognize the end result of his corrupted life."

Scrooge must ask. "Since you are sent to minister, why do you not simply prevent us, somehow, from doing ourselves and others harm? Could you not have kept me from discovering the details of Peter's death, for instance? Since you tried to warn me off, you surely knew what a mess I would make of things, and how I made my dear Rebecca suffer. Surely you could have placed a roadblock in my path that would have prevented me from pursuing the case."

"Had I done that you would be nothing more than a pawn on a chessboard, with someone else making the moves. No, man has been given free will and that is what you exercised when you insisted on going your own way. Yet, the Almighty is well able to make things work together for good, at the end of an honest mistake, or even at the end of a stubborn pursuit. It is only required that man acknowledge his error and seek Divine intervention."

As usual, it was the spirit who determined how and when the meeting would end, and it was now that time. Scrooge knew he would most likely not "see" the spirit again, but he did not know what a person should say to a departing spirit. It wasn't quite the same as waving adieu to an acquaintance who is pulling away in a coach.

The spirit looked at Rebecca for a moment, obviously pleased, then back at Scrooge. He nodded his head in affirmation, and was gone.

The next morning Mrs. Haiter prepared her usual excellent breakfast for the couple and Scrooge found he was ravenous.

All of that talk the night before must have given him an appetite, particularly the information about Jacob Marley.

Just as he took a drink of coffee Rebecca commented, "You must be relieved to learn that Jacob Marley is not, after all, suffering the flames of Hades."

Scrooge coughed, spewing the mouthful he meant to swallow. He quickly wiped his mouth and clattered his cup back into its saucer. "Rebecca! Are you saying you were awake the entire time the spirit was speaking?"

"No, my dear, I do not think I was, entirely. I believed I was dreaming until this very moment, as you just now confirmed that you were actually communing with a spirit. So, I did hear it rightly? Jacob had a deathbed conversion?"

Scrooge was clearing his throat, but he finally managed to say, "He did, and I must say, yes, I am extremely relieved. I think that has brought on my enormous appetite this morning. But what else did you hear, not that I mind if you heard it all."

"Well, I heard all that was said about Jacob, and I believe your conversation was mostly about him, at any rate, was it not?"

"It was, although he did answer a few questions I had about spirits, in general. I was surprised to learn that Marley was visited by this same spirit as you and I. The fact that Marley never mentioned his dream about Carter to me is testament to the pitiful shallowness with which we both approached life in those days. Even if he had taken the spiritual visit seriously, I'm certain he would not have broached the subject with me. He would most likely, and rightly, have assumed that I would say it was all humbug and not to bother me when I was busily counting the day's profits."

Scrooge must ask Rebecca. "How are you taking in all of this communication with ethereal beings?" He smiled as he added, "Since it seems you have been initiated into the club."

"I evidently have been, and I must say I feel somewhat privileged. It is an exclusive sort of group I'm certain, but I believe, from what was said last night, that we may never again meet with our spiritual friend."

"I suspect so. In fact, he said as much."

"Ebenezer, I would most likely have believed you, had you told me earlier of these visits of yours on Christmas Eve 1843, if for no other reason than the extreme change that occurred in your character that night. Even though I didn't know the 'Old Scrooge,' many people could have attested to the difference between you then and now, so I would have known that either you were dreaming a very vivid and poignant dream which turned your world on its ear, or you had a true heavenly encounter. Either way, you were a changed man by Christmas morning." She continued.

"I would not, however, have expected to experience anything of the sort, myself." She chuckled softly before saying, "I must admit, Ebenezer, that meeting and marrying you has been a breathtaking whirlwind of an adventure, and I would not have missed it for anything!"

CHAPTER FORTY-TWO

Christmas Eve 1846

S crooge was determined that once again Old Fezzywig would live on in a Christmas Eve celebration at the Scrooge home, and what a celebration it would be! Even better than two years ago, mostly due to the presence of the new Mrs. Scrooge, bless her!

Both Mr. and Mrs. Fezzywig would have been proud of their apprentice Ebenezer Scrooge and how he was now keeping the spirit of Christmas in his heart. Years ago, Fezzywig had definitely shown both Scrooge and Dick Wilkins how to enjoy a Christmas Eve gathering, and neither would ever forget the love and joy of that evening.

People had been important to Fezzywig and he would never have them miss out on a chance to celebrate. He surrounded his guests with rich delicacies to eat; warm drink; a fiddler by which to dance, and laughter enough to shake the rafters. Nor did he skimp on candles. There was enough light in the warehouse on Christmas Eve to make it shine like the Christmas star, itself!"

Rollo Norris was of course invited to join the Scrooges on Christmas Eve, and he certainly was welcome to bring a guest, but this year he decided to celebrate downstairs in the Symons' kitchen and servants' hall. He had chosen to spend the evening with Lily as she helped prepare the Christmas Day feast that would be hosted by Fred and Catherine Symons.

By now, Rollo had spent many hours downstairs at the Symons home, and Lily had gradually become a very important part of his life. He was actually hoping, to his own amazement, that she might someday be with him permanently.

The Symons' servants, and Rollo, went upstairs earlier in the evening for the Christmas toast with champagne. Then the servants were given their gifts before Fred and Caroline left to celebrate with Scrooge and Rebecca. After they departed, there was a lull in the preparations for tomorrow's feast, which gave Rollo and Lily time to themselves.

The two of them sat at the servants' table drinking a lovely spiced hot chocolate that Cook had made especially for them, and they began to recollect their first meeting. It had been long enough now, and they knew each other well enough that they could both laugh at the incident. Lily was recalling sitting on the sidewalk, in tears, while constables all around her swung their truncheons and knocked heads together, when Rollo suddenly interrupted her story. "Lily, do you think you could ever be a policeman's wife?"

Lily's heart skipped, but she was learning not to expose her thoughts and emotions too quickly, so she replied with a question of her own. "Why are you asking?"

"Because, a man has to think of his future, doesn't he? I'm doing just that, am I not?" *Does that mean I am part of his plans for the future?* Lily was taken by a slight shiver of delight but would certainly not do him the favor of appearing to be overly eager.

"Well, I must say 'no,' I have not thought about it." That was not entirely the truth, although it was true that she dared not actually hope for such a thing, for fear of disappointment. He knew she was playing a sort of game, and he could play it as well as she.

"Then when, exactly, would you would be willing to think about it?"

She sat a moment before answering, cocking her head to one side. "February 14th. I'll think about it on Saint Valentine's Day."

"Do you promise?" Now she had backed herself into a corner, but she really didn't mind. She was enjoying the chase since she, too, had hopes. There were worse things than being cornered by Rollo Norris, who had, over the past months, become a proper hero to Lily.

"Yes, I suppose I do promise. I will think about it on that particular day. So, if you want to have further conversation on the topic, come around then. I'm certain Cook will have prepared a number of lovely pastries, and you know she always saves some for you!"

He would see her many times before February, but he would definitely be there on Valentine's Day, perhaps with one of those elaborate Valentine cards, but definitely with a formal proposal of marriage. Knowing Lily, she might still put him off a bit, but she was seriously considering him, and that was enough encouragement for now.

Rollo held up his cup of chocolate as if to offer her a toast, and she raised her cup in return. It was the closest she was willing to come to an outright acceptance of his suggestion, at least until Saint Valentine's Day.

While Rollo and Lily were enjoying their time together, the festivities were gaining momentum at the Scrooge home. Mrs. Scrooge had managed the decorations with the able assistance of Mrs. Dilber, and even the Crown Prince would have been comfortable in the setting. A huge Christmas tree stood in the drawing room, decorated with glowing candles and small packets of candies. Popcorn was strung and wrapped around the tree with the occasional fabric and lace figure, or glass ball, peeking out from among the branches.

Green garland with holly was everywhere on mantles, mirrors and any flat surface, plus the stair railings. Although gas lighting was available, candles served to illuminate the garlands with an effect that better served the event. There were several kissing balls made of mistletoe and greenery, tied and hung by a bright red ribbon. They hung in doorways mostly, but occasionally a couple might find themselves standing beneath such a ball in an out-of-the-way alcove that lent itself to a more lingering, kiss. It was under just such a decoration the previous year that Scrooge had finally made a decisive romantic move toward Rebecca, and he was determined to give the same opportunity to any man who was so inclined!

At 7:30 of the clock the guests began to gather at the Scrooge home. In came Fred, Catherine and Flora, followed by the Cratchits – every one but Martha, whose absence occasionally brought a tear to her family's eyes. Mr. Brownlow and Oliver had been invited to the festivities but declined with sincere regrets since they were to celebrate Christmas with the Maylies and Dr. Losberne in the countryside. They begged Scrooge and Rebecca to visit them for the New Year, if possible, and the Scrooges were seriously considering it.

Among many other guests were Rebecca's mother, Mrs. Sotherton; Homer's parents, Mr. and Mrs. Probert, who wished to celebrate with the Cratchits because they were now "family;" Fred and Catherine's particular friends Julian and Marian Thorne; Rector Colin Gifford; Dick and Priscilla Wilkins; Rebecca's cousins the Purtell-Smythes, who stopped in to say hello and remained until the last few guests departed; newly wedded Tobias and Honora Blythe; the very capable Sergeant Clarke; Scrooge's housekeeper Mrs. Dilber and her husband Ollie, and Mrs. Haiter the cook, who had been the principal organizer of tonight's feast. Constable Stagg had been invited, but he was on duty and said he would attempt to stop in for a few moments sometime during the evening.

Mrs. Haiter and her accomplices had outdone themselves. There were specialty breads; roast beef, poached salmon and roasted poultry; vegetables such as new potatoes with cream sauce, mushroom pudding, buttered peas and vegetable salad; and a variety of fruits. Desserts included trifle, lemon tart, egg custard, sponge cake and apple charlotte. No one would be allowed to return home with anything less than a bursting stomach.

Naturally, there were drinks to accompany the food. A flaming rum punch was the favored standby of the season and there was also plain fruit punch for the children, or those who preferred something lighter. One could have a brandy smash, gin, or even champagne. There were no rules as to what a guest might sample, and there were fewer rules with regard to toasts, since many of the guests were inclined to offer one.

Glasses containing all sorts of concoctions were raised throughout the evening to congratulate, remember, wish good luck, and to merely appreciate. More than one toast was offered to Homer and Martha, and the Carters, who were certainly in

America by then. They were terribly missed, but it was prayed that they were having a Happy Christmas in New York!

No Christmas Eve gathering at the Scrooges' would be complete without musicians. Instead of Fezzywig's lone fiddler however, tonight there was a violin, a piano and a woodwind instrument, in this case a flageolet. The players not only entertained but also provided music for those who wished to dance.

The musicians were proficient, and they generated enough energy for the guests to dance the Galop, during which several of them did just that, galloping right into each other and bringing on a good deal of laughter and jibes as to their dancing proficiency. The Polka produced even more levity, after which women sat and fanned themselves until they could catch their breath. The Mazurka, as it was played that evening, proved to slow things down a bit, but it was the Waltz, with its wonderfully smooth movements, that allowed the women who had been resting to finally fold their fans and again accept their partners' requests to whirl about.

When the musicians took time from their playing to share in the bountiful food, Rebecca suggested that Flora sit down at the piano and accompany anyone who might volunteer to sing a Christmas carol.

Rebecca announced, "Flora has accepted my request to accompany anyone who would like to sing for us. Is there someone who would care to do so? I know we would all enjoy it."

No one stirred, so Sergeant Clarke stepped forward and said he would be very pleased to sing, and would Flora please play "Silent Night." She agreed and began the introduction. When it was time for him to join in, he began, not timidly, but with the finest and clearest tenor to ever grace the walls of the old house.

"Si-i-ilent night. Ho-o-oly night . . ." Within three measures everyone was gathered around, having been pulled in by the unexpected talent. By the end of the first verse there were several guests wiping their eyes at the stirring of emotion. Then, before Clarke began the second verse, Honor Purdy Blythe slipped quietly in beside the Sergeant, to bravely join him. No one knew how much courage it had taken to do such a thing, but she had become more willing to display her talents since her marriage to Tobias.

In what could only be described as an amazing alto, Mrs. Blythe provided the perfect harmony. The duet was astonishing, and the applause was long and loud. Before they were allowed to quit, Clarke and Mrs. Blythe were coerced into singing two more carols. It would be remembered as a highlight of the evening.

The guests were awed by the impromptu performance, especially since few of them knew Sergeant Clarke, and not many had ever paid any serious attention to Honora Purdy Blythe, even though they had known her for years. Most of them had heard her braying and snorting, but no one had ever heard her sing. Such a voice!

Some of them wondered how one person could have the ability to emit so much equine racket on the one hand, and such splendid music on the other. Since Honora could not do both at the same time, she would certainly be asked to sing again at other gatherings. It was a sure thing that Sergeant Clarke would also receive a number of invitations.

Tobias Blythe had been proudly standing by as Honora displayed a talent no one suspected she possessed. His life was greatly altered when she became his wife and, without realizing it, he no longer felt invisible. He was more accepted for himself and was far more amiable because he was finally loved by the woman he had adored for years.

Anyone paying attention would have seen that Tobias Blythe now stood taller and displayed a presence that made people actually want to talk to him and become better acquainted. Nor were they disappointed, because he proved to be quite an engaging conversationalist, and their dialogues invariably left them both with the impression that they had each made a delightful new friend.

As Scrooge and Rebecca made their separate ways around the home, ensuring that everyone was served and comfortable, they met in the entry hall where Scrooge took her hand and guided her to the kissing ball. He gave her a quick but meaningful kiss and commented, "You know, I am amazed at how little I am annoyed by Honora's braying these days. Perhaps she is no longer doing it, or I suppose it is also possible that I simply no longer hear it!" Just then a small, gleeful "*hee-haw*" echoed from the other room, but no one seemed at all disturbed by the sound.

When the last dance had finished, the final toast been offered, and most of the food been eaten, the guests began to disburse. At the door they gathered their wraps, scarves, hats and gloves and congratulated their hosts on a memorable and most enjoyable celebration. Then they wished each other a Happy Christmas as they departed.

The celebration had been a rousing success and both Scrooge and Rebecca were jubilant, but quite fatigued.

That night, as they lay their heads on their pillows, Rebecca immediately fell soundly asleep. Scrooge, however, stared into the darkness for some minutes, recalling the spirits who had visited him here. He knew a part of him would miss them.

Then he recalled that they are always about, ministering and protecting. Wasn't it true, too, that people often entertained them unaware? It was even possible that he might bump into one, perhaps his own personal guardian, and not know who it was! For some reason the thought comforted him.

Scrooge lay still, listening to the delicate whisper of Rebecca's breathing and thanked God for her, as well as for the rest of his family and dear friends. Mostly, he was grateful for the Grace that could save reprobates such as he and Marley had been for so much of their lives.

Soon Scrooge was softly snoring, unaware of the dazzling light emanating from angels that filled the room. They sang heavenly praises with music that could never be replicated by human voices, then they departed. As they glided gracefully away, their wake was charged with brilliant beams that flashed and sparkled with the indescribable glory of Divine promise.

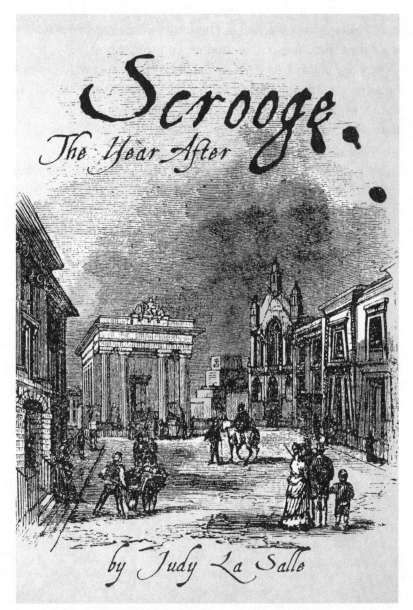

The first book in "The Scrooge Years" series

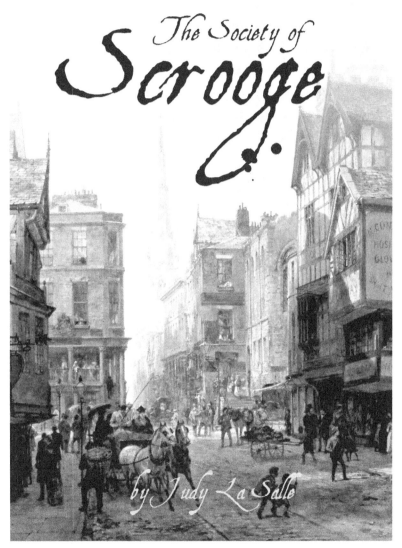

The Society of Scrooge

by Judy La Salle

The second book in "The Scrooge Years" series

Made in United States
Orlando, FL
07 December 2024

55107896R00178